TWO TRUTHS

AND

A LIE

Book 1 in the PRG Investigations Series

Ashley Stoyanoff

Ashley Stoyanoff Books

Published by Ashley Stoyanoff Books
www.ashleystoyanoff.com

Edited by Kathryn Calvert

Cover design by Sarah Hansen, Okay Creations

Also By Ashley Stoyanoff

Dedication

For Mom.
I'm so thankful to have you in my corner.

Chapter One

Elena

I lost my life on my twentieth birthday.

I suppose one could argue the truth of that statement. I know I have. It's probably more accurate to say that I lost my life four months prior, the day I climbed into the back of Officer Lawrence Peck's cop car. I just hadn't realized it at the time.

But my twentieth birthday marks the day that I made the choice to leave it all behind. It marks the day that I became a missing person.

Right before it happened, I opened a fortune cookie that read: *Your life will be happy and peaceful.* I'm starting to think that cookie was meant for someone else.

I took it as a sign then, but it's been exactly three-hundred and sixty-five days since I read that fortune, twelve full months, and happy and peaceful has not come my way yet.

I thought running was the answer. If I could just get away from that man, I'd find my peace. I'd find my happiness.

Turns out running from a police officer isn't as easy as I thought it would be.

Today my fortune says: *A new environment makes a world of difference.* I'm not sure if that's true, but I'm hoping it might be.

Because today, I'm facing the nightmare that has become my

life. Today, I'm done hiding. I'm done running.

Today, I'm going to take the step that I should have taken a year ago. I'm going to take my life back.

I stare at the words on the small piece of paper, pinched between my fingertips. A new year, a new fortune. It was a tradition from my old life. A fortune cookie on your birthday sets you on the right path for the year that lies ahead of you. That's what my mom used to tell me. She believed them, followed them. If she were here right now, I'm certain she'd be packing my bags and pushing me out so I could discover a *new environment*.

But I'm already in a new environment. A shady bar in a shady part of a city I've never been to before.

The bar itself isn't exactly *new*. The tables are scratched and gashed. The leather-covered booth I'm sitting in has more duct tape on it than leather. The lights are low, hiding most of the wear and tear on the establishment, but it can't quite conceal the blistered and peeling paint or the layer of grime on the windows.

The music isn't quite loud enough. It's almost a strain on the ears to hear the lyrics over the rowdy banter of the other patrons. It's rock music. That much I can tell, but what song, what artist, I have no idea.

The men in this place look a little rough around the edges, so do the women. But there's something real about them. They laugh too loud, talk too loud. They aren't hiding behind polite conversation or fancy clothes. They are just … real. Genuine.

It's refreshing.

It's comforting.

If you asked me a year and a half ago where I'd be on my twenty-first birthday, I would have said at a club. Somewhere with pop music. Somewhere I could dance. Somewhere I could be with friends and drink and flirt.

But that was a year ago.

It's different now. That life, the one where I was a carefree girl, where I actually had friends, is gone. I don't know that girl anymore, but then I don't really know who I've become either.

But I do know that I want to be someone. I want to have a

life that's not full of fear and running. I want to live in one place long enough to make friends. I want to finish college, get a job. I want to see my family again.

Most of all, I want to see Officer Lawrence Peck rotting away in a prison cell.

Sighing, I fold the tiny piece of paper in half and tuck it into my pocket. I take a sip of my beer and glance around. The air is thick and stuffy, and I'm tempted to head outside, just for a quick, fresh breath, but I don't.

I can't.

I know the breath will turn into ten, and ten will turn into twenty, and once I hit twenty, I'll start to second-guess myself.

And then I'll end up running—again.

I cut my eyes to the table where the man I've come to see sits.

It's him. I know it is. I studied his picture for hours before I came here. He's tall, and solid in a way that says he spends a lot of time working with his hands. A black tee hugs his torso and he wears a pair of blue jeans. His jaw is square, strong, with a dusting of black stubble, and his nose, straight and smooth. His black hair isn't long, but it's not short either. It curls slightly at the ends, and looks as though he just rolled out of bed and ran his hands through it a few times.

He sits there, nursing his second beer, and laughing with another man—a friend, I assume. Maybe it's one of his partners from PRG Investigations; I'm not sure. I wasn't given pictures of them. He has two that I know of, though, Wesley Gates and Vance Rutherford.

As I contemplate how to approach him for what has to be the hundredth time, my heart races, each beat almost painful. They've been here for about forty-five minutes, and I'm still not sure what to do, or what to say exactly. It would be so much easier if the guy had an office. I could just call, make an appointment.

But he doesn't have an office and his number isn't listed. He works by referrals only.

I almost feel like a stalker.

A third beer is set in front of him.

Oh God, I can't. I can't …

I have to do this. I can't keep running. And he knows I'm coming.

I watched Mr. Chapman send the email before he packed me up into a car with a GPS and a few hundred dollars in cash. The man has a picture of me, too. He knows why I'm here. He knows my story. He probably clocked me sitting here the second he walked in and is waiting for me to make the first contact.

Just get up and walk over there, I tell myself. Waiting is only making it harder, and with each minute that passes, my nerves fray a little more.

I take a deep, calming breath, let it out, and then, I slowly slide out of the booth and make my way through the bar. Anxiety mixed with excitement fills up my stomach. What if he won't help me? What if he does? In this moment, I'm not sure what would be the better outcome. Both seem just as terrifying.

The gap between us closes too quickly and I stop a couple feet away. I stand there for a moment, wiping my sweaty hand on my jean-clad thigh, and hold my breath, waiting for him to notice me.

It doesn't take long for him to glance my way, only a couple seconds. He's smirking, a confident and perhaps a little amused smirk, but there's also a sort of soft concern in his eyes as he looks at me.

It's kind of impressive, the mixture of confident and soft.

It's also a bit unnerving.

His eyes scan me, pausing on my breasts, before making their way down in a slow, thorough inspection, following my curves all the way to my toes.

Embarrassment heats my cheeks. Not only am I sweating, but I'm also wearing worn jeans that are too big and frayed along the edges, and a plain cotton top that's wrinkled and grungy from spending two days doing nothing but driving. My hair is wrapped up in a messy twist on top of my head because I haven't had a chance to wash it since I started my journey, and

I'm not wearing a stitch of make-up.

I feel exposed under his scrutiny.

Too exposed.

I didn't wear my usual hoodie, ball cap or sunglasses to hide under. I didn't want to chance him not recognizing me and taking off.

Suddenly, I wish I had worn them.

For a moment, I find myself fighting the urge to glance around and make sure no one else is staring, but then, his eyes come back to mine and he smiles, and good God, but that smile has my stomach doing flip-flops and my brain stuttering.

His picture was impressive, but up close and with that smile …

"Hi, darlin'." His voice is deep and husky. It's the kind of voice that calls for attention. Full of coolness and confidence, and matches the rest of him perfectly.

My entire body flames with heat and my throat dries up. I swallow hard, and attempt to smile back. "Hi."

"You gonna have a seat?" he asks, jerking his chin toward an empty chair.

I glance at the empty chair at their table, think about sitting, but don't. Anxiety makes me feel a touch sick, and I know if I try to sit, all I'll do is fidget.

Instead, I hold up my beer, showing it to him, and say the first thing that comes to mind. "Just having a birthday drink."

He cocks an eyebrow, and his smile deepens, revealing a set of perfect dimples and straight white teeth. He chuckles, a rich, deep sound that unleashes a swarm of nervous butterflies in my belly. "Celebrating alone?"

Shaking my head, I say, "No." I take a breath, let it out, take another, and blurt, "I'm here to meet you." My voice comes out strained, and although I know that I need this man, I'm starting to feel like this was a terrible mistake, especially when I watch his forehead crease with confusion and his smile falter.

It's intimidating.

He's intimidating.

Suddenly he doesn't look amused anymore. His gaze turns

hard and a touch cold. "You sure about that?"

Strained silence stretches as he waits for me to answer, but I don't. I just stand there, tongue-tied, shifting from one foot to the other.

His friend is watching me with cool amusement. His eyes are active, though, cataloging every inch of me. He's not missing anything. Not a twitch or tremble. It's almost too much. Invasive. A little scary. For the last year, I've worked on being a ghost, and now, under their scrutiny, I feel very much alive.

I'm not sure I like the feeling.

I want to run away, but I don't. Mr. Chapman trusts this guy. He wouldn't send me here if he didn't. He wouldn't put me at risk. I know it. I try to smile, but it feels flat and lifeless on my lips.

"You are Jason, right?" I ask. "Jason Pierce?"

He arches an eyebrow, but doesn't confirm or deny it. Is he testing me? I don't know what to say. I take a small sip of my beer, trying not to fidget. If I didn't know any better, if I didn't watch Mr. Chapman send that email to him, I'd think this guy has no idea who I am.

But I was there. I saw the email send. I listened to Mr. Chapman leave a voicemail, too, telling Jason to meet me here at Constant Pub. He may have been fifteen minutes late, but he did show up at the right place on the right day.

Sighing, I look away, and then back at him. "Yeah, I'm sure," I say. My voice surprises me. It's stronger, more certain, and makes me feel a bit more confident. I smile. "I'm here to meet you."

He considers this for a moment as his gaze sweeps the length of me again. The moment feels like a year as I try not to hide myself from his eyes, before he finally meets my gaze once more. "Who are you?"

Who am I? I laugh, a nervous little bubble of sound. I could give him the standard answer. My name is Elena Reed. I'm twenty-one, live in New York. That's what you'd find if you glanced at my driver's license.

But that's not what I tell him. I give him the real answer, the honest answer. "I don't know."

Jason

I let out a light laugh. Her answer is an interesting one. Clever. Clever enough to peak my curiosity. She may have meant it to be cute, but there's truth to it, too.

I'm good at reading people, always have been, but she's easier to read than most. I wonder if this girl has any idea how transparent she is. She's attempting not to show it, but she's nervous. I can see it. I can sense it.

It's written in her coiled muscles, and the way she unconsciously fidgets with the hem of her shirt, rubbing it between her forefinger and thumb. She lifts her glass to her lips and it trembles ever so slightly as she takes a sip.

The poor girl actually looks close to terrified, but yet, she doesn't retreat.

She's watching me, her expression blank, completely devoid of emotion. But those eyes ...

Pretty, soft blue. The most soulful eyes I've ever seen. Her expression may be sealed up tight, but those eyes give everything away.

She's not just nervous. She's desperate.

Wes makes a choking sound, fighting off a laugh. His lips are pressed in a tight line, hiding the shit-eating grin that's trying to push its way onto his face, although he can't quite hide the laughter in his eyes.

Bastard. He's loving every second of this, whatever the hell this is.

I consider telling her to go. I should just tell her I'm not interested. It would be the smart thing to do. Young and hot doesn't always make for a fun night. She can't even hold my gaze without fidgeting.

But ... for the first time in years, I find myself curious. The girl's been sitting in a booth across the bar for the last forty-five minutes watching me, and despite the fact that she's obviously uncomfortable, she figured out my name, got up the guts to approach me ...

"Have a seat, darlin'," I say, gesturing to a chair across from me. "Let me buy you a birthday drink."

She takes a step closer, small and hesitant, and then she drags her teeth over her bottom lip and shakes her head slightly. "I think I want to stand, um, if that's okay with you?"

I shrug a shoulder, leaning back in my chair. I don't even know what to say to that. She doesn't want to sit? Fine. Whatever.

"What's your name?" I ask. "And don't give me any of that *I don't know* bullshit."

She shakes her head again; a few blonde curls that have worked their way loose from the knot of hair piled on her head bounce against her shoulders. Her eyes flick to Wes, and then back to me. "I want to know who he is first."

A pang of irritation hits me at her question. I try to push it back, but it seeps into my voice anyway. "Yeah?" I say, sitting up straight. "And why the fuck would you want to know that if you're supposed to be here to meet me?"

She looks at me as though she wants to both devour and strangle me. I chuckle softly. She's fucking adorable.

"Because," she says, the word shaking slightly on her lips. She grimaces, no doubt she heard it, too, and clears her throat. "I do."

Wes takes a sip of his beer, considering her for a moment, and then lifts a shoulder in a half shrug. "I'm Wesley Gates."

"Oh, hi," she says, sounding startled. She stares at him, and this sweet, timid smile graces her plump lips. "It's really nice to meet you, Wesley."

Laughing, Wes folds his arms over his chest. "I'm guessing you've heard my name before."

She flushes an adorable shade of peach and nods. "Yes, well, I know you work with Jason."

Annoyance hits me fast and hard. Goddamnit she's flirting. She's fucking flirting with Wes. Is that her angle? Figure out my name as some sort of an icebreaker, an opening so she could meet him?

"You seem pretty confident that I'm Jason," I say, coolly, barely hiding my annoyance.

She makes a face at me, aggravation with a mix of fury. "I know who you are." It comes out like a growl, throaty and raspy.

"What's your name?" I ask again.

She glares at me. "You know who I am. I wouldn't be here if you didn't."

I grit my teeth, stopping a frustrated groan from passing my lips. I don't even know what to say to that. She may have a tight little body, but goddamn, this innocent, timid game she's playing ... Not worth the headache.

Sighing, I shake my head. "Don't know what game you're trying to play here, babe," I say. "But you can take it somewhere else. I'm not interested."

The girl is silent for a moment, gawking, before she finds her voice and whispers, "Asshole." As soon as the word slips out, the color drains from her high cheekbones and her pretty eyes widen. Obviously, she hadn't meant to say it out loud and she looks at me, horrified. "This was a bad idea," she says, taking a step back, and then another. "I think I'm just going to go now."

"Yeah," I say right away. "You should probably go on and do that."

She freezes, stalling out on her retreat, and looks at me with big, hurt-filled eyes, before her expression morphs into something blank and cold and distant.

Suddenly, there's no indication of what she's thinking or feeling, and when I search her face closely, I realize that those expressive eyes of hers are completely free of everything. It's as though she just simply stopped feeling—anything.

My chest tightens, and I don't know why, but that look ... it guts me.

In that second, I can't imagine anything that could be worse than seeing that look.

Realization slams into me like a runaway freight train. She

isn't some young girl looking for a fun night. She isn't playing a game. She expects me to know who she is.

I'm here to meet you.

Goddamnit! Someone sent her to me.

I stand up quickly, my chair teetering, before clapping back in place against the floor. I take a step toward her, and she takes another back. "Someone referred you, yeah?"

She flinches, as though she felt my question physically, but doesn't say a word. She inches back another step.

And another.

And another.

I follow; my mind works fast, trying to think of something, anything, to say that will stop her from leaving. "You want to go somewhere?" I ask. "We can talk for a bit."

"No," she says, her voice cold and harsh. She raises her hands, indicating for me not to come any closer. "I'm just going to … It was good to meet you both." And then she turns, sets her glass down on the nearest table, and she runs.

Chapter Two

Elena

"Hold up there, darlin'," his voice calls from behind me.

I don't stop. I can't. I'm ten seconds away from full-out running. I push the door open, rushing out into the humid night air.

A small group of people stand just outside the doors, smoking. They barely glance my way as I skirt around them, and cut through the dimly lit parking lot toward my car.

The sound of heavy footsteps follows me. Faster. Louder. My hands are trembling, my fingers tingling. I don't know if it's from anger, or disappointment, or from the ever growing fear that maybe, just maybe, the guy really isn't Jason.

Maybe the guy chasing me is his brother or a cousin. It's possible. Someone close enough to him to know his friends. Someone blood-related that could share similar features. It would explain why Wesley looked so amused during our brief interaction.

But maybe it is Jason. Maybe Mr. Chapman didn't get a chance to fill him in as he was supposed to. Maybe Jason didn't see the email.

Maybe Jason Pierce is just an asshole.

I expected him to be a dick. Mr. Chapman warned me that he wasn't the most agreeable person, but I didn't expect him to act as though he doesn't have a clue who I am. He could have just told me he wasn't interested in the job.

I might be disappointed, but I wouldn't blame him for it. It's not as though I can pay him. At least I can't pay him until I get back home.

"Stop," he shouts, the sound of his shoes hitting the pavement coming faster. "Just stop for a minute."

Quickening my stride, I keep my eyes on my car, as I rifle through my purse for my keys and call out, "Stop following me."

Where the hell are my keys? Pushing back a swell of anger-fueled anxiety, I keep searching. My fingertips brush against the metal ring. I clasp onto it, pulling them out, just as a large hand wraps around my bicep and I'm jerked to a halt. I yelp, and stumble, rocking on my heels, and dropping the keys. Another hand settles on my hip, steading me.

Then, I'm pulled around to face Jason. His eyes flicker over my face a few times, doing what looks like a silent assessment, and whatever he sees makes him draw his lips tight and his brow dip in a frown. "Are you okay?"

Am I okay? I laugh. I don't even know how to answer that question. I probably should be. I know that. I've waited a year for this chance, to have someone like him help me, but right now, after the exchange in the bar, with his hand locked around my arm and another on my hip, I don't feel okay. Not even a little.

"Yes, I'm good," I stammer, taking a hasty step back, yanking myself free of his grasp. "Everything's just fine."

He doesn't look reassured by my answer. Actually, he looks a little annoyed. He arches a questioning brow and folds his arms over his chest.

I stand there, hesitating, contemplating whether or not I should turn around and run. My car isn't far. Another twenty, maybe thirty steps. Will he chase me again if I do it?

"Can I go now?" I ask, not ready or wanting to endure another chase.

He shakes his head slowly. "If you want to make a lie

believable, you gotta weave it with the truth."

My brow furrows, confused by the comment. "What?"

"Two truths and a lie, babe," he says. "Makes the lie harder to pick up on."

Is this guy for real? He looks it, serious, a little brooding. He's watching me, waiting for … I don't even know.

"Okay, fine." I throw up my hands, exasperated, and sigh, long and loud. "I'm fine, just in a hurry to find a hotel and grab a shower." I bend down and snag up my keys; then, I meet his eyes. "Better?"

He laughs under his breath, but there is not a stitch of humor in the sound. "Yeah, but I'd rather you didn't bother with the lie."

I scoff. "Well, I'd rather you didn't chase me through a parking lot."

He's quiet for a moment, giving me a peculiar look, as though I'm some sort of an anomaly and he wants to figure me out.

"Why won't you tell me your name?" he asks.

Why is he doing this to me? Am I just a joke to him?

The thought burns through my throat as I try to swallow the pent up anger and frustration and the growing ache in my chest that seems to double with each second that passes by.

"Stop it," I hiss. "Just stop pretending you don't know who I am. If you don't want the job, then fine. But you don't have to be an ass about it."

He lifts his hands in a peace offering. "I honestly don't have a clue who you are," he says quietly, sounding a little uneasy. "I get you think I'm supposed to, but I don't."

"If you didn't come to meet me then why are you here?"

He lets out a light laugh. "Come here with the boys pretty much every Friday night, darlin'."

He looks serious, but I'm not sure. He's hard to read, but his eyes are soft, concerned, and a little confused. Jesus, I think he's telling the truth.

The realization should make me feel better, but it doesn't. My stomach is in knots, and the uneasy thought that maybe he really isn't who I thought he was slams into me again. But he looks so much like …

"Let me see your driver's license," I demand.

"Why?"

Why? The words 'because I'm freaking out and I'm starting to feel a little crazy' are on the tip of my tongue, but it feels like there's way too much truth in that statement to actually spit it out.

"Because Jason Pierce is supposed to know my name," I say. "He's supposed to know why I'm here and he's supposed to be here to meet me."

"I'm Jason Pierce," he says. "But I don't have a fuckin' clue who you are or why you're here."

"Prove it," I say. "Show me your driver's license."

He stares at me for a moment, contemplating, and then shrugs. Giving me an amused smirk, he reaches into his back pocket, withdraws his wallet, and pulls out a small stack of plastic cards from the bill area, shuffling through them before handing one over.

I snatch it up quickly, scanning the details under the dim light in the parking lot. Last name: Pierce. First name: Jason. Address: Sacramento, CA. Date of birth: June 19th, 1986.

I think I'm supposed to be relieved. It would be a rational feeling to have, the expected one.

But I'm not.

All I feel is flustered.

This isn't me.

I'm not this girl. I never used to be and I don't want to be her now. Over the last year, while I've been on my own, I've fought, I've struggled, and I've survived. I don't want to be nervous, and stress, and jump over the littlest bumps and thumps.

It's crazy how scared I've been since I walked into that bar. I know that.

I think I'm going crazy.

The idea—the hope—of not having to run any longer is driving me insane.

Scratch that. I think it's probably the solitude over the last year that's made me crazy.

Hesitantly, I hand the card back to him. He takes it, stuffs it back in his wallet, and puts it back in his pocket. Then, he gives me a look and says, "Will you please tell me your name now?"

I shake my head. "Did you, or did you not, receive an email from Richard Chapman two days ago?"

He stares at me, unblinking, eyes scanning my face as his expression turns serious. "Who are you?" he asks, his tone suddenly low, threatening, unnerving.

My breath hitches. Warning bells sound in my head, urging me to move, run, vanish, hide, but my feet are glued to the pavement. Unmoving and frozen.

A door squeaking open draws my attention to the bar where Wesley is exiting.

"Who the fuck are you?" Jason demands. His voice is scathing, almost a shout. His hand jumps out, gripping my bicep in a surprisingly gentle hold.

The gentleness confuses and terrifies me. It doesn't pair with his heated glare or his tone. My heart hammers hard in my chest. *Don't tell him,* a part of me screams, the small, scared girl inside wanting to run fast and far, but I swallow it down. "Elena Reed."

And then Wesley is there, pulling Jason away. He says something to Jason, his voice so low that I can't make out anything other than the furious, whispered tone.

But I don't wait to find out what's being said. I turn tail and run for my car.

Jason

"What the hell are you doing?" Wes growls, dragging me away from the girl—Elena Reed. "You're scaring the shit out of her."

"I don't give a fuck," I say, yanking out of his hold.

Turning my head around, I scan the parking lot for the girl. She's already running. Fucking running. Her heels slapping against the pavement.

I move to go after her, only making it a step before Wes is in front of me, both hands pressing against my shoulders, holding me in place. "You need to calm the fuck down," he says.

Calm down? Calm down! What is it about those two words that makes the fury inside me burn hotter? It's as though a match is lit, setting every muscle, every nerve ending in my body, in flames. *Calm down.* Those simple words cause an entirely different response in a person than they should.

I grit my teeth, watching as she yanks open a car door, hops in, and slams it shut. A rattle, a grind, her Honda sputters, and then turns over. She reverses, her tires squeal, and then she's pealing out of the parking lot.

I watch as the beat up car takes off down the street. My muscles are taut. I can feel them straining, clenching. Goddamnit! I shouldn't be this pissed off. Richard fucking Chapman shouldn't be able to get under my skin like this anymore.

But he does.

Just hearing the name sets me off, and I feel like I'm spinning … Spinning out of control.

"Jase, the girl was just looking for some help," Wes says calmly. He's watching me carefully, closely, and after a moment, he drops his hands from my shoulders, taking a step back. "You said it yourself before you ran after her. Someone sent her. She's a referral."

"A referral." I laugh, but there's nothing funny about the way I'm feeling. That girl, young, seemingly innocent … Sending her was low even for him. "Richard Chapman sent her." The name tastes like acid on my tongue. Pure acid.

He eyes me warily for a moment. "Your dad sent her?"

"Yeah," I say. "My dad sent her."

Cursing, he shakes his head. "I guess that explains why she was so nervous talking to you."

"Yeah, I guess it does."

"She's not what he usually sends to get your attention," Wes points out. "Did you get her name?"

"Yeah," I say. "It's Elena Reed."

He pulls out his phone, but doesn't go to use it. Instead, he stares at me, studying me, as though maybe he's not sure if I've got my shit together enough to deal with her. "Maybe we should just leave this one alone."

"No," I say, shaking my head. "I'm fuckin' sick of this shit."

Chapter Three

Elena

"Come on, come on, come on," I whisper as the phone rings and rings and rings in my ear.

God, my chest is going to explode. The pressure ... the unbelievable pressure is too much. Who would have thought disappointment would hurt so badly. I really believed Mr. Chapman. I believed him so thoroughly, so fully. *Jason's a good guy*, he told me. *He'll help you. He doesn't know how to turn away someone who needs help. He ain't built that way.*

And I believed him. I believed every word. I needed to. I needed that hope that there really were people out there, good, kind people, who wouldn't look the other way. Who wouldn't let greed or fear or anger stop them from doing the right thing, the decent thing.

Believing was stupid. Stupid, stupid, stupid.

What's wrong with me that I actually thought Jason Pierce would help me just because I needed helping?

It shouldn't hurt this badly. It just shouldn't. Not after everything I've faced over the last year. I should be stronger than this. More resilient to the disappointment.

But I'm tired. So, so tired.

Why? Why! Why can't I ever catch a break?

I feel sick. Sick with nerves. Sick with anger. Just sick and shaky and cold.

Voicemail clicks on and I promptly hang up, only to call again.

The phone rings.

And rings.

And rings.

I rest my head on the steering wheel, listening to the ringing, and waiting for the voicemail to pick up once again. The line clicks and I'm about to hang up and redial when a groggy, rough voice answers. "Hello."

Relief washes over me in a hot wave of emotion. I sniffle. I try to say hello back, but it only sounds like a louder sniffle. Good God, what's wrong with me? Ten minutes of sitting at the side of the road, calling the same number over and over, and the only sound I can make when I finally get an answer is a sniffle?

"Is that you, baby girl?" Mr. Chapman asks, sounding instantly alert. "Elena?"

"Yes," I say, my voice coming out as an angry whisper. I clear my throat and swallow. "It's me."

"What's wrong?" he asks. "What happened?"

"He didn't know I was coming," I say, accusingly. "I trusted you. If Peck finds me. If I have to go back there—"

"Elena," he says, cutting me short, his tone firm, controlled. "Peck ain't gonna find you. Now tell me what happened."

"Jason was an ass," I say. "Or I guess, maybe he wasn't really. I thought he was jerking me around, but I don't know …" I pause, suck in a deep breath, and let it out. "I don't think he listened to your voicemail or read the email. When I mentioned you sent one, he got all pissed off."

Mr. Chapman lets out a light laugh. "I'm not surprised. Jason doesn't like me much."

I stall at those words, feeling ice freeze my blood. "You're not surprised? How did you even know he'd be there?"

"He's there every Friday night, baby girl," he says and laughs again. "I knew you'd find him even if he didn't know you were coming."

"Why did you send me here?" I demand sharply. "Why would you do this to me?"

He makes a sound somewhere in between a grunt and a sigh. "Let me talk to him, baby girl."

"I can't do that," I say. "I ... uh, he grabbed my arm and started yelling and then Wesley pulled him away and I, well, I sort of took off."

He's silent for a few breaths. "Wes was with him?"

"Yes, he was," I confirm.

"Good," he says. "Here's what you need to do, baby girl. You go find somewhere to sleep for the night. Let Jason clear his head. He'll get it together. He always does and then he'll come find you. I promise you. Wes will make sure of it."

Before I can respond, the line goes dead and my phone begins to beep. I sit there hesitating, contemplating, before I start my car and ease back onto the street. I'm not entirely sure I want Jason to come find me, and I'm not sure I want Wes to, either. But I do need sleep. And a shower. I could really use a shower.

Jason

Elena Reed is a missing person.

It's all here. Easy enough to find. Article after article. Pages and pages of search results.

Except, she didn't seem *missing* to me. She was shy, nervous, and yeah, she even seemed desperate, but nothing about her screamed *see me*. If anything, I'd have to say Elena Reed doesn't want to be seen.

So she ran ... Ran from someone or something.

I'm not going to lie, this isn't what I expected to find. I thought there would be something incriminating. Something that would shed some light as to why that timid girl would team up with my old man. But she's clean. No record. Not even a parking ticket.

Finding my dad's email, which promptly landed in my junk

mail folder, hasn't added any insight. He found Elena living in our family's cottage two months ago. Other than a picture of her taken outside the cottage confirming she was actually there, he gave me a link to a missing persons article and said: She's scared. Help her.

But Dad doesn't help anyone. Not without getting something in return. The bastard is probably using her fear. Using it against her? Using it against me?

Shit, I don't know.

It could be either. She seemed so genuine (even if she was freaking out) in the parking lot, as though she really was looking for my help. As though she truly was there about a job.

Picking up the missing persons report, I read it again …

Authorities Searching for 20-year-old Woman

NEW YORK, NY – The New York Police are searching for missing 20-year-old Elena Reed.

Reed was last seen by her fiancée on Thursday evening, July 25th, 2013, celebrating her twentieth birthday at Vilnius Grill in Brooklyn.

Description
Name: Elena Ann Reed
Age: 20-years-old
Racial Identification: White female
Height: 5ft 6
Weight: 130 pounds
Hair Color: Blonde
Eye Color: Blue

Further Identifying Information: Reed was last seen wearing a knee-length black dress, and was carrying a tan cloth purse. She has a flower tattoo on the lower part of her back.

Efforts have been ramped up in the past couple of days to try and locate Elena Reed. Her friends, family, and authorities have all been searching for her.

You are urged to share this article and information on any social media that you use to alert others to her disappearance.

Anyone with any information is urged to call 911, or if you have any information, you can submit an ANONYMOUS tip to Crime Stoppers.

I groan, rubbing my neck, and replace the article on the table, switching to the engagement announcement. It's dated two days prior to her disappearance. She's engaged to a cop, Officer Lawrence Peck. So why did she run? What happened that her cop fiancée couldn't protect her from? It doesn't make a whole lot of sense to me, unless it's the cop she's running from.

She's smiling in the photo, a small smile, not much different from the scared, timid one she gave me tonight.

And the cop, he's smiling, too. A big, wide smile, looking down at her as though she's a prize.

The best prize.

I drop the announcement and lean back, resting my head on the back of my chair. It's closing in on five in the morning. Almost six hours since she ran from the parking lot.

I feel terrible. Fucking terrible for yelling at her. When she mentioned his name, I figured my old man was up to his usual bullshit. I thought he sent her to clean me out, take back what he says is rightfully his. I thought ...

"Found her," Wes calls as he walks into the room. "She checked into The Broken Bottle Inn about five hours ago. Room sixteen."

"The Broken Bottle Inn," I echo, shaking my head. I'm too exhausted to even try to make sense out of why she'd get a room at that disgusting place. Pushing myself out of the chair, I stand up. "Let's go get her."

Wes gives me a look. "You can stay here."

"Not a chance," I say, waving a hand in the direction of the door. "Let's go."

Elena

The Broken Bottle Inn.

Out of all the places in Sacramento, I have no idea why I chose this one. Perhaps it's because it's cheap, or maybe it's because the parking lot is around the back, hiding my car from the street. I don't know.

What I do know is that I'm not sure I can sleep on the bed.

Sleep … Who am I trying to kid? Even if the sheets and mattress are clean, which is definitely questionable, the concept of closing my eyes and allowing myself to be vulnerable is not an idea I'm fond of right now.

I guess the place is still a step up from my car or my trusty tent, and the shower was amazing even if the water pressure was lacking, but …

The rooms are rented by the hour here. I found that out when the guy at the check-in desk advised me of both, the hourly and nightly rates. Then, when I told him I wanted a room for the night, he informed me it would be fifteen minutes before one would be free. That's one of the reasons why I question the cleanliness of the bed; the other is the large stain in the center of the worn out comforter. I think it may have been blue once, but it looks more gray now than blue.

But like I said, it's cheap and since I have exactly three-hundred twenty-eight dollars and nineteen cents left, I figure cheap, even if it means sleeping on the floor or in the bathtub, is still better than my car. A car both Jason and Wesley saw me drive away in.

I'm sitting on the floor in between the large picture window and the door, my back pressed against the wall. It's seven minutes after five. Six full hours since I ran from Jason, and aside from the shower, all I've done is sit here, constantly lifting the drab brown curtain, peeking out the corner as I attempt to figure out what the hell I'm supposed to do now.

I can't stay here. Can't stay in Sacramento. Not when I was stupid enough to give Jason my name. My real name. Not that I have a fake one, but I probably should have made one up.

But, good God, he was angry, and that anger mixed with concern; it was flustering. Confusing. For a moment there, I swear my brain just shorted out.

And besides that, he was supposed to already know who I am.

I shouldn't have trusted Mr. Chapman. I know that. But there is just something so kind about him even if he is a little sad. I really thought he wanted to help me. Hell, the man let me stay with him and fed me for two months before he managed to convince me to come here. Who does that if they don't really want to help?

I guess this is just another mistake to add to the long list of mistakes I've made. There's no point in self-pity. No point in regret. The two are lonely companions in this life and they lead you nowhere but to further regret and self-pity.

Maybe I should try to change my name again. I tried to do it once. It was nine months ago. I found a guy who promised to get me new identification and layout a paper trail for that new identity. I spent every dime I had for it. Every single penny.

I thought it was a good investment. With a new identity, I could get a job. I could replace the money, get a place to live.

It didn't quite work out that way, though. The guy took my money and then took off.

Closing my eyes, I take a deep, calming breath that does nothing to soothe my jittery nerves.

"Yo, Elena," a male voice calls out, followed by three swift knocks against the door. "Open up, babe, food's gonna get cold."

I yelp in surprise and my hands fly up to my mouth in a pointless effort to staunch the sound. It takes a second or two to place the voice, and another two seconds for the surprise to ebb, replaced by a sense of foolishness.

Of course they'd come find me. Mr. Chapman told me that. He told me to find a place to sleep, told me to wait. And Jesus, that's exactly what I did.

Does that make me completely crazy?

Yes, it probably does.

"Wesley, is that you?" I call out. The question is pointless. I recognize the voice. I know it's him. The words do nothing more than confirm that I am, in fact, here.

"Yeah," he says. "It's me."

I shift to my knees and push the curtain aside. There he is, dressed in blue jeans and a light blue tee, the same things he was wearing at the bar. He has a ball cap on, his light brown hair flipping up around the sides. He seems taller, all around bigger, although that could be because I'm kneeling.

I look around, scanning the street in front of the inn and the sidewalk. He's alone, or at least I can't see Jason lurking anywhere. I'm not sure if I'm relieved or disappointed about that.

I look back to Wes. His green eyes are warm, smiling, as he holds up a brown paper bag and a cardboard carry tray with two large coffees.

"You gonna open up?" he asks.

His voice is muffled, distorted through the thick glass. I reach down, cracking the small sliding portion of the window open, only half an inch, before I answer, shaking my head, "Probably not, no."

He laughs, clearly amused. "You can let me in or I can pick the lock," he says. "I'm coming in either way. We gotta talk and I ain't gonna do it through a window."

I hesitate. I don't know this guy. I don't know anything more than what Mr. Chapman told me. Wes is the nice one (supposedly). But since I'm thinking I should have never trusted Mr. Chapman in the first place ...

I can tell Wes is getting impatient, the smile fading from his eyes, and dropping from his lips. He doesn't look mad, though. Not at all. If anything, he almost looks like he expected this. He jerks his chin toward the door. "Does that door have one of those chain locks?"

Really? He tells me he's going to pick the lock if I don't

open the door and now he expects me to tell him what other security features the door has?

"Why would I tell you that?" I ask, narrowing my eyes.

"Just answer the question, babe."

His tone isn't really sharp, but it's most definitely not amused. I roll to my feet, my gaze locking on to the chain, which I secured the second I closed the door. I wonder if it would stop him. It looks flimsy and the bolts are loose.

Sighing heavily, I look back to Wes. "Yes, there's a chain lock."

"Good," he says. He balances the paper bag on top of the coffee cups, and reaches around to his back, pulling out a Taser and a cartridge. "I want you to put it in place, unlock the door, and stand back. I'm going to open the door just enough to slide this Taser and cartridge in. You know how to use one of these?"

I shake my head in disbelief. "Yes, but why … why would you do that?"

"Because I wanna have a chat with you and you don't trust me," he replies as though the answer should be obvious. "I figure this might make you feel a bit safer."

My first instinct is to refuse, but I'm thrown off by his offer. Besides, something tells me that he isn't kidding about picking the lock. I suspect that he'll walk in here no matter what I say, and he's right; having a Taser will make me feel safer.

Taking a deep breath, I close my eyes for a second.

Good God, I hope I don't regret this.

Chapter Four

Elena

Wesley hasn't said a word since I let him in. It's only been a few minutes. Five ... six at the most, and he just stands there, leaning against the wall, watching me as he eats an egg and bacon breakfast sandwich. He looks relaxed, paying no attention to the Taser I have trained on him.

I'm sitting on top of a desk across from him, a coffee on the surface beside me. Somehow, I'm even more nervous with the Taser. The small laser dot jumps around his chest as I try to hold it still and eat the egg and bacon breakfast sandwich that he brought for me.

There's something so ... unsettling about seeing him this relaxed. My finger shakes over the trigger. He sees it, I know he does, but he doesn't react. It doesn't ruffle him at all.

I can't imagine Peck being this calm. But then, Peck would have never given me the security of a Taser.

Peck likes control.

Peck likes intimidation.

Peck likes ...

"So ..." Wes says, dragging the word out as he rubs a hand over his chin. He glances around the room, his lips curling in a grimace as his eyes settle on the bed. "Please tell me you didn't actually sleep on that bed."

I don't want to laugh. Really, I don't. I don't want to lose any of the tension between us. Losing that would no doubt lead to me lowering my guard. But it happens no matter how hard I try to swallow it down. I laugh at his question, feeling some of my anxiety ease out of me.

"Uh, no," I say laughing again. "Actually, I didn't sleep at all."

His perfectly straight teeth flash as he smiles. "Me neither."

"Up all night digging up the dirt on me?" I ask, feeling steadier, less shaky, at the sight of his easy smile. It's warm, concerned, even caring. The tremors in my trigger finger recede and my hand stops vibrating with nerves.

"Something like that," he says.

"Find anything good?" I inquire, feigning disinterest. Truly, I want to know everything. What he found, and more so, what he didn't. I shift on top of the worn desk, uncrossing my legs only to cross them again.

His light green eyes crinkle as his smile grows and he cocks a brow in question. "Is there something good to find?"

I pop the last bit of my sandwich into my mouth, chewing slowly, stalling. I know he had to have found something. If not, then he's a horrible private investigator. I've done a few searches myself since I left New York, and the internet is filled with results on my disappearance. So I can only guess that he's fishing, hoping I'll slip up and enlighten him with the details that cannot be found. The details that nobody knows but Peck and me.

I swallow down the food and take a long sip of coffee. "Where'd you get the breakfast?" I ask, shifting the subject. "This is the best egg and bacon sandwich I've had in a long time."

He sighs and his smile fades with disappointment. I'm not quite sure what he expected from me. Last night at the bar was an epic fail. He can't really expect me to be forthcoming, can he?

"Sunnyside Eatery," he answers, the disappointment from his expression seeping into his tone. "It's about five minutes down the street. I'll take you there sometime."

His gaze drops from mine to my hand, resting in my lap. It's just a quick look, down then back up, but I catch it, follow it, and I realize that the Taser is in my lap as well.

Good God, I didn't even notice I'd put it down.

"Thanks," I say quickly, flustered, bringing the Taser back up, aiming it at his chest. "But I'm heading out soon."

The words sound like a lie. Saying them out loud doesn't add another layer of concrete to the idea of leaving like I thought it would. Instead, the lie acts like a sledgehammer smashing through the layers I've already laid out.

I swallow thickly; a lump in my throat makes the action almost painful. It took me a year to take this step, to find help. Am I really going to walk away from it just because Jason is intimidating and a little scary?

"About that ..." Wes pushes away from the wall and steps toward the small garbage can in the corner by the window, tossing his wrapper in. "I'm not sure I can let you run off just yet."

"I don't think you really have much say in that," I say, waving the Taser around.

He glances between the Taser and me, and for a second I think I see amusement flicker in his eyes before the disappointment settles back in place. "No, I guess not," he says quietly. "But I'm asking you to stick around for a little while."

"Why?"

He watches me, his eyes scanning my face as a sad smile lifts the corners of his lips. "Because I think you want to," he says. "I think you need to. I think you're sick of running."

I'm taken aback. I'm not sure why hearing him say it makes me freeze for a second. He's right. I'm sick to death of running. Staying here, well, not *here* exactly because this inn is disgusting, but in this town, in one place even if it's only for a little while is exactly what I want.

But I don't tell him that.

"You don't know me," I say, carefully keeping my tone nonchalant. "You don't know what I want or need, and you have no idea what I'm sick of."

"No, maybe not," he says seriously. "But I'd like to know it all. So would Jase."

I shrug noncommittally. I'm not sure how to respond to that. If Jason wanted to know me, I'm pretty sure he'd be here, not Wes. He didn't strike me as a sitting on the sidelines kind of guy.

Wes sees my shrug, takes it in, and leans back against the wall. He sighs. "Something you should probably know is that Jason and his dad don't talk. They haven't spoken in five years."

"Okay," I say slowly, confused. "Why exactly do I need to know this?"

His brow furrows, his gaze filling with question. "Because he didn't listen to the voicemail and the email went to his junk mail. Jase doesn't acknowledge any attempt his dad makes to contact him." He speaks slowly as though he believes I already know this, and the fact that I don't is perplexing to him.

He pauses for a moment, letting his words sink in. And when they do, when my slow, tired brain starts to piece it together, I don't say anything. My mouth falls open. Mr. Chapman is Jason Pierce's father?

"So that's why Jase didn't have a clue who you were," he adds, and then pauses again, giving me more time to absorb his words.

I just keep gaping.

He continues, "The last time that asshole sent someone to *meet* Jase, it wasn't because that someone was looking for a private investigator."

"What were they looking for?" I ask meekly, dreading the answer.

He shakes his head and lets out a loud, frustrated breath. "That's Jase's story to tell. I just thought you should know that he had a reason for being an ass, and he feels like shit about it."

"He was an asshole before I mentioned his father's name," I point out.

Wes chuckles and cocks a brow. I can feel my face flushing. He doesn't have to say it. I know what he's thinking. I wasn't a welcoming ray of sunshine either.

I laugh once, stamping down the unwelcome bloom of embarrassment. "Where is Jason anyway?"

Jason

Twenty-eight minutes.

I don't have a fucking clue how I ended up sitting in the car waiting outside The Broken Bottle Inn for twenty-eight goddamn minutes.

Actually, that's not entirely true. I know exactly how I ended up here; I'm just not too sure as to why I agreed to wait here or why I'm still sitting in the car.

Somewhere in between getting Elena coffee and food and pulling up to the curb outside the rundown building, Wes got me to agree to wait in the car. At first, I thought it was probably smart. She's already run from me twice in the last seven or so hours, once in the bar, once in the parking lot. There's really nothing to gain from scaring her into running again, especially if that means she'd be running back to my old man.

Fucking disaster. That's exactly what that would be.

Then I'd have to follow her, because there's no way I could let my father ruin someone like her. She's too sweet, too naïve, to get messed up with his bullshit. And after hunting her down, I'd run the risk of seeing the man himself.

But it dawns on me ... If she were really trying to run from me, she probably wouldn't have stayed in Sacramento. She would have hit the road, driven as fast and as far as she could.

And that brings me back to the desperation I sensed in her. It was there, living, breathing; pushing her to walk up to me, a stranger, after running for a year. Even if my old man is using it against her to get to me, it's still there, glaringly clear. The girl needs help.

Which leads me to believe that she wasn't running from me exactly, just the situation.

I drum my fingers on the dashboard.

Thirty minutes.

The sun is just starting to rise, lightening the sky, and I'm tired, exhausted, and downright miserable. I haven't had a wink of sleep in twenty-four hours. I can't even begin to guess what's taking Wes so long to collect Elena. She can't possibly want to stay in this shithole, can she?

I sigh, exasperated, as I run my hands down my face and close my eyes. Who knows what kind of places she's been staying in for the last year. The cottage isn't bad, but it's far from luxurious. And there were months before she found her way there. Months of God knows what. For all I know, The Broken Bottle Inn is a step up from the other places she's hidden away in.

I swallow back the sickening twist in my gut. My skin prickles, and the coiling in my stomach wraps up tighter. The only reason she's in there now is me.

I won't let her stay in a place like this.

I can't let her stay here.

Goddamnit! Why am I still sitting in the car?

I pop the door open, and fold out of the car. Jamming my hands in my pockets, I cross the weed-ridden lawn, scanning the inn. It's L-shaped, with the office in the center and a line of rooms on either side. Most of the windows on the left side are boarded up, the glass broken and never replaced. The trim around them, rotting or gone all together. A fresh coat of paint wouldn't be enough to revive the exterior. The place should have been torn down years ago. The only thing in good repair is the lit up sign.

The door to room sixteen is hanging open about a foot. Wes trying to make her feel comfortable, I guess.

I pause outside the door, listening to Wes chuckle, and then Elena asks, "Where is Jason anyway?"

Her voice is annoyed, bordering on angry.

I don't wait for Wes to respond. I reach out and grasp the door handle, pulling it open.

As soon as the door is fully open, I realize my mistake. I should have knocked. I should have called out.

Elena screeches and her hand leaps up. I barely process the fact that she has a Taser before she pulls the trigger.

Pain, hot white pain, hits my chest and my body seizes. I go down, landing hard in the doorway. My muscles twitching, contracting, screaming.

Thirty seconds—it only lasts thirty seconds—but it feels like a goddamn lifetime.

Chapter Five

Elena

Oh my God.

Oh my God.

I didn't. I couldn't have. No. No, no, no.

Holy crap, I did. I just shot Jason Pierce in the chest with a Taser.

My eyes bug wide open as I watch Jason fall. "Oh my God," I say out loud, dropping the incriminating device. It tumbles to the carpet, the thump sounding louder in my ears than possible.

Wes is laughing. Not the small, amused chuckle from before, but a loud howl of a laugh. He laughs as though it's the funniest thing he's ever seen.

My cheeks flame, my heart races. Clicking fills the air, each one sending another shock into Jason. A small grunt of pain escapes from his lips, but he doesn't move, frozen in place as the shocks keep coming.

I can't look away. I want to. I want to get up and go to him, but I can't. All I can do is watch.

Thirty seconds. Thirty excruciatingly long seconds tick by before the awful clicking stops.

Jason lets out a loud breath, and slowly pushes himself back to his feet. He glowers, first at me, and then at Wes.

Wes doesn't seem bothered by the furious glint in Jason's

eyes. He only laughs some more and says, "Told you to wait in the car."

"You didn't tell me you were giving her a fuckin' Taser," Jason grumbles.

Glancing down at his chest, his jaw clenches as he looks at the barbs and wires. He takes hold of one of the barbs, wincing as he yanks it out, and then does the same with the other.

I want to say something, anything, but I'm mute. Stunned silent. Good God, I can't believe I did that. Why the hell did Wes give me a Taser?

Minutes pass. Long drawn out minutes of Wes chuckling and Jason scowling down at the barbs and wires clutched in his hand.

Finally letting the wires fall to the floor, Jason asks, "You two about done in here?"

He doesn't look up as he speaks. I think I should probably be thankful for that. His tone carries an undercurrent of hostility and the sound is more than enough to freak me out, without seeing it mirrored in his eyes, but still, I wish he would look at me.

"I'm sorry," I blurt, ignoring his question. "I'm really, really so sorry. You startled me and I …"

Jason's gaze snaps to mine, freezing me mid-sentence. He lowers his chin, glaring at me. His hands open and close by his thighs. "It's fine. Forget it ever happened."

It's not fine, though. I can see the annoyance lurking in his eyes. I can feel his tension radiating through the room.

"Don't think I'll forget that," Wes says, grinning wide. "Shit, I wish I took a picture. Fuckin' priceless."

Jason cuts a dirty look at Wes, before returning his heated gaze to me. It's uncomfortable, invasive. It sears through me, seeing too much, and at the same time, not enough. There's a question there. I can see it burning in his eyes, but I have no idea what he's looking for. It pins me in place. Has me dreading to hear the question and dying to answer it.

He sighs, shaking his head, as though banishing whatever thoughts were invading him only moments before.

"Let's go," he says, waving a hand toward the door. "You're not staying here."

My spine snaps straight but other than that, I don't move. I don't even breathe. Has he lost his ever-loving mind? I just shot him with a Taser and he's obviously pissed about it. Why in the world would he think I'd go anywhere with him right now?

Leaning back ever so slightly and sucking in a deep breath, I shake my head.

Jason closes the distance between us in a few short steps, still glowering, his dark eyes burning right through me. He looks as though he wants to throttle me.

He stops right in front of me, and with gentle fingertips that I do not expect given the fiery look in his gaze, he reaches out and tucks a loose piece of hair behind my ear.

It's just like the parking lot. Anger and gentleness. A confusing mixture that twists up my stomach with a mix of hot and cold. The man is a walking contradiction.

I flinch, or jolt. I'm not quite sure which one. Whatever it is, it happens before I can stop it.

Jason's face falls along with his hand. He stands there for a moment, jaw clenching and unclenching, before he huffs, and bends down to retrieve the Taser.

"I must be out of my goddamn mind," he mutters under his breath, before turning to Wes. "You got another cartridge?"

Wes nods and digs a hand into his pocket, retrieving a new cartridge and placing it in Jason's outstretched hand. He's still grinning, although he's pressing his lips together in an effort to hide it.

Jason huffs and rolls his eyes. "Give us a minute, yeah?"

Wes's smile dies a little. He stares at Jason, and I get the funny feeling that there's some silent conversation, or battle of wills going on between them.

Jason must have won because suddenly Wes's smile comes back. He glances at me, winks, and then, darn him, he walks out the door.

My stomach flips over. What? No! No, no, no. Pleas for

Wes not to go tingle my tongue, but I don't let them out, because Jason is staring right at me as though he knows exactly what I'm thinking.

As soon as Wes is gone, he smirks and starts fiddling with the Taser.

My heart revolts in my chest as I watch, stunned and unblinking, as Jason ejects the used cartridge and replaces it with a fresh one. For a second, I have this ludicrous idea that he's going to shoot me with it. An eye for an eye and all that jazz.

It is ludicrous, right?

Then, he shocks the hell out of me by placing the Taser in my hand and closes my fingers around the handle.

"What are you doing?" I ask. "I just shot you with this."

"I know," he says, his smirk growing, "and I'm really hoping you won't do it again."

I'm flabbergasted. I almost wish he'd shoot me with it. Almost. I think that would be easier to deal with than the trust he's giving me.

I want to drop the device, throw it far away so there's no possibility that I could shoot him, or anyone with it again, but he doesn't let me. He keeps the pressure on my fingers, forcing me to accept his trust. Trust that I've done nothing to earn.

"I'm gonna help you, darlin'," he says quietly. "Whatever you're fighting so hard to hide from, I'm gonna do everything I can to fix it."

My heart races with his declaration. "Why?" I ask, my voice coming out breathless. "Why now?"

My skin tingles with awareness as his eyes rake over me. His face holds the most open expression I've ever seen. It's confusion and anger. Heat and frustration. Coolness and attraction. It's contradicting. It's confusing. Every speck of emotion he's feeling shines through. It's too much. It makes me blush, makes me glance away.

He reaches out, sliding his hand to the back of my neck and pressing his thumb on the underside of my jaw, and lifts my chin back up to meet his eyes again. "It's what I should have said when you first walked up to me."

I don't know if it's the tone of his voice, or the sheer determination glinting in his eyes, but I believe him. Call me stupid or crazy or whatever, but I believe every word.

And he sees it, that moment of belief and trust. He sees it and smiles, a tired twitch at the corners of his mouth.

"Let's go, yeah?" he says. "I'm fuckin' exhausted and you look like you could use some sleep, too."

His fingers linger on my neck. The soft touch is a direct contrast to the rough, calloused tips. I stare at him, taking in his sleep deprived, red-veined eyes, the tired lines around his mouth, and the slight droop to his shoulders.

Slipping off the desk and out of his grasp, I say, "Okay. Let's go."

And so I go. I follow Jason to the office as he returns my room key. I trail along as he stalks out, and I don't utter a single protest as Wes takes my keys and tells me he'll follow us in my car, or when Jason throws open the passenger side door of his car and waves a hand for me to get in.

I just go along.

Not because I have to. Not because I'm tired or because I feel threatened, or even because he gave me the Taser.

I do it because I want to. Because at one time, I might have been okay with running. I might have thought it was a good way to protect myself, my family, and my friends from Officer Lawrence Peck.

But the last year has strengthened me. I'm no longer ready or willing to go down without a fight.

Chapter Six

Jason

I'm not an impulsive person. I never have been. I think things out, scrutinizing every possible consequence, positive or negative, that could come from any given action.

But this ... I didn't think this out.

I let my goddamn emotions drive me.

First, it was anger. As soon as I heard my old man's name, I didn't think. I reacted. Can't say that it was one of my finer moments, but it happened. I lost my temper, acted rashly and harshly.

Then I found out Elena was on the run, and that was it. Everything shifted. I let ... Sympathy? Concern? Protectiveness? I don't even know. Maybe it was a bit of all of it. Maybe it was something else entirely. But whatever it was, I let the emotions drive me forward. I didn't think any further than collecting her. And I most definitely didn't think about what I would do with her once I had her with me.

But here we are now, sitting at the curb, waiting for Wes to bring her car around. I'm curious as to why Elena gave up her keys so easily and got into my car. She may have started the night by seeking me out, but then ran from me twice and shot me with a fucking Taser. Honestly, I figured she'd fight me, at least a little, when I came to get her.

I do have a few thoughts on why she didn't fight me, though. It could be because she has nowhere else to go, or maybe she thinks I'll just keep hunting her down if she runs from me again.

But I worry that her reasoning isn't so simple. What if she's gotten herself snagged up too thickly with my old man and if she doesn't help him with whatever plan he's working on now, then she thinks she'll find herself running from two men instead of one.

I should probably be concerned about her ties with my old man. It complicates things. Makes helping her harder, messier.

Except, I'm not worried.

Instead, I find the whole situation really fucking amusing. Especially the part about her shooting me with a Taser. And what do I do after that? Reload the damn thing and give it back to her.

Maybe it's exhaustion.

Or maybe I'm out of my goddamn mind.

Elena is quiet in the seat beside me. I'm not sure what to make of that. She hasn't asked where we're going, or given any indication that she cares for that matter. She seems relaxed enough. She seems comfortable.

I glance over at her. Her head is tilted down and her blonde hair, now hanging in loose waves, hides her face. I think she's staring at the Taser, which sits on her lap. She's not touching it, her hands are pressed palms down on the top of her thighs, framing the damn thing.

She must feel my gaze, because after a moment she slowly looks up. She smiles, that timid smile of hers, and reaches for the center console, opens it, and carefully places the Taser inside, before closing it again. She doesn't say anything about it, just shrugs, and turns from me, staring out the side window.

I almost tell her to keep it. Almost. If it'll make her give me a real smile instead of that timid, unsure one, I think I'd be fine with her shooting me with it again.

My insides instinctively tense at the thought of her doing it, and just like that, all of the amusement I was feeling seconds ago is gone.

Jesus fucking Christ, I need to get my head checked. And a drink. I really need a drink.

Not having a clue what to say to her, I rub my face roughly, and turn my gaze back to the rearview mirror.

Strained silence chokes the car.

And it stretches.

And stretches.

And stretches.

A few minutes pass—five, maybe less—before I spot Wes pulling up behind us. I blow out a frustrated breath, shift my car into gear, and ease out onto the street.

"You made a pretty big commitment back there," she says as we start moving, her voice low and cautious, as though maybe she's just waiting for me to take it back.

I don't respond right away. What can I say? She's right. It's a big commitment, especially when I only have a small glimpse of her problems.

I let out a heavy sigh. "Yeah. I guess I did."

From the corner of my eye, I see her turn to look at me. Her lips are pursed and her brow dipped. "Don't you think you should know what I'm running from before you make promises like that?"

I shake my head. Yeah, it probably would have been smart to confirm my hunch first. I can't believe that I didn't. But, Jesus, the way she looked at me when I gave her the Taser back. Eyes so wide, filled with shock and awe. It's the kind of look that could make a man do incredibly stupid things.

I pull in a deep breath and let it out slowly. "You're running from your fiancée, the cop."

She laughs to herself, turning back to the window. "You found the engagement announcement."

It's not a question, but I respond anyway. "I did. Found a few other things, too. You were a history major at NYC. Your parents own a small bakery in Brooklyn. You've got a brother ..."

Letting my voice trail off, I glance at her quickly, gauging her reaction. Her expression is blank, but she nods. The action seems to be more to herself, as though she's accepting what I've found, understanding that I've been looking into her over the last few hours, and not necessarily confirming my statements.

Eyeing me warily, she asks, "How did you figure out it's him I'm running from?"

"I didn't," I say, shaking my head. "It was a guess."

"Good guess."

I can hear the anger in her voice, and it makes me pause. I gaze at her curiously for a second, wondering if the emotion is directed at me or if it stems from the topic.

I consider dropping it, but what the hell? I need to know more about her, and I figure she's got to know that, so I push on.

"How long were you with him?"

"Uh …" Her brow furrows and she hesitates, pulling a hand through her hair. "Four months."

"Quick engagement."

"Yeah," she says. "It was."

Her short answers make me stumble. "You know you're gonna have to talk to me, yeah? Can't help you if I don't know what I'm dealing with here."

The color drains from her face, and she shifts in her seat nervously.

"I can't pay you," she whispers. "I mean I can, when it's over. When I can get back home again."

"I ain't doing this for money, darlin'," I admit, surprising myself by how much I mean those words.

She gives me that look again. Shock and awe. Like I'm some kind of superhero. "Then why are you?"

I can't help but laugh. "I haven't really thought any of this out, but when I figure it out, I'll let you know."

Elena

I blink and blink again. He's not doing this for money. He hasn't thought this out. His confessions leave me at a loss.

The air in the car is charged with a nervous energy and scented with his rich, woodsy cologne. My heart is pounding, keeping my exhaustion at bay.

A part of me can't believe that this is even happening, that he's really going to help me just because he wants to. It feels unreal, like a dream, and at any moment, I'm going to wake up and find myself shivering and alone in my tent somewhere.

"I hope you still feel that way after you think this out," I whisper.

A muscle jumps in his jaw and he reaches over, taking my hand in his. He squeezes, just a light, reassuring squeeze, and although he doesn't say a word, that squeeze says enough.

A feeling hits me, a really good one. It quivers through me, spreading over my skin in a burst of warmth, and I squeeze back, a silent thank you.

I expect him to let go, but he doesn't. Instead, he rests our joined hands on my thigh. I feel the pad of his thumb stroking up and down my wrist. I can't explain it, but the lazy swoop of his thumb causes a whole new shuddery-shivery feeling to tear through me like a shot of adrenaline.

I look down at our clasped hands, and my entire body focuses on the spots where we're touching. His hand is warm, rough, calloused, engulfing mine, and his thumb continues its lazy trail along the sensitive skin, heating it, licking like flames.

"Um … Where are we going?" I ask a little breathlessly.

His head angles my way while still keeping his partial gaze on the road. One of his incredible dimples shows with his smile. "My place for now," he says, in a deep, toe-curling voice. His smile slowly fades and his gaze warms. "We can figure the next step out after we get some sleep, yeah?"

My breath catches. His place. We're going to his place. My heart pounds faster as I sit motionless in my seat, my body hyperaware of his closeness. I can feel his gaze watching me and I get the feeling that he doesn't miss much that goes on around him.

My cheeks flush, and I quickly bob my head up and down. "Okay."

Ugh, my voice sounds squeaky and raw. I cringe. This is ridiculous. I'm being ridiculous. He is not *taking* me home. He's just giving me a place to crash for the day. That's it.

Jason doesn't miss the squeak in my voice. He probably doesn't miss my flaming cheeks, either. His lips are pressed together in a firm line, but I can see the dimples again. And his shoulders are shaking with silent laughter.

My cheeks flush hotter. I'm mortified. I feel like a total fool, sitting here, while he fights to suppress his amusement at my reaction. I start to pull my hand from his, but he doesn't let me.

"Maybe you should have kept that Taser," he says on a chuckle.

"Yeah," I say, laughing at myself. "Maybe I should have."

It takes us another ten minutes to reach his house. I spend the time staring out the window, trying and failing to not think about what happened over the last several hours.

By the time he pulls into a driveway, my nervous energy is gone and all I feel is drained. Physically and emotionally drained.

Jason pulls his car right up to the two-car garage, slips it into park, and turns off the engine. He gives my hand another light squeeze before letting it go, and he folds himself out.

He doesn't give me a chance to hesitate, coming around the car and opening my door. He holds out a hand and I take it, climbing out.

As soon as I do, I catch sight of Wes shutting my car door. He walks past us, barely even looking our way as he tosses my keys to Jason and grumbles something about needing sleep and the couch, before disappearing into the house.

"You want anything from your car?" Jason asks, already walking toward it.

I shiver. I'm not sure if it's from overtiredness or the fact that I'm about to sleep in Jason Pierce's house. A man who in the last few hours has made my heart pound and my skin flush for several different reasons, and not all of them pleasant.

My heart starts pounding so hard that I'm scared he can hear it.

"Um, yeah, my bag and I ..." I stall for a second, hesitating, and drop my eyes to the ground. "I have a tent so I can just set it up in your backyard. I mean, if that's okay. I don't want to be a problem."

Jason laughs and his dimples come out in full force. "You're not sleeping in a tent, darlin'."

"It's ... it's really not a problem," I say, stammering a bit. "I've camped out a lot over the last year."

He shakes his head and laughs again. "You'll stay in my guest room."

Before I can object any further, he's at my car, pulling out my bag. Then, he's back beside me, taking my hand and leading me into the house.

The two-story house is large. He tugs me along, pointing out the kitchen, living room, and bathroom. My eyes scan the rooms as I pass them by, but other than the fact that there's furniture and Wes is sprawled out on a couch in the living room, my brain isn't taking in much.

We reach a set of stairs and he pulls me up. At the top, Jason points out another bathroom, and leads me down a hall, stopping at the second door on the right. He pushes it open, and sets my bag inside.

"I'm at the end of the hall," he says, pointing to a set of double doors. "You need anything, come get me, yeah?"

"Okay," I say with a small nod. "Thank you. Really, thank you for this."

"Don't mention it, darlin'," he says softly, smiling warmly at me, before he turns around and starts down the hall toward his room.

I stare after him for a moment, pondering the change in him from our meeting at the bar to the parking lot to now. I'm suddenly regretting not saying anything to him about Mr. Chapman, and before I can stop myself, I call out, "Um, Jason." He stops moving, glancing over his shoulder at me and giving me a chin lift. "I just wanted you to know that I didn't know Mr. Chapman was your dad."

Jason turns back to me and regards me for a moment, a hard

look coming into his eyes. "Huh."

"Huh," I echo, furrowing my brow. "What does that mean?"

He shrugs. "I can't tell if you're lying to me about that." And then he turns away, leaving me alone in the hallway.

I stand there for a moment, staring at his closed bedroom door, feeling slightly lost. The house is quiet. So quiet that I can hear the rustle of Jason's clothing through the door as he strips, most likely getting ready for bed, and the soft snores coming from Wes downstairs.

It strikes me then that Mr. Chapman, though he had a crappy way of going about it, delivered exactly what he said he would.

I'm with Jason Pierce.

He's going to take my case.

I'm going to get home.

Smiling, I step into the bedroom and close the door. I go to lock it only to find that there's no lock.

My stomach sinks and twists.

Glancing around the room, I spot the large window and I rush over to it, pulling the curtains aside.

No lock.

There are no locks in this room.

How am I supposed to protect myself without any locks? What if Peck finds me?

I look out the window. I'm on the second floor. He'd need a ladder to get in. That would make noise, right? It would wake everyone up, right?

That's when it hits me. I'm alone in a house with two men that I don't know. Two men who could easily call the police and turn me over.

Oh God.

I pull in a sharp breath, let it out, take another.

What am I doing here?

Okay.

Okay, okay, okay. Calm down. Just breathe. Think about this logically. If Mr. Chapman wanted to screw me over, he would have done it already. He wouldn't have kept me safe and fed me for two months.

And he wouldn't send me to people who would turn me over to Peck.

He would have done it himself already.

And Jason … he wouldn't have brought me to his home if he were just going to call the cops. No, he would have taken me to the police station.

My head races, so does my heart. Maybe Jason was right. I should have kept the Taser.

I glance back at the door, considering if I should retrieve it.

Okay, stop. I need to stop. The front door is locked. The window is too high up for someone to climb in unnoticed.

I'm safe here.

I'm safe.

I close my eyes, willing my heart to slow, and when I reopen them, I feel slightly better.

And exhausted.

Padding over to my bag, I get ready for bed, forcing myself not to think. If I just don't think about it, perhaps I can sleep. Sleep will help. Sleep always helps to put things in perspective.

Right. What I need is sleep.

Leaving the light on, I climb into bed. My muscles relax instantaneously as they sink into the soft mattress, my weary body urging me to close my eyes.

I let them drift close, reminding myself that I'm safe here. I'm safe. I'm safe.

Chapter Seven

Jason

Vance is trying not to laugh.

Wes stopped trying not to laugh twenty minutes ago.

I'm trying not to punch them both in the face.

Wes and Vance are sitting at the table, Wes with a coffee in his hands, and Vance with a beer. I'm standing over the stove, flipping strips of bacon while listening to Wes fill Vance in on the Elena situation.

I love my partners. They're like brothers to me. But the more I listen, the tighter the knot in my gut coils. If I have to hear either of them say Richard Chapman's name one more time …

Jesus, I'm a fucking mess.

I feel pulled, twisted, knotted, and utterly useless.

I've got a beautiful girl upstairs, who's technically engaged. Who's on the run from said fiancée. Who looks at me as though I'm her personal superhero. And she was sent to me by my asshole of a father.

I don't know if she's really here for my help, or if she's here for my old man. I just don't know. Why the fuck would he send her? Her. Someone who so obviously needs help.

Because you won't say no.

Goddamnit. Why'd she have to bring him up this morning?

Another loud burst of laughter fills the room, and I spin around, glaring. "Keep it the fuck down. She's still sleeping."

Wes stops laughing and grimaces, glancing at the stairs. "Shit, right, sorry."

Running a hand down my face, I groan, as a sudden quietness settles over the room.

I don't even know what to say.

I need to take this case. *Need to.* And I want their votes on it. I want them in.

We've never taken a case without everyone voting in.

We're not just partners, we're a team.

And if they think I'm losing my shit over this, I know damn well they'll back out and try to shut it down.

"So, your old man sent her," Vance says eventually, his tone bland and unamused. He leans back in his chair, stares at me for a moment, shifts his gaze to the stove, and then back to me. "And now you're cooking for her."

"Yeah," I mutter. "That's right."

Vance shakes his head, an apprehensive smile playing at his lips. "I don't know what to say about that, Jase."

I chuckle, but it's without humor. "Say whatever you're thinking," I tell him. "We both know you have an opinion. You always fuckin' do."

Vance answers me with a worried silence. He seems taken aback and is trying to make sure I'm serious. He studies my face, and I can tell he's looking for some kind of crack. Something to tell him that my head isn't where it should be.

I wait quietly, so does Wes.

After a moment, Vance sighs and slowly nods, "Fine. I think sending a girl who's on the run from her cop fiancée, knowing damn well you won't turn her away, is pretty fuckin' smart."

"She didn't know the relationship between them," Wes says, shaking his head.

"Huh." I rest my hip against the counter. "She said as much to me this morning, but something was off. Couldn't tell if she was lying or not."

"I'm telling you," Wes says, "she didn't know." He stares at me pointedly, eyes narrowed in challenge.

I don't know what to say. I don't even know what to think.

I want to believe him.

I really do.

Taking a deep breath, I look up at the ceiling, asking myself why this shit with my old man is getting under my skin like it is. It shouldn't. It's been five years since I cut ties with him. Five goddamn years of him sending people to poke around in my business. I should be used to it by now. But never, *never,* has he sent someone like her.

"Whether she knows about the relationship or not doesn't change the fact that she could be here for the photos," Vance says. I watch him take a sip of his beer, his movement casual, but his eyes intense. "He could be promising her the same help you are in exchange for those photos. Can't see any other reason why he'd help her. It'd be stupid to ignore that."

"I'm not ignoring it," I say. "But I'm not gonna let him jerk her around like that, either. You two can back me on this, or not. Doesn't matter. I promised her my help and I'm gonna give it to her."

Silence.

We survey each other.

I can see the shock in their eyes, maybe a little doubt, even. I've never considered taking a job without them. But this isn't just a job. It's personal.

I turn back to the bacon, flipping the pieces again, before going to the fridge to retrieve the eggs. Deciding to do scrambled simply for ease, I grab a bowl and start cracking eggs over the edge.

"Shit, I can't believe I'm agreeing to this," Vance mutters, cutting through the silence. "Okay, why'd she run?"

I spin back around, glancing at Vance, then Wes, and then back to Vance. Despite myself, I grin. I have their votes.

"Don't know," I say with a shrug.

Vance's eyebrows go up and his tone turns from questioning to exasperated, as he grumbles, "Right, so you don't know if it's something the fiancée did, or something she did."

"If it were something she did, there'd be a warrant and not a missing persons report," I say.

"Unless she decided to run before he found out whatever it is she did," Wes points out.

I scoff. "You met her. You can't tell me you think she's the lawbreaker type."

He's quiet for a moment, contemplative, as he looks at me. "Your old man never struck me as the dirty cop type, either."

Elena

My eyes drift open slowly and I blink a few times, clearing the sleepy haze from my vision. The bedroom light is still on, despite the daylight that is pouring into the room. I don't know if it's late afternoon, or perhaps it's early. I'm not really sure. I feel as though I've slept for days. My muscles are stiff and sore, my arms and legs heavy, and a slight headache pinches behind my eyes.

I glance around the room, searching for a clock. There isn't one. There really isn't much of anything. A bed, a cherry wood night table and dresser. Everything else is blue. Gray-blue walls, light-blue sheets, bold-blue comforter.

With a heavy sigh, I let my eyes fall shut again, listening for any sounds of movement from within the house. Off in the distance, I can hear shuffling footsteps and muted voices, and I wonder if Wes is still here, or if it's someone else.

Rubbing my eyes, I sit up in bed, letting the blankets fall and gather around my waist. I should probably get up. Go talk to Jason. Figure out what I'm supposed to do now.

But I don't want to. Not yet. I need me time. Centering time. Thinking time.

I can already feel the stress creeping up on me, choking me, at the thought of telling him everything. I know I have to and I also know I'm going to feel like a fool doing it. What's worse, he's going to think I'm a fool.

Good God, I don't want him to think of me as a fool.

There's something exciting and alarming about him.

The way he can be so angry, and still so … gentle with me.

My skin prickles, remembering the way it felt when he held my hand, and stroked his thumb along my wrist; the way it made my heart race and my body heat.

Groaning, I toss the covers back and stumble to my feet. I need to focus on my motivation. My parents, my brother, my freedom.

And I need to not think about the way Jason Pierce made my heart race.

Exhaling a flustered breath, I quickly get dressed, pulling on jeans and a violet tee, and hurry out of the room and down the hall to the bathroom, locking the door behind me.

The bathroom is large, bright, and white. I take care of business, splash water on my face, brush my teeth, and tame my hair back into a ponytail.

By the time I'm finished, I feel better—a little less sore, a lot more stable. After putting my toiletries back in my bag, I hurry out to find Jason, telling myself not to worry about whether or not he'll think I'm a fool, because it doesn't matter. The only thing that matters is stopping Officer Peck and getting back home to my family.

I find Jason in the kitchen. He's standing over the stove, cooking what smells deliciously like bacon. He's barefoot, wearing a pair of jeans, and a dark-gray tee.

Wes is here, too, sitting at the table with a bunch of papers spread out in front of him. He looks like he just woke up, hair mussed, shirt wrinkled, and he's totally engrossed in whatever he's reading.

There's another guy beside Wes, reading as well. He's hunched over the table, scowling, and I give him a quick once over. Hard jaw, high cheekbones, tanned skin. His hair is short, dark brown, and he's tall, broad shouldered, not quite as broad as Jason's, but broader than Wes's. He's dressed in jeans and a green tee. I wonder if he's Vance.

I hesitate, feeling awkward and a little unsure. Now that I'm here, I'm not sure what to do, or what to say. At the moment, hovering in the doorway, I'm not sure of anything.

After a few seconds of none of them noticing me in the doorway, I clear my throat. "Um … hi."

Jason turns around, catching my eye. Our eyes lock and hold. His gaze drills into me before he sweeps it over the rest of me with such thorough intensity that my insides quiver. The corners of his mouth curl up, revealing his dimples. "Hi, darlin'. Sleep alright?"

"Yes, great, thanks," I say. "Thanks again for letting me stay here. I really appreciate it."

He smiles and nods, as his eyes scan me over again, making my cheeks flush. He cocks an eyebrow at me. "You gonna come in and grab a seat, or just stand in the doorway?"

"Uh, yes. Okay, sure, I'll sit."

Swallowing down the awkward feeling, I make my way over to the table. I can feel him watching me, feel his eyes glued to me. His stare makes me so nervous I feel like I'm going to trip over my own feet. I take a seat quickly, fiercely trying to block it out.

"No Taser this morning?" Wes asks, giving me a lazy, uneven smile. He sets down the paper he was reading, and leans back in his chair.

I laugh, shaking my head. "I figured it's safer for all of us if I don't have it."

The man beside him laughs, a real, belly-shaking laugh. He glances at Jason and says, "I get it," before leaning across the table, sticking out a hand to me. "I'm Vance."

I shake his hand. "Great to meet you, Vance. And what is it that you get?"

His lips curl up slightly and he shrugs as though it doesn't matter. My brow furrows in confusion and he laughs again at my reaction. "So, Elena Reed, what is it exactly that you think we can do for you?"

I blanch and swallow thickly. Unease chokes me at the blunt question and I glance at Jason. He's still watching me, an expectant look on his face.

Okay. Okay, okay, okay.

I force myself to focus. I guess there is no easing into this. Best to get right to it.

"Right to it, then," I say, shifting in my seat. I take a deep centering breath, let it out, and take one more. "Okay, I need help finding something that will put Officer Peck in jail."

"You want to put your fiancée in jail," Vance says, regarding me curiously. He motions toward the pages littering the table. "Since I haven't found a thing that would explain that, you wanna tell us why?"

I stall, leaning forward and glancing down at the papers spread across the table. My heart races in my chest. There's picture after picture of me. Me with my brother. Me alone. Me at my parents' house. Me with friends. Me with Peck. They're from my Facebook profile. All of them.

Good God, these guys have been busy.

Mindlessly, I reach out and begin shuffling through the pictures and papers. My missing persons report. My college transcript. Tweets, Facebook statuses ... They haven't been just looking into my disappearance, but me overall.

My gaze falls on my engagement announcement, and I pause for a few heartbeats, feeling my skin grow clammy and pale.

"Wow, I hate that picture," I say, deceptively calm, glancing up. "He always looked at me like that. Even the first time we met, like I was a prize, a toy, something to be owned."

"Why'd you say yes then?" Wes asks, looking at me with complete openness and interest. He's smiling, it's not overly warm, but it looks genuine.

"I didn't," I say, shrugging. "I found out I was getting married the same way you did. I read the announcement."

My statement makes them both hesitate, glancing from me, to the announcement, to me again. They start stacking up all the papers, staring at me, but they don't speak.

It's awkward and my hands start to sweat. I'm not sure I want to explain how I got engaged, that Peck had the article printed, threw it down in front of me while shoving a ring on my finger, so I just stare back.

After a moment, they have the papers cleared away, and

Jason is setting plates down, heaped with bacon, eggs, and pancakes. Once everyone has food, drinks, and utensils, he joins us at the table, taking a seat right beside me.

I wipe my sweaty palms on my jeans, and pick up my fork. The guys dig in, but I'm not all that hungry anymore, so I shift my food around on my plate.

Closing my eyes, I try to forget everything.

Just for a few minutes, I don't want to be nervous.

For a few minutes, I don't want it to be awkward.

I just need a few minutes.

"So it was a shitty proposal that made you decide to run," Jason says, around a bite of eggs. "Is that why you want him in jail, too?"

I don't know what I expect from him, but it's not that. I turn to Jason, frowning. "You're a bit of an ass, you know that, right?"

His eyes shine with amusement and he reaches under the table, giving my knee a small, reassuring squeeze. He laughs, shaking his head. "I know, darlin', you've told me."

Is he joking? I think he is. I hope he is. I take a deep breath, trying to relax, and he squeezes my knee again.

Sitting quietly, I take a bite of eggs, stalling for a moment, and consider what to say. I briefly wonder if this is a mistake, but I can't know that, not until I give them a chance. Sighing, I glance down at my plate, not able to look at them. "I spent four months dealing with Peck's abuse, blackmail, and coercion, and I couldn't do it anymore. I didn't decide to run. Nobody chooses to run if they have other options. I was out of options. He took them all away from me. Shelters didn't keep me safe. The police didn't believe me. Going home wasn't an option; neither was hiding out with friends. They'd only end up suffering just as much as me for helping."

Jason brings his hand up, cupping the back of my neck. He tilts my head, raising my gaze to level with his. "Abuse, as in he was physical with you?"

I nod slowly, taking in the protective, bordering on possessive, look he wears. It chills me, and warms me. Creeps me out, and makes me feel safe. I don't know whether I love it, or hate it.

Oh crap ... I'm screwed.

I'm so totally screwed.

How the heck am I going to work with him?

Pulling my eyes away, I look down at my plate once more, but Jason doesn't move his hand from my neck. Instead, he keeps it in place, rubbing small passes with his thumb on the side of my throat.

It's strangely soothing, and I find myself leaning into him.

"The first little bit was okay," I say. "He was nice enough and my parents were so happy that I hooked up with a cop, especially him. He's pretty well respected in my neighborhood. But after a couple weeks, things changed. He got angry, yelling at me all the time for ridiculous little things. I told him I was done and that was the first time he hit me. He broke my nose."

Jason curses under his breath, so does Wes, but Vance says nothing. He just watches me, his face remaining open, taking everything in. "Did you go to the hospital?" he asks.

I laugh coolly, remembering the first hospital visit. "Yes. He took me, flashed his badge around, and told the doctor that I walked into a door. No one would believe me when I tried to tell them what really happened. They didn't even listen to me. It was like I wasn't even there. They treated me, and then sent me home with him. I ended up in the hospital one other time with a fractured wrist."

"How'd you get tied up with him?" Wes asks quietly.

I turn to him, swallowing thickly. "I made a mistake. Peck caught me doing it and gave me a get out of jail free card. It was supposed to be dinner. One night, a single dinner, that's it. He wanted more, and when he realized I didn't, he put me in a spot where I couldn't refuse."

Jason squeezes the back of my neck lightly, and brings my eyes back to his. "What did I say about lying?"

I blink. Seriously? It stuns me how easily he sees through me, how easily he picks up on my lies. I stammer for a moment, and then answer, "Two truths and a lie. Weaving it with the truth makes the lie more believable." Which is exactly what I did.

"What else?" he coaxes, rubbing his thumb up and down the side of my neck.

"You'd rather I didn't lie to you."

"Whose mistake were you covering for?" His voice is tentative, like he's afraid to hear my answer.

I hesitate, staring at him, and he just sits there massaging the back of my neck, watching me. I let out a sigh, and drop my eyes. "My brother. Peck pulled us over. He'd been drinking. It was his second DWI so he would have gotten jail time. Peck was checking me out, my brother noticed—"

"Jesus Christ," Vance mutters, cutting me off. He presses his lips together in a tight line. "You've been gone a year, yeah?"

I nod. "That's right."

"You have any idea if he's still looking for you?" Vance asks.

"Yes, I think he is," I say. "He almost caught up with me a few months ago, just before I met up with ... um ..." I stop, glancing at Jason as his hand lightly flexes against my neck.

Right, okay, don't mention his dad.

Taking a deep breath, I push on. "I was in Portland and made a stupid mistake. I was hungry, out of money, and I tried my debit card. I hadn't used it for months. Not since I first left and took as much money as I could out. Anyway, two days after I used it, I saw him. He saw me, chased me, and I managed to dodge him." An involuntary shudder passes through me. "There have been a few other close calls, but that was the closest he's come to finding me."

The room falls silent. It's tense and uncomfortable, and I start to sweat as all three of them look at me, studying me, as though they're trying to see if I'm lying or leaving anything out.

After a painfully long moment, it's Wes who breaks the silence. "Do we have anyone in New York?"

Jason's hand on my neck tightens, a light squeeze, and then it drops. "Liam's still there. I'll give him a call. Vance, get copies of those medical records, yeah?"

Wait! What?

"Sure," Vance says, and then he shifts his gaze to me. "Gonna need the names of the hospitals he took you to."

I blink. Oh God. If they start digging around in that kind of stuff, Peck will know. I'm sure of it. "I don't think—"

"You're gonna need to trust us, darlin'," Jason says, stopping me mid-protest. "You're safe here. I swear it."

My brow furrows. He stares at me for a moment and I hope he's reading the questions in my eyes. His expression softens a bit, but he says nothing more. He stands up, giving me a small smile, as he fishes his phone out of his pocket, and heads out of the room.

Chapter Eight

Jason

I clench my teeth against a fresh swell of anger, but it does nothing to help. It just builds and builds, multiplying and compounding with a heavy dose of frustration. I can feel myself growing hot again, and I close my eyes, take a deep breath, trying to keep my anger from showing.

Liam is going to look into Peck. He's going to track him down, start tailing him. Vance is working on getting her medical records, and hopefully they'll show something. Suspicion, doubt, proof that her injuries were not accidents. It shouldn't take them too long to get me something.

I need to relax.

I can't let her see how much her story is getting to me.

I won't scare her into running from me again.

Elena has been talking for hours. *Hours.* She's trying not to cry and it fucking kills me. Guts me. Shreds me up from the inside out.

Peck was careful, she says. He'd keep her hidden until her bruises faded, and made up creative stories for her folks when he couldn't.

He has enough on her brother to put him away for years. He has a health inspector that will shut down her parents' bakery.

He threatened her with it. Blackmailed her. Bullied her.

I sit in the living room, my feet propped up on the coffee table, and Elena tucked into my side. My arm is curved around her shoulders, my other hand, curled around a beer bottle. I'm not sure when that happened, really. Sometime between us sitting down on the couch and the guys taking off. She perched herself beside me when we first came into the room and as she talked, the space between us lessened and lessened, until she was leaning on me, and my arm was around her.

I want to pull her closer.

I never want to let her go.

Especially when I hear the tremble in her voice.

It's really fucking hard listening to it.

Over the last year, Peck's been searching for her, tracking her. It sounds like most of his leads in the beginning were from people spotting her and reporting it. When those dried up, his leads came from her mistakes.

And she made a few of those. Using her debit card, credit card, her real name when she found odd jobs or checked into hotels.

She's been running, hiding ... She hasn't been able to settle anywhere for more than a few weeks before he'd show up, chasing her to her next place.

The most shocking part of her story, the part that has me the most furious, is that she did seek help. Before she vanished, Elena actually went to a shelter and those idiots released her to Peck when he showed up to get her.

She tried to go to the cops, too, but they didn't believe her. Told her she was telling stories. Made her sound like a vindictive housewife.

That's when he started using her parents and brother against her. It's also why she never went to her parents for help. She was scared. Scared Peck would ruin them if she did.

The whole goddamn thing makes me sick.

I'm not surprised Vance *got it* as soon as he met her. There's just something about this girl, small, sweet looking, innocent smile. It makes you want to protect her, slay dragons and lay their heads at her feet.

But there's also fight in her. It's dwindling, but it's there. And goddamnit, I don't want to see that fight burn out.

My eyes are trained on the television, on some romantic comedy that I don't know the name of, or care about.

I put it on to distract her.

It hasn't worked yet.

It's past midnight. We've only been up for about five hours, but she's getting tired. I think the stress is getting to her. She's rambling on about her brother now, between yawns. I think she's trying to make me believe that he isn't a complete fuck up.

It puzzles me.

Even if I can look past the fact that it was her brother who traded a date with his little sister to get out of a DWI charge, which I can't, she's also told me that her brother's a drunk. That he can't hold down a job. That he barely finished high school, and at three years older than her, he's still living with their parents.

It's a lost cause.

She can say whatever she wants, and I'm still going to think he's a fuck up.

"You're something else," I mutter, adjusting my arm around her, snuggling her closer in the crook of my arm.

She cuddles into my body, a little tense at first, but slowly, she melts, settling her cheek on my chest.

"I don't know what that means," she says, peering up at me with big blue eyes.

I brush a strand of hair from her forehead. "It means you're amazing. You're strong, you're loyal. You gave up everything you love, everything you want, for someone who doesn't deserve it, and still, you smile, you survive."

It seems like hours pass, both of us staring into each other's eyes. I have no idea what she sees that holds her, but I can't look away either. She's giving me the look again, the one that makes me feel like a superhero.

"He deserves it. My brother's a great guy. He deserves it." The words are whispered and she chokes on them like she can taste the lie and it's too bitter to swallow.

She wants to believe them.

She wants them to be true.

"If he knew what that asshole did to you," I whisper, my voice raw from emotion, "do you think he'd agree?"

"No," she says. "Probably not." She pauses, lips parted, and I wait for more, but all I get is a soft sigh. She looks at the television and laughs quietly. "I love this movie."

I take a long pull of my beer, finishing it off, and careful not to disturb her, I reach down, and place the empty bottle on the floor. She shifts a little, laughs again, and I'm struck by how the sound of her laugh loosens the knot in my chest.

After a while, her head starts to fall, her breathing begins to even out and deepen, and I realize she's falling asleep.

As I watch her, I find myself hoping Liam takes his time tracking down Officer Peck.

Elena

A ringing phone startles me awake.

I jolt, blinking away my blurred vision, feeling disoriented and stiff. Really, really stiff.

The phone rings again followed by a vibration against my hip. Groaning, I move to stretch, and twist to dig it out of my pocket, when I realize I'm not alone.

Oh my God. I'm not alone.

There is an arm, a thick, strong arm wrapped around me. There's also a hand on my ass. A hard body beneath mine. A blanket over the top of me.

My heart starts pounding as I stare down to find Jason underneath me. "Oh God."

The ringing cuts off, only to start right back up again. I try to shove away from him, but his hand on my ass tightens, and the arm around my waist pulls me closer.

I can't move.

I'm pinned.

Stomach to stomach. Chest to chest. One of my legs is

cocked up, pressing into his side, and the other is locked between his thighs. My hands are trapped in between us.

I fell asleep on the couch?

We were talking. I was talking, telling him about Peck and my parents and my brother. We were watching a movie, and …

The ringing stops.

It starts again.

"Answer your phone, babe," he grumbles in a deep, raspy voice. His arms tighten around me, squeezing me close, and he nuzzles into my neck.

My heart is frantic, thumping like a bass drum in my ears. I struggle against him, trying to reach for the phone, but I can't move. He's holding me so close I can barely catch my breath.

"Let go," I say, trying again—unsuccessfully—to pry myself out of his grasp. "Jason, you need to let go so I can reach it."

He grunts, loosening his hold, not a lot, but enough for me to wiggle one of my arms free and dig out my phone. I'm not even sure if he's fully awake, or if maybe he's in that in between place, not quite dreaming but not quite conscious, either.

Sighing, I bring the phone to my ear, answering with a mumbled, "Hello?"

"Hi there, baby girl. How are you holding up?"

Mr. Chapman. The moment I hear his voice, a smile lights up my face. "I'm good."

And stuck.

And kind of nervous.

Actually, I'm freaking out a little bit.

"Did Jason wise up and pick you up yet?" he asks. His voice is cautious as though he's not sure if he believes that I am, in fact, good.

"Um, yes, he did."

I move to sit up, my elbow digging into Jason's ribs hard. He grunts, snatching a hold of my elbow, moving it. He opens his eyes—finally—and laughs, flashing his dimples. God he looks good, just waking up. Hair mussed-up, sleepy smile, dark stubble along his jaw. His eyes are half-mast, peering up at me, flashing with amusement. "Hold still, darlin'."

Rolling my eyes, I jiggle his hand loose from my elbow, and I wonder how I even managed to end up in this situation. I think I should be annoyed about it, but I'm not. I just can't drudge up the emotion just yet. I laugh, swatting at him. "Jason, let me up."

He does. Thank goodness he does.

Jason knifes up to a sitting position, pulling me up with him, and I slide off his lap. He leans over, elbows on his knees, looking at me.

"Elena," Mr. Chapman barks out. "What's going on?"

Suddenly, Jason shifts his gaze to the phone and every inch of him tenses. "It's him, isn't it?" he asks, hard bitterness spilling into his voice.

I'm not sure how to respond to either of them. I start stammering, looking away from Jason, but his gaze follows me. I can feel it—tormented and angry—burning through me, waiting.

"Yes, um ..." I stammer into the phone. "Nothing's going on. Everything's fine."

"Hang it up, Elena," Jason says, voice low, cold.

I risk a look at him. The corners of his lips are twitching, but it's not with a smile. He's scowling at me, or more accurately, he's scowling at the phone pressed to my ear. He looks as though he might snatch it away if I keep talking.

A chill runs down my spine as he stands up. His eyes burn into me with some unspeakable emotion. He glares at the phone for a long moment, his hands fisted, and hanging rigidly by his sides, and I watch him warily.

I don't hang up.

I should. I want to. But I don't.

Why did I even answer it?

I feel so incredibly stupid. I should have just turned it off. Mr. Chapman is the only person who has this number. And with Jason ...

Oh God, I shouldn't have answered it.

Mr. Chapman is shouting in my ear, demanding to know what's going on, but I hardly notice.

I stare at Jason.

He closes his eyes and lets out a harsh breath. Then, he turns from me and heads for the stairs.

"I've got to go," I say and I hang up the phone, tossing it down, and jumping up. "Jason, wait a minute."

"Not now, Elena," he says quietly, stopping at the top of the stairs. He glances over his shoulder, his jaw working hard, but his eyes have softened. "Just give me a few minutes, yeah?"

He doesn't wait for me to respond. He steps around the corner, and a second later, I hear a door slam shut, and then the sound of a shower turning on.

I sit back down, folding myself up on the couch. Guilt presses against my chest until it's hard to breathe as I stare at the stairs, giving him the few minutes he asked for.

Jason

I need to get myself together.

Exhaling, I start the shower, letting the water warm up, as I strip out of my clothes, dropping them in a pile on the floor.

Fuck.

I'm losing it.

I can still hear his scratchy voice yelling through the damn phone.

I climb into the shower, pulling the curtain closed behind me, and step right under the warm spray of water.

Elena looked so adorable, waking up laid out on top of me. The sweetest smile, nervousness mixed with what looked like contentment.

And she was soft. So fucking soft and warm in my arms. I didn't want to let her go. I think I could have laid there with her all goddamn day.

But my old man has a way of ruining things. He ruined his marriage. Destroyed his career. Ripped apart his family.

And this morning, he shattered the sliver of trust I'd managed to build with Elena.

If he were here, he'd blame me for all of it.

I don't place the blame on myself, though. I never have. He's the one who committed the acts. I'm just the one who shone the light on them.

I groan, resting my forehead against the cool tiles. She can't be talking to him. Not while she's here. Not while I'm helping her. If it were in my power, I'd never let the bastard speak to her again.

I need to get the photos out of the house.

And the flash drives.

And the tape.

It's obvious, I think. I can't leave her here with it, any of it, even if it is locked up tight. I'll stress. I'll worry. And I'll wind up resenting her for it.

Right, get the stuff out of the house so I can focus my attention on her case and not stress the fuck out.

I wash, taking my time lathering up and scrubbing my hair, trying my damnedest to not think, not feel. Then, I stand under the spray for a while, letting the water rain down on me, before finally reaching over and turning off the taps.

Pulling the shower curtain open, I climb out and snag a towel off the rack. I need to get out of here, get some work done, and finish up the last pieces of a case we've got going, so I can focus my efforts on her.

And I need to move the stash.

What to do with Elena?

I can't leave her here, and I can't take her with me.

An idea strikes me and I smile, toweling off quickly, before digging my cellphone out of my discarded jeans pocket. I bring up my contacts and tap on the number I need. It rings twice before she answers. "Mom, I need a favor."

Chapter Nine

Elena

"Where are we going?"

I'm sitting in Jason's car, pulling on my seatbelt. It's half past eight, and I'm still in the clothes I woke up in—jeans and a violet tee. I wanted to shower, or at the very least, to change my clothes, but Jason claims we don't have time for that.

Jason puts the car in reverse, and starts backing out of the driveway. He looks my way and gives me a quick smile. "You'll see when we get there."

The smile isn't real.

There are no dimples.

No amusement in his eyes.

He's forcing it.

It's uncomfortable. The whole morning's been uncomfortable from the moment I woke to find myself nestled in his arms.

I scowl at him as he pulls out onto the street, trying to ignore the coiling in my stomach. I was waiting at the bottom of the stairs when he came down, his hair damp, freshly washed, and he'd changed into faded blue jeans and a gray polo shirt. I was worried about what to say to him when he came back downstairs, so I planned a speech. I had questions and I wanted answers. I opened my mouth, but before I could say so much as a word, he shook his head and said, "Let's go. You've got somewhere to be."

That was all he said.

Then he grabbed his keys and ushered me out the door.

"Don't give me that look, darlin'," he says, chuckling softly. "It's a surprise."

Sighing, I glance out the window. A surprise. I don't know what to think about that. This whole morning has been such a mess that I want nothing more than to rewind time and go back to the moment we woke up. The moment my phone was ringing, before I answered it. If I could do it again, I'd turn the darn thing off.

And if I turned it off, if I didn't answer it … well, I'd probably still feel uncomfortable and awkward, but it would be for an entirely different, and not a completely horrible, reason.

I turn back to him cautiously, wondering if he'll talk to me about the whole *dad* thing. "Can we talk about what happened this morning?"

"Sure," he says, his voice taking on a playful tone, and he reaches over, taking my hand. "You fell asleep cuddling into me during the movie. You looked so damn cute I didn't want to wake you, so I stayed put."

I blink a few times, shaking my head. Although it's good to know how we ended up sleeping together, it's not what I meant and I'm almost certain he knows that. He's watching me from the corner of his eye and his thumb is tapping against my palm, agitated.

I let out a deep sigh. "That's not the part I want to talk about and you know it."

His eyes come my way, landing right on my face and holding for a long second before going back to the road. "If I'm gonna help you," he says, "I'm gonna have to ask you to stop talking to my old man."

His tone is sharp, all traces of the playfulness gone, and it's most definitely not leaving room for any creative interpretation on whether it's a request or a demand. He might have phrased it as a request, but with that tone, it's a clear-cut demand.

Eyes wide, I watch him warily. I don't know how to respond to that. "I ... uh ... I ..." I stammer for a second, and then spit out, "What?"

After a moment of silence, Jason looks at me again, his eyes scanning my face, before he fixes them back on the road. "Can't have him knowing my business, Elena."

I'm taken aback. "Who I talk to has nothing to do with your business."

"Yeah, darlin', it does," he says. "The minute I decided to take your case and move you into my house, you became my business."

He cannot be serious.

I eye him for a moment in silence, debating on whether I should push the topic and pry into what his issue is with his father or not.

I want to point out how ridiculous he's being.

I want to tell him how wonderful his father is. How he took care of me. Gave me a place to stay. He knew who I was from the first time he saw me, but he didn't call the police. He brought me food, supplies, clothes. I want to tell him that it was his father who gave me hope again.

And most of all, I want to ask why he hates the man so much.

I want to.

I really, really want to.

But I don't.

We hardly know each other and I'm worried that if I push too much, too fast, he'll decide that I'm not worth the hassle.

He'll decide not to help me.

I'm agonizing over what to say when I pull my hand from his and fold my arms over my chest. Maybe I can just send a text message to Mr. Chapman, let him know what's going on. I probably should have already done that after hanging up on him like I did. I'll ask him why his son hates him so much, too, while I'm at it.

I slouch back in my seat, looking out the window, and instead of pushing it, I go with a safer response. "Um, about that moving in thing ... I think I should probably find somewhere else to stay."

Jason exhales loudly. It's a frustrated exhale, one that seems as though it stretches for minutes, rather than a second or two. "You're staying at my place and if you say one fuckin' word about putting up a tent in my yard, I swear I'll burn the damn thing."

I guess I misjudged the whole safer response thing.

But his words do make my skin tingle. I don't know if it's from anxiety or excitement. I'm not sure I care either. I give him a look. "You're being really bossy this morning."

He laughs. "I guess that's better than being an asshole."

I could argue with that. Right now, the two are feeling pretty similar.

But he's laughing, and his smile is real, full dimples on display, so I don't.

Despite myself, I laugh with him, relaxing a bit.

A couple minutes later, Jason swings the car into a Starbucks drive-thru and rolls his window down. He glances my way and asks, "You want anything?"

"Um ..." I hesitate. He didn't give me time to grab my purse, but even so, Starbucks isn't cheap and I don't really have the money to spare, even if I'm supposedly staying with him now. I shake my head. "No thanks."

Ignoring my decline, Jason orders me a black coffee with cream and sugar on the side, as well as half a dozen muffins in assorted flavors, and hands them to me with a wide grin. I thank him and he nods, telling me to dig in.

I do. My stomach is grumbling, and the coffee smells so good, I can't resist it. I quickly add three creams and two sugars to it, stirring it in, and I pluck a banana chocolate chip muffin out of the box.

We drive for a few more minutes, and I'm still nibbling on my muffin when Jason pulls the car into a parking lot, and stops in front of Mona's Salon and Spa.

"We're here," he says, turning off the car and opening his door. "Bring the muffins and coffee with you. You'll be stuck here for a few hours."

I stare at the sign, puzzled, as he folds out of the car. He comes around to my door, opening it, and I rush to unclip my seatbelt. "You're taking me to a salon?"

He nods, his eyes settling on my hair, looking torn. "You should have changed your hair a year ago."

He's right. I should have. I know that. It probably would have helped with the sightings that led Peck closer to me, but I didn't venture out in public too often, and aside from meeting Jason in the bar, I always wore hoodies, ball caps, large sunglasses. I thought it was pretty brilliant, myself. I saved a lot of money that I didn't have to spend, and by doing so, I was also able to keep my blonde hair.

"I don't want to change my hair, Jason," I say. "I can just wear a ball cap and sunglasses when I'm out." *And I can't afford it.* Splurging for a drugstore hair color is one thing, but a salon … It's too much.

He leans into the car, cupping my cheeks in his palms, bringing his face close to mine. "Don't want you hiding behind a ball cap and sunglasses when I take you out to dinner tonight."

My eyes widen. Is he serious?

I can feel my body flush and butterflies, those pesky little things, try to take flight in my belly. "You're taking me out to dinner tonight?"

He smiles widely, taking the muffins in one hand and mine in the other, pulling me out of the car. "Yeah, I'm taking you out to dinner."

The salon is closed.

I notice the sign in the window showing that it won't be open until eleven as the car door closes behind me. I tug on Jason's hand, pulling him to a stop. "They're not open yet."

He laughs under his breath, amusement touching his eyes as he looks down at me. "They are for you. I called in a favor."

"Right," I say, starting to walk again. "Jason, I can't do this. I don't even have my purse."

"You don't need your purse, darlin'," he says, brushing me off. "Like I already said, I called in a favor."

How does a private investigator get favors for salon appointments?

Jason pulls me along the side of the building, through an alleyway, to the back. He strolls right up to the back door, knocking.

The door opens almost instantly, and an older woman appears in front of us, her expression light and happy. Long black hair brushes her shoulders, with wispy layers framing her face. She's dressed in a floral sundress and flip-flops. She looks at us, her warm brown eyes shifting between the two of us, before settling on Jason.

"Hi, Mom," he says, leaning in and kissing her on the cheek. "Thanks for coming in early."

Mom? I blink a few times, caught off guard, and I watch, dumbfounded, as Jason embraces her.

I guess the favor makes a little more sense now.

"No problem, honey," she says, stepping back, and motioning for us to come in. She smiles at me. "You must be, Elena. I'm Mona."

"Hi," I say, with a little wave, as Jason leads me into the back room. The walls are lined with shelving, filled with supplies. A wall of hair dye. One with cleaners. Mops and brooms rest against another wall, neat and tidy.

She leads us through to another room, the washing station, and then out to the main part of the salon, and without any preamble, she gestures for me to take a seat at what I assume is her station.

Setting down my coffee on the counter, I glance at Jason. He nods encouragingly, and with a sigh, I sit down.

I'm really going to do this, aren't I?

I guess I need a trim. It's been over a year for that, but I've never colored my hair.

Mona spins me around so I'm facing the mirror, and asks, "So what color were you thinking of?"

"I don't know," I mumble, shaking my head. "Um ... I didn't know until just a minute ago I was coming here."

Her brow furrows, and she looks at Jason in question. He

sets down the box of muffins, smirks, and shrugs. "It was a surprise."

They stare at each other for a moment, and a soft smile spreads across her lips. "We'll go through the colors and pick something out," she says, walking across the room, and picking up a large black book. "Do you have any ideas on what style you want?"

I shake my head, and she gives her son another *look*. It's questioning, but also knowing, and I wish I knew whatever it was that was making her smile like she is.

Jason hovers over my shoulder for a few minutes as his mother flips through a book with loops of colored hair, pointing out different colors that she thinks will suit me, before he pulls away. "I've gotta get going."

My brow furrows. "Wait, you're leaving?"

"Yeah," he says. "I've got some work to do."

My heart jumps to my throat. I'm not scared, but nervous? Yes, I'm nervous. He can't mean to leave me alone with his mother. What if I say something wrong? Does she know that I know her ex-husband? Are they even divorced? I know that they're separated, but I don't know if I'm even supposed to know that. And what does she know about me?

I look at Jason, eyes pleading. "But—"

"You'll be fine," he says, cutting me off before I can form my protest. "Enjoy this. Get your hair done. Your nails, too, if you want. I'll be back in a couple of hours to pick you up."

I offer him a small nod and a smile, trying to get myself under control. It's crazy, really. I barely know the guy, and he's scared me more often than not since we met, but the thought of being alone with his mom ...

He frowns, regarding me carefully. "You've got that about to bolt look again."

I can feel my face heating with embarrassment. What's wrong with me that spending some time alone with this man's mom—a man that I only just met—makes me so nervous? "Just ignore me. Honestly, I'm good. I'll see you in a few hours."

He doesn't look convinced. "Give me your phone."

I pull it out of my pocket, handing it to him, and watch as he presses a few buttons, and then hands it back.

"You need me to come back sooner, you call me, yeah?"

I shift my gaze to my phone, and then back to him. "Okay."

He squeezes my shoulder lightly before turning to his mom. "Thanks again, Mom."

"Sure thing, honey," she says. "Now go on and get out of here."

Giving me one more smile, he turns away and disappears out the door.

Chapter Ten

Jason

I swear that look is gonna kill me.

I wonder if Elena knows what she's doing when she looks at me like that. When her eyes get wide and all that sweet innocence in her just spills out, and even though she's nervous, she looks at me as though she's certain that I'll keep her safe no matter what.

It's a goddamn form of torture; that look.

It makes me think I can do anything.

It makes me want things I shouldn't be wanting.

It's that look that has me kicking myself for leaving her with Mona, and anxious as hell to get back to her.

No. Wait. What the hell am I thinking? She's just a job. It might be a personal job, but still, just a job.

I'll get the shit she needs, get her away from my old man, and then she'll be gone, back to New York.

But this morning … Holy shit, this morning. I could get used to waking up to her soft body curled around mine, and seeing that sweet, sleepy smile of hers. She was so damn beautiful just waking up. Never have I wanted to kiss a woman so badly. But it wasn't just a kiss I wanted. I wanted more. I wanted all of her.

As I pull up at Heaven Here Coffee, I'm about ready to say

the hell with the meeting and head back to the salon. For a woman like her, I don't think the guys would blame me. I could just turn back …

No. Stop it. None of that matters. It can't matter. She's a job. Just a job.

But yeah, it kind of does matter, doesn't it?

So what the fuck does that mean?

I don't have a goddamn clue.

Sighing, I pull up beside Wes's truck and cut the engine. Vance is parked on the other side, and the two of them are leaning against the hood, waiting.

I close my eyes and take a deep breath.

I can't deal with Elena right now.

I'll figure it out later.

I don't have much choice but to be here anyway. The client is one of my referrals. He'll want me here to deliver what we found.

Yes. I just need to finish up this case, and then I can deal with Elena.

When I open my eyes again, I'm slightly more focused. Wes and Vance are watching me, their expressions, curiously blank. I run a hand down my face, and take another deep breath, before I climb out and head over to them.

"You made it," Wes says. His eyes study me for a moment before his lips start to twitch as though he's fighting off a grin. "Thought maybe Elena had you tied up cooking for her again."

I glance at my watch. I'm on time. Uncommon for me, I'm always five minutes early, but still, I'm not late.

"It's nine-fifteen," I say and shrug. "What can I say? I like being punctual. You two should try it. It'll save you time on this waiting around shit you're doing."

Shaking his head, Vance gives me a considering look, a hint of amusement in his eyes. "You look like shit. What's up?"

An involuntary chuckle escapes my throat before I can swallow it down. I have no doubt I look like shit. I sure as hell feel it.

I don't bother denying it.

They wouldn't believe me if I tried.

I shrug, smoothing my face out into an impassive mask. "Is he here yet?"

Vance narrows his eyes. He's not buying the mask. Neither is Wes. How the hell am I supposed to look indifferent when I feel anything but?

"Yeah," Wes says, pausing for a second to stare at me before continuing, "he went in a few minutes ago."

"Then let's get this over with," I say, motioning toward the shop.

Neither of them moves. They say nothing. They just stare at me.

They wait.

They watch.

They want an explanation.

I have no idea what they're looking for, but they want something. Knowing these two, I'll be standing here all morning if I don't give it to them.

Sighing, I rub my hands over my face. "Got woken up by a call from my old man."

"He called you?" Wes asks, disbelief thick in his voice.

"No," I say, shaking my head. "He called Elena's cell."

Vance cocks a brow. "And how exactly did that wake you up?"

Internally, I groan. How did her phone wake me up? Vance isn't a stupid guy. He could piece it together. He was there last night, he saw her pressed into my side on the couch before he left. He's probing, fishing for information that I don't particularly want to give him.

A lie is on the tip of my tongue, but I hold it back. I've never lied to Vance before, and I'm not going to start now. "We passed out on the couch last night watching a movie."

Cursing under his breath, Vance pushes away from the car. "Hope you're being careful, Jase," he mutters.

I don't need to ask what he means.

I know, because I can hear it in his voice.

He's not just talking about being careful with Elena, but also myself.

Uncomfortable and not in the mood for this conversation, I shift irritably from one foot to the other. "Yeah, I'm being careful."

Vance holds my stare for a long moment, and then gives me a small nod, and asks, "You leave her alone at your house?"

Right, so he doesn't believe me.

He knows I'm not being careful with any of it.

Fair enough.

I don't believe me either.

I shake my head. "No. Dropped her off at the salon. She's getting her hair colored and cut."

Wes laughs. "You left that poor girl alone with Mona?"

Rolling my eyes, I turn away and start for the door. "Mona's not that bad," I say. Then, on second thought ... I glance back at them. "Maybe we should hurry this along."

Not surprising, neither of them disagree, because, yeah, my mother can be a bit ... abrasive? Brash? Pushy?

Okay, another thing I didn't think out.

Shit. What's that girl doing to me?

Elena

Chocolate brown ...

I like chocolate. It's delicious, especially when you heat it up and drizzle it over vanilla ice cream, or dip strawberries into it, but never have I consider the color before.

Not once.

Until today, anyway.

That's because Mona has declared chocolate brown to be the perfect color for my hair. She is not wrong. It is perfect. It's dark, really dark, but it has a slight reddish hue to it that I love.

She's in the back mixing the color right now, and while I'm alone, I pull my phone out of my pocket. I want to send Mr. Chapman a message. Let him know what's happening here while I have the chance.

Except, I'm not really certain if I should.

I'm baffled, entirely unsure of what to make of what happened this morning.

Truth is, I'm unsure of what to make of everything that's happened since I arrived here.

Okay …

I just have to think about this. I need to figure out how to deal with this.

Yeah, right.

My brain is so muddled right now that I don't have a clue what I'm supposed to do here. Cut off Mr. Chapman? Hide our conversations from Jason?

I don't know.

Neither option feels good. Neither feels right.

Both men have gone out of their way to help me.

Neither of them has been completely honest with me, but I'm not sure I can blame them for that. I haven't been entirely open and honest either.

One thing I know for sure is that I'm willing to do just about anything to see Peck behind bars and get back home.

So what am I doing?

Ugh, I don't know.

This whole situation is a mess.

Sighing, I tap the power button, waking up the phone, and glance at it. I thought I'd see missed calls, messages, something from Mr. Chapman, but there's nothing.

He hasn't even tried to contact me since I hung up on him and put the phone on silent.

I contemplate for a moment, my fingers hovering over the keyboard, and I glance over at the doorway, making sure Mona is still in the back, before I type out a message.

Me: So everything's fine and sorry for hanging up on you, but I've got some bad news.

I hit send and close my eyes, hoping that he'll respond quickly, and I wait.

And wait.

And wait.

My gaze darts from my phone to the doorway, watching and waiting for Mona to come back, and I'm about to put my phone away when the screen lights up with an incoming message.

> Mr. Chapman: What?

> Me: Jason has declared that I can't keep in contact with you.

> Mr. Chapman: Not surprising.

Really? I suck in a breath. His response pisses me off and I instantly want to strangle him. If it's *not surprising*, then why didn't he tell me?

Most likely for the same reasons he didn't tell me that Jason is his son, or that Jason wouldn't be too thrilled that I was sent by his father.

But don't I have a right to know? It's my life he's screwing with here.

> Me: About that ... I think you need to explain. I think you should have explained before you sent me here.

> Mr. Chapman: He's going to take your case, right?

> Me: Yes, but ...

> Mr. Chapman: Then there's nothing to explain.

Okay, I kind of expected that response. The man has never been incredibly forthcoming with information. Actually, he's always been fairly quiet when it came to personal details, but still ...

Me: Uh, yes there is.

Mr. Chapman: What did he tell you?

Me: Nothing. He gets scary angry when your name comes up. I need to know why.

Mr. Chapman: All you need to know is that he's a good man. He has his reasons for hating me and I deserve it.

Me: This is crazy. I don't understand any of this. Why did you send me here?

Mr. Chapman: Because I can't help you, baby girl, and he can. His team is good. Better than me.

Me: Better than you? What's that supposed to mean?

Mr. Chapman: If it'll make him breathe easier and focus on you, then do what he's asked.

I look at the text and feel my jaw tighten. I read it a second time, slowly, shaking my head, completely confused.

I was *so* not expecting him to say that.

But I don't have time to respond. Mona comes back, rolling a small cart in front of her holding a green plastic bowl full of hair color and brushes. She comes close; stopping right behind me, and with a soft touch, her hand brushes the back of my hair.

My phone lights up again, and I quickly shove it in my pocket as I compose myself, sitting up straighter and forcing a bright smile.

She sees it. Her eyes follow my phone as I put it away, but she doesn't mention it. Instead, she smiles, a cautious, muted smile.

"So," she says softly. "What should we talk about?"

I sit here, uncertain. I feel so out of place. I don't know what's left to talk about. We already covered the basic small talk while picking out the color, and I feel like a ball of frazzled nerves, trying to make sense out of Mr. Chapman's response.

"Okay," she says after a moment, dragging the point of the color brush along my part, baring my roots. "I'll start. What's a girl like you doing moving in with my son?"

I blink. I'm stunned at her bluntness.

Stunned and also slightly impressed.

"I ... Uh ..." I stammer. My stomach is so knotted that I can't even form a thought. Jesus, it's been in knots since I arrived in this darn town. This amount of nervous anxiety can't be healthy. I swallow hard. "A girl like me?"

"Yeah, honey," she says, quickly swiping the brush back and forth along my roots. "A girl like you."

I meet her eyes in the mirror. She's smiling, a genuine smile. It's sweet, caring even. She looks completely at ease.

It's confusing given her question.

Confusing, just like her son.

I laugh sharply, my nerves clawing at my throat. "I'm not sure I know what you mean by that."

Using the pointed end of the brush, she flips the painted portion of my hair over, and starts applying a new layer of color. "You're not his usual type."

What's his usual type?

No. I don't even want to know.

Okay, maybe I kind of do want to know, but I'm not asking.

I won't be here long enough for it to matter anyway.

"It's not like that," I say. "We're not seeing each other. I'm just a case."

Mona laughs barely loud enough for me to hear. "I saw the way you were looking at him, honey," she says. "You have a very expressive set of eyes on you."

I'm caught off guard by her response. Am I that transparent? I thought I was hiding it better than that. She stares at me in the mirror, the color brush swiping at my hair. I feel her gaze burning through me just as hot as the flush staining my cheeks, waiting.

I hesitate before repeating myself. "I'm just a case."

She laughs again. "Jase doesn't move his cases into his house. He doesn't call me to give them a new hairstyle, either."

Okay, she makes a valid point there, but I imagine I'm not like his usual cases.

I drop my gaze to my lap, muttering, "I'm thinking most of his cases aren't homeless."

She lets out a deep sigh. "I'm not trying to hurt your feelings. I saw the way he was looking at you, too."

She stares at me for a moment, waiting for a response as I try to come up with something that will reassure her. I don't get the feeling that she's opposed to the idea of me staying at her son's, but I also know she doesn't love it.

But it's more than that. There's something else here, hidden in her questions.

I can feel it.

It strikes me then, that Jason must have told her something about me. Why else would she come in early to give me a new look? She seems too inquisitive to just say yes without hounding him for details. I wonder if this has something to do with the person that sent me here.

I meet her eyes in the mirror, hoping mine convey calmness that I don't really feel. "I know what you're really looking for," I say evenly, hiding my nerves as best as I can. "It's so much easier if you just come out and ask."

"Oh, yeah?" she says, her lips curving up with an amused smile. "What exactly do you think I'm looking for?"

Taking a deep breath, I state, "You want to know why Mr. Chapman sent me here."

Mona curves an eyebrow judgmentally, her eyes scanning me slowly in the mirror, picking me apart. After a moment, she laughs. "Am I that obvious?"

"No, not really," I say. "It's just a lucky guess." I pause for a moment, gathering my thoughts, before I continue. "I don't know what Jason told you, but I didn't know he was Mr. Chapman's son. They have different last names and they don't look alike at all. I didn't know anything other than that he was sending me to a private investigator that could help me sort out my life so I could go home."

A legitimate look of surprise crosses her face. I don't think she was expecting me to be open. I wasn't really expecting to be either. She looks as though she has hundreds of questions so I'm surprised when she says, "Jason changed his name when I divorced his dad. He didn't want any ties to Richard."

"What happened?" I blurt.

"We just weren't good together," she says with a shrug. "Divorce isn't that uncommon, honey."

That's not what I meant and she knows it. I can see it in her eyes.

I say nothing, hoping she'll keep talking.

But she says nothing, and focuses all her attention on my hair.

Chapter Eleven

Jason

I'm seated at a rectangular wooden table with Wes, Vance, and our client, Gary. My elbows rest on the tabletop, my chin in my hands, and I watch as Wes taps the screen of the iPad. The video surveillance footage immediately begins to play.

We're tucked away in a small alcove in the back corner of Heaven Here Coffee. The alcoves are one of the reasons we meet with clients here. They give a semblance of privacy, blocking out other patrons from seeing us. The soft sounds of a rainforest are coming through the speakers and the rich scent of coffee floats in the air.

To his credit, Gary's expression doesn't change as the video plays. There's a moment of silence when the feed ends, before he looks up at me. "I can't believe this."

This is not an uncommon reaction for a client. It happens more often than not. People see the proof and they don't want it to be true. It's so much simpler to suspect than to know.

Except Gary had his doubts in the first place. That's why we were hired. But like most clients, he wanted to be wrong.

He wants us to be wrong, too.

"I'm sorry, Gary," I say, purposefully keeping my voice steady and cool, as to not make this any harder on him than it has to be. I slide an envelope containing photos and a written report of our findings across the table to him. "I know seeing this can't be easy."

His features begin to crack as he picks up the envelope and dumps the contents onto the table. He shuffles through the photos. I'm not sure if he thinks what we found is better or worse than he suspected.

His wife isn't sleeping with the gardener.

But his seventeen-year-old daughter is.

I'm not sure which is better.

I think I'd want to kill the gardener either way.

He laughs, shocked and uneasy, and he shakes his head. "I don't know what to do with this."

It's not my business how he handles it from here.

It can't be.

"What you do with this is entirely up to you," I reply. "We'll give you all copies of everything we've collected."

My phone rings, distracting me from the conversation. I fish it out of my pocket and glance at the call display.

Liam.

I stare at it for a moment, seeing the name flash back at me, before pressing the button to silence the ringing and placing the phone on the table.

He found something already.

He wouldn't be calling yet otherwise.

I don't know how I feel about that.

"So you don't keep anything on file?" Gary asks, sorting through the photos and shoving them back in the envelope. "What about the negatives?"

I understand his worries. It's all about image. People with money always worry about their image. How others perceive them.

Looks like Gary is no different from the others.

"We keep a shortened report," Wes says. "And enough info on you to bill you for our time. You can have the negatives or we can destroy them along with the video file after we send you the copy."

Gary nods, seemingly content with this response. He should

be. Our image is just as important as his. Leaking cases would ruin us. He knows that.

My phone starts ringing again, and once again, Liam's name flashes across the screen. Calling twice in under two minutes, not leaving a voicemail …

My stomach coils.

That's not good.

"Gotta take this," I mutter, snagging up my phone and standing up quickly. Vance narrows his eyes, so does Wes, but they don't say anything. Gary is still muttering over the photos as though if he says this has to be a mistake enough, the images will change to whatever it is he wants to see.

Stepping away from the table, I press the answer button and bring the phone to my ear. "Yeah."

"Jase." His voice sounds terse, annoyed maybe. Tired for sure, but that's the nature of our work. Late nights, early mornings. It catches up to you quickly.

"Yeah," I say again, walking to the door. "What's up?"

"You just sent me to voicemail," he says. "If I didn't know any better, I'd say you're ignoring me."

Pushing the door open, I step outside and start across the parking lot toward my car. "I was in a meeting," I tell him. "What's going on?"

"Thought you'd like to know that I found him," Liam says.

"I figured as much," I say, stopping beside my car and leaning against it. "You find anything else?"

"Yeah. The cop's been having breakfast with that girl's parents daily," he says. "From what I got from one of the bakers, he's only missed a few days over the last year."

That doesn't surprise me.

From what Elena said last night, Peck had tracked her down a few times, the last being three months ago, just before she hooked up with my old man. He knows she's still alive. Knows she's still running. He's probably waiting for her to get sloppy again.

"He's probably hoping she'll call them at some point."

"Maybe," Liam agrees. "But there's more. After Peck left

the bakery, he picked up the brother. The guy was just standing there on the corner about two blocks away. Peck stopped, jumped out of the cruiser, and slapped cuffs on him. The guy didn't look surprised. Didn't say a word. Just went along with it. It was as though he were expecting it. He was taken to the station. Hasn't been released yet."

"Huh," I say. I'm not sure what to make of that. I'm not sure if I'm surprised or not. Maybe Peck's caught wind of Elena again and decided to follow through on his threats to lock her brother up?

"Yeah," Liam says. "That pretty much sums it up."

"Stay on him, will you?" I ask. "And let me know when the brother comes out."

"Sure, Jase, whatever you need." He's quiet for a moment, before asking, "You want me to run a check on the brother?"

"Nah," I say. "I'm gonna stop in at the station. I'll get Cruz to run it."

I hang up, slipping my phone into the pocket of my jeans. Sighing, I just stand there for a moment in silence, taking a minute to gather myself before heading back into the coffee shop.

Twenty minutes later, the meeting is finally over, and we head out the door. It's still early, nearly ten o'clock, and as much as I don't want to leave Elena alone with my mother any longer than needed, I know she won't be too thrilled with the idea of coming to the police station with me, and I'm not too keen on the idea either. I should have another half an hour before her hair is done. Enough time to stop by the police station, but probably not enough to move all the stuff I have on my old man from my house.

Standing beside my car, I turn to Wes. "Can you—?"

"Nope."

I stall, my hand on the door handle, taking in his annoyed expression. "I need you to—"

"Nope," he says again, this time shaking his head.

"Fine," I bite out, pulling open the car door. "See you guys later."

I don't know what's gotten into him.

Okay, maybe I do know. He's pissed I walked out of the meeting. Looking at Vance, I'd have to say he's not too impressed either, but right now, I don't care.

"Jase, stop," Wes says. "Give us a couple minutes, will you?"

Sighing, I pause and glance back at him. I don't have time for this. Keeping my words tentative, I say, "I got a lot to do before I pick her up."

"What did Liam say?" Vance asks harshly, ignoring my statement. He watches me with an eyebrow raised—waiting.

He's unhappy.

I don't blame him. He has every right to be unhappy with me right now.

I close the door, leaning my arms on the roof of the car. "Peck's keeping in touch with her family—daily. He also picked up her brother this morning."

"How are you planning to deal with that?" he asks, folding his arms over his chest.

"I'm not sure yet," I mutter, dragging a hand through my hair. "I'll figure that out later. Right now, I'm going to see Cruz."

"Okay," Wes says slowly. "What about Elena? How do you think she's gonna take this?"

I hesitate. I don't think she'll take it well. Actually, after listening to her last night, I think she'll probably crack over this.

"I don't think I'll be telling her," I admit. "At least not until I find out why he was picked up."

Shaking his head, Wes grins. "You think keeping this from her is a good call?"

No, probably not.

I shrug a shoulder. "There's no point in worrying her."

Vance full out laughs. "Heads up," he says. "That's probably a mistake."

"No different than any other case," I counter. "We get the facts, and then share them."

"This isn't like any other case," Vance points out. "The client is living in your house."

I grimace. Point received.

It doesn't change my mind, though. Actually, it only makes me more certain that keeping this quiet for now is for the best.

"Can one of you head to my place, empty out the safe?" I ask. "Won't be able to get that stuff moved before picking her up."

"Sure," Vance says and nods. "I'll handle it."

"You want me to come with you?" Wes asks.

"No, it's fine," I say. "I've got this."

Wes doesn't look happy with my response, but he doesn't protest it either.

In good traffic, the drive to the police station takes ten minutes. Today it takes me nearly fifteen. I park my car right in front of the building, and make my way in.

At the front desk, I have to wait a few moments to be noticed, as the young officer behind it finishes up whatever she's doing on the computer.

I smile when she looks up. "I need to speak with Detective Cruz."

She asks me my name and smiles at me warmly, before she picks up the phone, paging him, and tells me to take a seat.

I only wait about five minutes, before I see Cruz coming through a door off to the side of the reception desk. He smiles when he spots me and waves me over.

"What can I do for you, Jason?"

"Just in the neighborhood," I say casually, as another officer walks past us. "Thought I'd stop by and see how my friend was doing."

Cruz laughs, amused at my choice of words. We aren't friends. Never have been. We've known each other since high school, but never really crossed paths until he became a cop. We found ourselves working on the same case, for different reasons, with different targets, and ended up sharing information.

One thing led to another, and we've been working together—off the books—for a few years now.

It's been a slightly tense relationship, but it's a needed one.

For both of us.

He gestures for me to follow him and leads me down a hallway, stopping in front of an interview room, and pushes the door open. Wordlessly, I go in, and slip into a chair at the table.

Cruz closes the door behind us and gives me a look. "How about we cut out the friend bullshit and you tell me what you're here for?"

Straight to the point.

I've always liked that about Cruz.

There's no bullshit with him.

No dicking around.

"A friend of mine was picked up about an hour ago in New York," I say. "I need to know why and I need you to run a full check on him."

"Does this friend have anything to do with the girl you moved into your house?" he questions, keeping his face straight, as he takes a seat across from me.

I curve an eyebrow at him. "You're not watching my house again, are you?"

His smile freezes.

He hears the thinly veiled warning in my voice.

He knows I won't put up with that shit again.

He tried it once. Had me followed. Staked out my house. I clocked them right away and let it slide for a week before calling him out on it.

He thought I was feeding him fake leads on our joint cases. So he figured if he watched me, he'd be able to see it all first-hand. He'd be able to prove I wasn't being upfront with him.

But I wasn't giving him fake leads. He was just too slow on the uptake. He took his time verifying everything, and by the time that was done, the leads were cold.

I made it clear he'd lose my info if he ever tried that shit again.

"Savannah had coffee with Lynn this morning," he says quickly, explaining. "I guess she passed by your house on her way, saw a new car in the driveway and you getting into your car with some girl. She was upset."

Upset. I laugh. Savannah doesn't do upset. She has two emotions: saccharine sweet and raging lunatic. I took the woman out three times close to a year ago now, and I haven't been able to shake her yet.

"Nice. Savannah on a rampage again. Just what I need." I suppress a groan and wanting to get back on track, I cut him a look. "Thought we weren't doing the friend bullshit."

He doesn't look happy with my response.

But then, he wasn't thrilled when I hooked up with his sister-in-law, either.

If I'd have known who Savannah was to him at the time, I would have steered clear.

Can't rewrite the past, though.

After a moment, he sighs. "Okay, fine. Is this for a case?"

"Yeah."

"Give me the details," he says, his voice monotone, and he pulls out a notebook.

I rattle off the guy's name, age, and arresting officer, giving Cruz as much detail as I can, which really isn't a lot, but it's enough. The name, age, and location will give us a hit.

He jots it all down, and then glances up at me. "I'll call when I've got something."

"Thanks," I say, standing up. I head for the door, and then pause, looking back at him. "One more thing. Can you rein in Savannah? I don't need her spewing her shit right now."

He regards me warily for a moment, and then grumbles, "I'll see what I can do."

Chapter Twelve

Elena

A new environment makes a world of difference.

I think this year's fortune just might be true.

Or maybe it should have read: A new hair-do makes a world of difference.

At the moment, I believe that both could apply.

Unblinking, I stare at my reflection in the mirror, as I twist a dark strand of hair around my finger, scrutinizing it. In this light, it makes my skin look pale. Not unhealthy, just lighter than normal. The cut is shorter than I typically wear it, coming to rest just above my shoulders, and the tapered layers cause my natural waves to bounce up into soft curls at the back, though the front is still fairly straight.

The cut and color changes my appearance more than I thought it would.

My eyes look brighter, a sharper blue.

My cheekbones look higher.

Even my lips look different, fuller somehow.

It's remarkable.

Suddenly, looking at myself in the mirror, I feel free. Freer than I've ever felt before.

Mona is scuttling around the salon, packing up make-up, hairbrushes, shampoo, conditioner, and anything she can think of that I may need while I'm here. I tried to stop her, feeling completely uncomfortable with her generosity, but she wouldn't listen, telling me if I leave it to Jason to think of these things, I'd never get them.

I think she's even packed me a hairdryer.

"You like it, right?" Mona asks as she sets down a cloth shopping bag filled with beauty supplies by my feet.

I grin. "I love it. Thank you so, so much."

I mean thank you for more than just the hair. I think she knows that, too. Although she wouldn't answer my questions about Mr. Chapman, she didn't hesitate on giving me pointers on dealing with Jason.

Except, I'm not entirely sure why she thought that I needed to know that he's allergic to bleach, or that he hates floral perfume, but she did.

I believe she thinks there's more going on between us than there really is.

Is it completely crazy that knowing that makes me a bit giddy?

Yes, it probably is.

I catch a sight of Jason approaching me in the mirror, and my attention is drawn to his reflection. I feel a hum of excitement, mixed with trepidation, as he approaches me.

He has that look in his eyes. The one from yesterday. Protective, possessive. He moves toward me with confidence.

I freeze.

My thoughts freeze, my breathing pauses.

Good God, he looks sexy, looking at me like that.

Mona must see it, too, because she giggles, and wraps an arm around my shoulder, giving me a little squeeze. "You need anything, anything at all, you call me, okay?"

"Okay," I whisper, keeping my eyes fixed on her son.

She steps away, grinning, as Jason comes up behind me, stopping close. His eyes run down the length of me, then come back to rest on my hair. He reaches up, gently untwisting a strand of hair from my finger, studying me carefully, and I feel my cheeks heat under his gaze.

"Beautiful." There's something strange in his voice as he says it, a kind of unease or insecurity perhaps.

I stare at him for a moment, blinking. Good God, he just called me beautiful, didn't he? Something inside me flutters from the compliment. I blush, fiddling with the hem of my shirt, and swallow thickly. "Um … Thanks."

Straightening, he lets his hand fall from my hair, resting it on my hip, and he gently squeezes. "You ready to get out of here?"

"That depends," I say. "Are you going to stash me somewhere else?"

My eyes widen as soon as the words are out of my mouth. Oh God. Did I really just say that out loud?

He smirks. "Is that what you think I did here?"

Do I? I don't even know. Kind of, I guess.

"Um … no, well, yes, maybe." Jesus, I'm stammering— again. I sound like a fool. I don't want him to think I'm ungrateful, because I'm not. Really, I'm not. I was just surprised he left me here, alone with his mom for so long. "I mean no, I don't really think that. I just like it better when you're around is all."

Shoot, I don't think that was any better either.

He chuckles, shaking his head. "Sorry, darlin'," he murmurs. He looks me over intently, his dimples coming out with a wide smile. "I was thinking we'd go back to my place. That good with you?"

His gaze is thoughtful, and perhaps a touch staggered, but his tone is sincere, as though what I want genuinely matters to him.

Turning around to face him, I say, "Are you planning on staying there with me?" There's a hopeful note in my voice and my heart skips a beat as I anxiously wait for his answer.

His brow furrows, looking slightly less amused and maybe even a little guilty, but he nods. "Yeah, darlin', I'll be staying with you."

"Okay," I mutter quietly, letting my gaze fall to the floor, hoping to hide the fresh flush that's heating my cheeks. "Let's go."

After saying a quick goodbye, Jason leads me out through the back door, holding my hand and carrying the bag of goodies Mona packed for me.

He says nothing to me on the drive to his place.

I don't say anything either.

It's not an uncomfortable silence, though. If anything, this is the most comfortable I've felt in his presence so far.

He holds my hand. I think he enjoys the contact. I know I do. It's soothing. Relaxing.

How long has it been since I've found comfort in such a simple act as holding hands?

Before leaving home, I loved being touched. I was a hugger. A hug a day makes everything okay. And I loved cuddling.

I never realized how much I missed that contact until now.

He pulls the car into the driveway and cuts the engine, sitting there for a moment, before he eventually lets go of my hand, and climbs out of the car. I miss the contact instantly, the warmth of his skin against mine.

I follow him inside, closing the door and kicking off my shoes. My brain starts racing, full of questions I want to ask him. I'm curious. About my case ... About him ... About his father ... About everything, really.

He drops his keys in a dish on a small table by the door, and lets out an exasperated sigh. "This won't work if we don't trust each other." He mutters the words quietly, not looking at me, as though he doesn't actually want me to hear them.

But I do.

I hear them so clearly it's as though he shouted them.

I'm not really certain where this is coming from or where it's going for that matter, but my mind immediately flies to the text messages I sent his father.

He couldn't possibly know about them, could he?

My stomach coils.

My hands begin to tremble.

"Trust can't live with secrets and lies," I counter, feeling a bit defensive. Okay, more like guilty.

Yes, really, really guilty.

"You're right." He sighs again, and rubs a hand over his

head. He opens his mouth to say more, but I don't let him.

"Please don't get mad," I blurt, and he immediately shuts his mouth, cocking a questioning brow. "I sent some messages to your dad while I was with Mona."

"I'm not surprised," he says, except I don't believe him. He looks shocked. Annoyed, too.

I pull my phone out of my pocket, and tentatively, I step over to him, holding it out. He stares at the phone coldly, not making a move to take it.

It's my turn to sigh. I push the phone into his hand. "Read them. I'm going to go take a shower and change."

Then, before his expression can change from shock to anger, I turn from him, and jog up the stairs, hoping that giving over my phone was the right choice.

Jason

I did not expect that.

I stand here, staring at the phone, blindly. A few minutes pass, five, perhaps more, before I pull my eyes away from it and go to the couch, taking a hard seat.

When I mentioned trust, I'd been thinking about her brother. I thought about it in the car. Wes and Vance are right. Hiding it is probably not a good call.

I was going to tell her.

I was going to fill her in on Liam's report and my meeting with Cruz.

I glance back at the phone clutched in my hand. I'm curious as to why she bothered to tell me about the messages. She's been so nervous—unsure—around me, that I hadn't expected this kind of openness without my prying for it.

What's changed?

I'm not entirely sure, but something has.

For both of us.

I wake up the phone, coldness running through me, and I hesitate to bring up the messages, entirely uncertain that I want to read the conversation between them.

My old man is like a plague, infecting everything—everyone—I come in touch with. I don't want it to spread to her.

Shit, my chest squeezes at the thought.

I need to put an end to this shit with my old man.

I want to move on with my life.

I look back at the phone, every muscle in my body seizing up tight, as I bring up the messages.

I take a breath, and another, and then I read.

I read every word. Twice. Three times. I look for hidden meanings. I try to read what's being said between the words.

But I see nothing.

I slip the phone onto the coffee table, leaning back on the couch, and I close my eyes.

Perhaps she really doesn't know anything.

But if that's right, then what the hell is my old man doing?

Elena

I shower, careful not to get my hair wet. I take my time with my make-up, and then I stress a little over what to wear. I don't have much to choose from, and I end up settling on a pair of black boot-cut jeans, and an off-white scoop neck peasant top, with black floral embroidery.

When I come back downstairs, Jason is sitting on the couch, feet up on the coffee table, laptop propped on his thighs.

I edge toward him cautiously, studying him, attempting to judge his mood. I don't think he notices me. His fingers are flying across the keyboard.

I stand there silently for a moment, waiting, debating whether I should speak up or not. A part of me wants to shuffle back, before he notices me.

Hesitating, I glance back toward the stairs.

"Come here," he says. "I'll just be a second."

I guess he does notice me standing here.

I swing my head back to him. He's still staring at the computer screen. Still typing.

I don't go to him right away. I have the urge to fidget, so I quickly stuff my hands in my pockets, stopping myself before I can start. "Did you read the messages?"

His brow furrows at my question. "Yes," he says, a bitter bite in his tone, and still he doesn't look up.

I laugh nervously, unsure what to make of his one-word response. "Are you mad?"

"No."

That's it. That's all he says. Another one-word answer.

I don't know if I believe him.

Uncertainly, I sit beside him, leaving about a foot of space between us. I'm frowning, looking right at him, but he just keeps typing.

I sit quietly for a few minutes, before clearing my throat.

That seems to draw his attention. He glances at me, offering up a lazy one-sided smile and with a few clicks, he closes the laptop and sets it on the coffee table. He leans back, centering his gaze on me. He's so quiet, taking me in that I start to get a touch self-conscious, and I shift, fidgeting in my seat.

Slowly, he reaches out, tucking my loose hair behind my ear, his gaze following his hand as it brushes along my skin. I try to keep eye contact, but I can't. His gaze is so intense it has me squirming.

He notices.

Of course he notices.

Jason grins, chuckling under his breath, and in a swift motion, he wraps his arm around my waist and pulls me onto his lap.

I gasp, surprised, and my hands come up to his chest, steadying myself. "What are you doing?"

"I like touching you," he says seriously. "I like you in my arms, and I think you like being here, too."

I do. I don't deny it, but I don't admit it either. From the look he's giving me, I don't need to anyway.

He sees it.

He knows.

"And," he continues, "if I'm holding onto you, you can't run away when I tell you what I need to tell you."

Oh. That doesn't sound good.

I swallow thickly, and press my hands into my thighs. "What do you need to tell me?"

"I heard from Liam," he says. "Your fiancée—"

"He's not my fiancée," I grumble, cutting him off. "He never really was. I didn't say yes. I didn't want it."

Jason chuckles and his arms tighten around me, pulling me closer. "Good to know."

I roll my eyes, but I can't stop the smile that pulls at my lips. "What did Liam say?"

"Peck's been having breakfast with your parents almost daily since you left." His voice has a hint of anger behind it, a bitterness, as though his statement leaves a sour taste in his mouth.

I just stare at him, stunned. "You can't be serious."

Eyeing me warily, he nods. "He's probably hoping you'll call them at some point. If he stays in touch, they'll be more likely to let him know."

Makes sense, but still …

Suddenly, I feel sick. I left, not just for me but also to get that asshole away from my family, and all this time he's been playing the worried fiancée, checking in with my parents?

Before I can get out a word, he continues, "He also arrested your brother today."

Wait. What?

He arrested my brother?

No. No, no, no. He wouldn't do that, would he?

Oh God.

My eyes get hot, my breath catches, and my heart jumps into my throat. "No," I whisper. "No, that doesn't make sense. It's been a year. Why would he do it now?"

"Don't know why yet," he tells me calmly. "Could be he caught wind of you again and is trying to flush you out, or maybe your brother fucked up again. I've got a detective here looking into it. I should know more soon."

"I've got to go," I whisper.

"No." His arms tighten like a vice around me. "What you need to do is stay here."

He means that. I can tell from the tone of his voice that this isn't something that's up for discussion.

But I can't do it.

"I need to help him," I snap. "This is my fault." I push at his arms, trying to get up, but it's useless. Just like this morning, he holds me tight, snatching ahold of my hands, pinning them to my chest, keeping me still. His grip is strong, relentless.

"What you need to do is sit here and wait," he says, his voice strained. "I've got people watching Peck and looking into your brother. There's nothing you can do for him right now."

I stare at him a moment, baffled by what he's asking me to do. "So what you're saying is, you want me to just sit back and hang out here."

"Yeah, darlin', that's what I'm saying."

"But shouldn't we be doing something?" I ask. "Maybe we should go to New York. We could follow him. Isn't that what PIs do? Stalk people. Watch them. Dig around for evidence."

He laughs, a glint of amusement flashing in his eyes. "I've got someone following him. Taking you back there isn't going to do any more than what's already being done."

I shake my head. "I can't just sit here hiding."

"Yes, you can," he says right away, his tone sharp. "You've been hiding for a year. What's a few more weeks gonna change?"

"Exactly. I've been hiding for a year. I'm sick of hiding." I pause, eyeing him. "If I wanted to stay hidden, I wouldn't have come here. I need to do something. I need to help my brother."

What's left of his smile fades, and he loosens up on his hold, reaching up a hand and cupping my chin. "Elena, just give me some time," he says. "Please, I'm asking you to give me time to figure this out. I'll get you through this, I swear it. You just need to trust me, yeah?"

I hesitate, contemplating, and then I nod. I'm not really sure what else to do right now. It's not like he's about to let me go, and he sounds so sincere.

I believe him.

He laughs under his breath, and flashes his dimples. "You know, you're really cute when you're not running away from me."

And then, he leans forward and he kisses me.

Chapter Thirteen

Elena

I hesitate.

Oh God, I hesitate.

I don't know why. I don't mean to. I don't want to.

But my traitorous body stiffens, and nerves, those blasted nerves, fill my belly, jumping around worse than ever before.

What the hell is happening here? One second we're talking about my brother being arrested, and the next, his mouth is on mine. Not that I'm complaining. Just startled. Yes, startled, that's it.

When was the last time I kissed someone? One year and … three days ago?

Peck.

I shiver. The last person to kiss my lips was Peck.

Jason pulls back, leaning away from me, looking me over. His brow furrows. "You okay, darlin'?"

I bite my bottom lip and nod, not trusting my voice.

"You want me to stop?" he asks, bringing his thumb up to my lip, pulling it free of my teeth.

"No." My voice squeaks. Ugh, of course it has to squeak. I feel my face heating, my entire body heating.

He watches me for a second, his eyes half-mast, burning a path along my face as they fall to my lips. A hint of a smile takes over his face as he moves back in, claiming my mouth once more.

His lips are soft, warm, and his kiss is gentle, tentative. His hand curls around the back of my neck, tilting my head slightly, and he licks a path along the seam of my lips.

I open for him, slowly, shyly. I shouldn't, but I do. Everything in me tells me not to. This—whatever this is—can't go anywhere, no matter how much I'm beginning to like him.

But it feels so, so good.

I don't want to stop. My body doesn't want to stop.

His thumb sweeps along my jawline, and his kiss turns from soft to hard, taking my breath away. His tongue seeks mine out, explores my mouth, and I melt.

Completely dissolve, liquefying, in his arms.

I forget about everything. My brother, my parents, Peck. Nothing matters. Nothing but this moment.

Tiny jolts of electricity spread through me as his lips leave my mouth, dipping to my jaw, and trailing down my neck. He licks, kisses, nibbles at my skin, as his hand slips under my top, exploring the small of my back.

I'm panting, sucking in breath after breath. I squirm on his lap, wanting to get closer, and he brings his mouth back to mine.

Best first kiss ever.

Jason pulls back abruptly, stiffening, and before I can recover, he lifts me, placing me on the couch, and he's suddenly on his feet, striding toward the door.

I hear it then. A rattle. The click of a lock.

The front door swings open before Jason reaches it, and Wes strolls in with a case of beer tucked under his arm and a grocery bag, dangling from his hand.

Seeing Wes, that huge grin on his face, is like being doused with a fire hose. My skin cools instantly and although I feel a touch of disappointment at being interrupted, a rush of relief also washes in.

It's conflicting. I'm conflicted.

And I'm a little embarrassed, too.

That kiss got intense fast.

Too fast.

Wes looks right at me, lifting his chin. "Yo."

I wave. It's all I can do as I try to catch my breath and Wes chuckles, shaking his head, amused.

Jason glares at him, taking in the beer, the bag, and the huge grin on Wes's face. "What the fuck do you think you're doing here?"

I'm taken aback by the harsh tone, but Wes isn't. Not at all.

He laughs. "Barbeque," he says as though it's obvious. "We owe Elena a birthday drink and if she's gonna drink, she's gotta eat, too."

Jason glances at his watch. "It's barely one o'clock."

He's pissed. I can hear it in his voice. See it in his glare.

My breath is evening out, but my lips are tingling and I'm certain they're plump and red. I'm sure Wes notices it. His wide grin tells me he probably does.

Wes laughs and pats Jason on the back. "Perfect time for a barbeque. Vance will be here in ten."

Jason glances at me, before looking back to Wes. "I'm taking her out tonight."

Instead of responding, Wes heads for the kitchen. He pauses as he passes me, his eyes scanning me over. His smile broadens and he reaches over the back of the couch, tugging on a curl. "Your hair looks fuckin' hot."

I blush furiously at the compliment, and smile nervously. "Um, thanks?"

Jason is staring at Wes, unblinking, unmoving, his hands fisted at his sides, and for whatever reason, Wes finds this amusing. He laughs, a full rolling laugh, and drops my hair, shaking his head, and moves off, into the kitchen.

Sighing loudly, Jason steps back over to me. He reaches out, brushing a thumb along my bottom lip, before leaning in and kissing me gently. Suddenly, I feel warm all over again, and when he pulls back, I make a sound, a quiet whimper.

"Looks like we're having a fuckin' barbeque," Jason grumbles after a moment.

I shrug, attempting nonchalance. "I like barbeques, and I

think I could use a drink right about now."

Jason

"That was so, so good," Elena says, leaning back in her seat and rubbing her belly. Her words are slightly slurred, she's drank one too many beers, but she's smiling. She looks content. Happy. "I've missed barbeques."

I chuckle. "You're easy to please, darlin'. I like that."

She doesn't argue, sighing dramatically, and she reaches for her beer, taking a deep sip. "Yes, yes I am."

It's early evening, and we're sitting on the deck in my backyard with Wes and Vance. Elena is beside me; my arm is resting along the back of her chair. Country music plays softly through the speakers and the sizzling scent of cooked meat still lingers in the warm summer air.

Wes is stacking up the plates, moving them off to the side of the table. "So," he says. "What's the first thing you're gonna do when you get back to New York?"

Back to New York.

My muscles grow taut. I can feel them straining as I try to stay still, and not show any reaction. Goddamnit, I don't want to think about this right now.

Elena drains the last of her beer and sets the empty bottle on the table. "I don't know," she says. She keeps her eyes glued to the bottle and she starts picking at the label. "I haven't really thought about it."

"Come on," Vance says, leaning over and nudging her with his shoulder. "There's gotta be something you're dying to do. You've been away for a year."

"Okay, fine." She sits up straight, knotting up her hands in her lap, and she thinks about it for a moment. "I'm going to see my parents or maybe I'll go see Peck."

My eyes snap to hers and I stare at her, trying to figure out what the fuck she means by that. "You want to see Peck?"

"Um ... yes," she says, looking slightly uncertain. "I want to see him in jail. I want him to know it was me who put him there, too."

We stare at each other.

It's the truth. She really wants to see him.

I consider this for a moment. "Huh."

She purses her lips. "It's important to me."

Silence falls.

She raises an eyebrow at me, as though asking if I've got something to say, but at the same time, her expression tells me that even if I do, it doesn't matter.

And it doesn't, does it?

Once I sort out her shit, she'll be gone. Gone back to her life. Gone to another state.

Gone.

Shit, I don't like that.

Not at all.

I barely know her, but the thought of her leaving doesn't sit well in my gut. I want more. More time. More of her. And I think she wants that, too.

I see it in her eyes.

She's seen it in mine.

"You gonna start school again?" Wes asks and takes a pull from his beer.

Swallowing hard, she turns her attention to him, smiling again. "Maybe. Not history, though. It's really a pointless major. I don't know what I was thinking when I started with it. It's interesting, but I don't know what I'll do with that degree when I'm done. Business is much more practical, I think."

Her response makes me laugh, loosening some of the unease squeezing my chest. "You sound unsure."

She grins. "That's because I am. I'm not the same girl I was when I left. I want to go home and I want my life back. I just don't know how the new me will fit into all of that." She laughs under her breath, shaking her head ruefully. "Guess I'll find out when I get there."

Despite myself, I laugh with her. Goddamn, she's adorable.

Sighing, Elena shoves her chair back and stands up, swaying

a bit. My hand goes to her back, and she grasps onto the table, steadying herself. She closes her eyes for a moment and when she opens them again, she giggles, and picks up her empty beer bottle. "I need another drink. Does anyone else want one?"

I laugh again, so does Wes and Vance.

She doesn't need another.

We probably should have cut her off at two. But she's having a good time, and we aren't going anywhere tonight, so whatever.

"Yeah, darlin'," I say. "But why don't you sit back down. I'll grab it."

"No," she says, pointing a finger at me, waving it around. "You just stay put. You've done quite enough already. The least I can do is grab you a beer."

She spins on her heels, her arms coming out a little, keeping her steady, and watching her feet, she sways toward the house.

I watch her go, liking the way she looks in my space.

Fuck.

I like it too much.

"From the drinking, I'm guessing you told her about her brother," Vance says, as the patio door closes behind Elena.

I swing my gaze to his and nod. "I did."

He grins at me, a big ass, shit-eating grin, as though he knew all along that I would. "You hear anything on that yet?"

I shake my head, leaning back in my chair. "Nope, nothing yet."

"I like her," Wes says. "Sucks she'll be leaving."

"Yeah," I mutter, finishing off my beer and letting out a light laugh. "It does."

Chapter Fourteen

Elena

"Stupid," I mumble as I place my hands palms down on the counter and close my eyes. My head is buzzing, so is my skin. The booze-induced tingle is pleasant, but also distracting.

I'm entirely too comfortable here.

My eyes snap open and I glare at the countertop. I'm too comfortable with Jason and Wes and Vance. So comfortable that for a few hours I forgot.

I forgot about Peck.

I forgot about getting back home.

Being this comfortable isn't a good thing.

It isn't a safe thing.

It makes me sloppy.

Except I do feel safe here. Despite our rocky start, I feel safe with Jason.

I close my eyes once more and let out an irritated sigh. I should probably keep my distance from them. Go to my room and call it a night. I could avoid Jason for the rest of the evening, maybe even tomorrow.

That would be the smart thing to do.

It's exactly what I should do.

So why do I completely hate the thought of calling it a night?

Because this has been undeniably the best day I've ever had.

It was tense and nerve-racking, yes, but I had fun. For a few short hours, I was carefree.

And that kiss … I swallow hard. That kiss was the best kiss I've ever experienced.

I don't want it to end, but the question is, what exactly is it? What are we doing here?

I let out a long groan. Stupid hormones. As if things weren't complicated enough.

"I'm being really, really stupid," I say under my breath, pushing away from the counter. But oh God, I'm enjoying being stupid. So what if it hurts me in the end? I can handle it. I've dealt with worse than a fractured heart.

Right, I can deal with it. So what now?

Beer. We need more beer.

Opening cupboards, I search for a mixing bowl or a pot to fill with ice. I open and close half the cupboards in the kitchen before I finally find a large frosted plastic bowl. Using the ice and water dispensers on the fridge, I fill it up, and then pack it with bottles of beer.

With a sigh, I look at the bowl. An unexpected thrill passes through me. I don't give myself time to analyze it. I just smile, and walk back outside, juggling the bowl of ice and beer.

"Your beer," I say as I approach the guys. I set the bowl down in the center of the table and grin.

Jason smiles and his eyes smile, too. Oh God, I can get lost in that smile. He looks at the bowl, noting that I packed it to the brim, and chuckles. "Thanks, darlin'."

Taking a seat beside him, I reach for a beer and twist off the cap. After tossing back a quarter of the bottle, I set it down on the table and look around at the guys. It's then that I notice how quiet they are, contemplative, and slightly tense. I don't know what they talked about while I was gone, but it's pretty clear it wasn't a happy topic.

Not liking the shift in them, I think about something to say, but I come up with zilch, nothing, nada.

I take another sip of my beer, swing my legs, and drum a random beat with my fingers on my thighs.

The tension mounts.

The air is electric.

Maybe I'm just drunk.

I take another sip.

Then it hits me.

I giggle. It's perfect. My legs stop swinging, and I slap my hands on the table. "Let's play a game," I say cheerfully.

Wes smirks and takes a sip of his beer. "A game," he says, sounding intrigued. "What kind of game?"

Bobbing my head up and down, I giggle again. "Yes, a game. It'll be fun. It's called two truths and a lie."

Jason laughs under his breath and a hint of amusement touches his eyes. I wonder if he's thinking about the advice he gave me in the parking lot. "How do you play this game?"

"Simple," I say. "You have to tell three things about yourself, two of them have to be true and one has to be a lie. Then the rest of us guess which one is the lie."

Jason leans forward, resting his elbows on the table, and stares at me curiously. "Not sure I like the idea of encouraging you to lie to me, babe," he says. "You do that enough already."

Those words stall me and my stomach begins to sink. I gape at him. Is this man serious?

Ugh, I don't have a clue.

His eyes look serious, but his lips are pulled tight as though he's holding back a smile.

"I uh ... I don't ..." I stammer and shift in my seat, slinking away from him.

I take another sip of beer, and as I do, from the corner of my eye, I notice Jason's shoulders shaking with silent laughter.

My body grows still, and my eyes widen. The jerk is laughing at me.

Okay, so maybe this game wasn't the perfect idea after all. Obviously, I'll never be able to tell if one of them is lying anyway.

I can't even tell when they're teasing me.

I think he's teasing now. Maybe?

I blush.

Good God, do I blush.

It races through me, heating my skin everywhere, and I'm certain my face is a nice shade of lobster red.

All their eyes are on me and they notice my heated face. One side of Wes's lips goes up in a half grin, Vance's eyes crinkle in the corners, and Jason flat out smiles.

They probably think I'm being silly, the jerks. I straighten in my seat, lifting my chin, and I own that darn blush. "You're being an ass again," I tell Jason, and then I look at Wes and Vance pointing a finger at them, "and so are you two."

Wes laughs and he flashes me a big shit-eating grin. "The game sounds fun, babe."

"I'm in," Vance says. His lips twitch as he draws them tight, suppressing a grin.

I turn to Jason and arch a brow in question. His eyes are on me and there's something in them that I can't quite read. Something sweet, precious even. But there's something else there, too. Something I can't understand. No one has ever looked at me like this before, and I struggle to place the meaning, but before I can grasp onto it, the look melts back into subtle amusement.

"Sure, darlin'," he says. "Let's see if you're any good at picking up on the lies. I know you're terrible at telling them."

I swallow thickly, thrown off by the look. "Okay, um, good," I mutter. "I'll go first." Pausing for a moment, I fix my expression to what I hope is blank and take a deep, centering breath. "I've kissed exactly three people since the day I realized boys didn't actually have cooties. I love chicken noodle soup especially in the winter. And the first beer I ever drank was only a few days ago, on my twenty-first birthday."

Jason stares at me, his eyes scanning me intently, making my cheeks flush. A flash of amusement crosses his face that tells me he sees the blush and he reaches out, running his thumb along my bottom lip.

"It's the chicken noodle soup," Vance says. "It's definitely the soup."

I pull my eyes from Jason and give Vance a shaky smile.

"Um, yes," I say. "Your turn."

Jason slouches back in his seat, throwing an arm over my shoulder and pulling me into his side. I don't know what's going on with us and the reckless part of me doesn't care.

I've put living on hold for far too long.

I want to live.

I want to be reckless.

I don't care how stupid it is.

Vance grins and reaches for a fresh beer, twisting off the cap. "I've never been to Vegas, I'm afraid of birds, and I can play the guitar."

All three of them stare at me, waiting for my guess, and I consider each statement carefully. It's hard. Vance has an excellent poker face and he kept an easy, even tone, but I can't imagine him being scared of anything, especially not something as harmless as a bird. He seems like the kind of person who would face any fear head on and conquer it.

Okay, so it's the birds.

I lick my lips and give my guess. "I'm going to go with the birds."

Jason snorts. "I was with him in Vegas last year."

My brow furrows. "Wait, what?" I blink at Vance, surprised. "You're afraid of birds?"

"Yeah, they freak me the fuck out."

"But they're just birds," I say. "Cute, harmless—"

"They aren't harmless," Vance interrupts. He shudders visibly. "Haven't you ever seen that Alfred Hitchcock movie, *The Birds*?"

Jesus, he's serious.

This gives me pause. "I don't think I want to see that movie."

"No," Vance says seriously, "you don't." Then he grins, lifting his chin toward Jason. "Let's hear them, Jase."

Jason turns to me, catching my eye. He stares at me for a moment, thinking, and he smiles. He has a great smile. Full lips, dimpled cheeks, perfect teeth. It's a genuine smile, not forced or half there, but full and real.

"I was married and divorced within a year, I never write with a pencil because it's too easy to change, and I don't like clowns."

Whoa.

Whoa, whoa, whoa.

Stop right there.

Married? He's been married!

I gape at him. Full on, open-mouthed, gape at him.

Wes and Vance both burst out laughing. "Relax, babe," Wes says through his hysterics. "Jase has never had a serious girl in his life."

Seriously? My eyes round, and then they narrow.

Is that supposed to make me feel better? Because it doesn't. Not that I want him to have a serious girl, or that I want to be that girl, but ...

Oh God.

I shake it off, and purposefully not looking at Jason, I declare, "I suck at this game."

"Yes, you do," Wes agrees. "But I'll be nice and make this one easy on you. You ready?"

I nod, rubbing my hands together and focusing all my attention on him. "Ready."

"I can fit a whole lemon in my mouth," he declares. "I enjoy gardening, and my favorite movie is *Scarface*."

That was supposed to be easy? I glare at him. He has a better poker face than Vance does. Instead of even trying to guess, I say, "I love that movie."

Jason gives me a peculiar look. "You love *Scarface?*"

I laugh at his baffled tone. "Of course. It's a classic."

"I pegged you more for a *Pretty Woman* kind of girl."

I laugh again. "Well, Jason Pierce, you would be wrong."

Jason's eyes change from amused to soft and sexy. "It's the lemon, darlin'," he murmurs. "He hates them. He wouldn't even try to shove one in his mouth."

Wes makes a sour face and I laugh. It feels so good, real, not forced or strained. It winds through me, so raw and powerful.

I instantly feel hungry.

Hungry for more laughter.

Hungry for more of ... everything.

The evening slips away, the sky darkening into night. We joke around, drinking and talking. It's strange, being this carefree and relaxed around other people. And happy. I'm so, so very happy.

As midnight creeps in, we head inside and not long after, Wes and Vance call it a night. I say my goodnights and stand in the living room as Jason walks the guys to the door and locks up behind them.

When Jason comes back, he moves in close. He doesn't say anything as his eyes scan me, settling on my mouth as I nervously lick my lips.

I shuffle my feet. I'm tired, but I don't want the night to end yet.

"That was a lot of fun," I say, breaking the quiet. "I'm glad we stayed in."

"It was fun," he agrees.

He watches me for a moment, seemingly torn, before a gentle smile pulls at his lips, and he takes my hand. "Come on. Let's go to bed."

Jason doesn't wait for my response, pulling me over to the stairs. He releases my hand when we reach the bottom and I clutch onto the banister, keeping myself steady as I make the climb. I walk down the hallway heading to the blue room, but as I reach it, he takes my hand once more pulling me on.

I stop moving and turn to him. "Where are we going?"

Jason stares at me for a moment before a one-dimpled grin touches his face. He squeezes my hand and starts forward again, pulling me along the last few steps down the hall and into his room. Once we clear the doorway, he drops my hand and closes the door.

A short-lived feeling of surprise washes over me, but it's quickly lost to my nerves as I watch him step toward me.

Um ... Oh God.

I start backing up, my breathing growing rapid and shallow. The urge to chew on my nails or perhaps my lip is strong, but I don't want him to see it so I find myself gnawing on the inside of my cheek. "What am I doing in here?"

His grin widens, giving me the second dimple, and he keeps advancing. "Going to bed."

My belly flutters and my pulse kicks up a notch. I continue backing up. "Where are you sleeping then?"

He moves in closer, his eyes sliding past me. "Same place as you."

My gaze follows his, and with the butterflies in my stomach and my skin buzzing with both alcohol and desire, I stop retreating.

I stare at the bed, swallowing a lump in my throat. It's large, covered with an olive green comforter that looks thick and irresistibly soft. The pillows look fluffy and I bet they would be cool against my heated cheeks.

My frazzled nerves jump all together, and in different directions. I try to breathe calmly, but my breaths come in short, sharp pants.

What am I doing?

What are we doing?

I've only ever *been* with one person—Peck—and those memories are far from stellar. Before him, I'd only had one other semi-serious boyfriend. I was in grade ten and we messed around a bit, but it was all relatively innocent.

But whatever it is that's happening between us right now is nothing like what I felt with Peck. Jason rouses something inside of me. Something electric and thrilling, that stirs warmth in my lower belly.

I hesitate before slowly pulling my eyes away from the bed, and back to him. He's grinning, dimples on full display. The sudden urge to lick those dimples strikes me.

Wait, what?

Lick his dimples?

Ugh! Stupid hormones.

What the heck has gotten into me?

It's not that I'm against sex, especially not sex with Jason. Actually, I like the idea of it, but I don't think I have the right emotional equipment right now to handle the consequences.

Slowly, I shake my head. "I'm not going to sleep with you."

He laughs under his breath, taking another step toward me. "Yes, you are."

"I'm serious, Jason," I say, inching back further into the room. "We just met a few days ago. Buzzed or not, I'm not that kind of girl."

He chuckles, cocking a brow. "What about last night?"

My eyes round. I think I should be offended. The insinuation isn't only in his words, but also burning in his heated, liquid brown eyes.

But his voice. Oh God, his voice.

It's low, intimate, sending a brush of heat across my skin, making me feel delirious.

I like it.

I like it a lot.

But I dislike the tingle of insecurity that follows even more.

"Last night was a mistake," I scoff.

"A mistake," he repeats, his eyes still on mine as he takes one more step, planting himself into my little bubble of personal space.

"Okay, maybe that was the wrong word," I mumble and my gaze involuntarily slides back to the bed. "It was an accident."

Jason takes my hand, tugging on it, and I topple into him, breasts to chest, as his other hand winds tight around my waist. "Relax, darlin'," he says softly, his nose brushing against my ear. "We already covered this. I like having you in my arms and I want you in my arms while I'm sleeping."

Right, sleep. He intends to sleep. I don't know if I believe that.

I flush and decide to stay quiet, sucking on my bottom lip. Clearly speaking isn't doing me any favors here. My heart is thumping and my blood pumping.

I don't like the effect he has on me.

No. Wait. That's not true. I love it; I just don't know what to do with it.

It scares me, but it also feels good. Great, in fact. The way he can turn me into a trembling babbling mess with just a smile or a light touch. And his dimples. Good God, those dimples have the power to make my body boneless in less than a second.

"So you're gonna sleep here," he continues, "with me, in my bed."

I'm stunned by his words, by the confidence in his tone. He leans back slightly, keeping his arm firmly around my waist just above my hips, and as he watches me, his eyes slowly change. It's not a concerned look or a sexy look. It's deep, seeing all of me, seeing through me. It touches something deep inside and I feel my discomfort edge away.

He sees it. At the moment, I don't know if I love his perceptiveness or loathe it. He grins, leaning forward and brushing a barely there kiss on my lips, before he lets me go and crosses the room to the closet. He pulls open the door and grabs a dark tee from a shelf, tossing it to me. I catch it— barely—and hold it up, raising a brow in question.

"You can sleep in that."

"Okay," I whisper, but he doesn't wait for my answer. He's already pulling off his shirt, and shucking off his pants, and then he's standing in front of me, wearing nothing but a pair of gray boxer briefs.

I'm stunned as I look him over; my grip on the T-shirt he tossed me tightens as I get my first real look at him.

My God.

He's gorgeous.

He's lean and long. Slim hips, narrow waist, broad shoulders. He's muscular, defined in a way that doesn't come from going to the gym for hours on end, but from hard manual labor. A light smattering of hair dusts his chest. And that sexy V that dips into his boxer briefs ... I lick my lips as something hot and wild shifts through me, settling into my core.

Jason's eyes drop to my mouth and then back up. One eyebrow cocks and a glimmer of amusement returns to his gaze. "Darlin'," he says, his voice impossibly deep, "you keep licking your lips like that while staring at me the way you are, and you'll find that tongue of yours playing with mine."

Oh my God.

I want that.

I really, really want that.

Heat spreads over my skin as though flames are licking me all over. I'm speechless. There's no teasing in his stare. My legs wobble and it's all I can do to keep my tongue from swiping across my lips once more.

I say nothing. Good God, I'm so worked up I can barely think as I cross the room to the master bathroom and quickly close myself in.

I go straight to the sink, turn on the taps, and splash cool water on my face, before resting my hands on the counter.

What the heck was that?

No.

Don't think about it.

Don't agonize or analyze.

Just get ready for bed.

I take my time stripping out of my clothes and pulling on the T-shirt. It's large, falling just above my knees and I fiddle with the hem for a moment, before heading back out into the room, my steps slow. I'm in no rush to face him again, not knowing exactly what I'm getting myself into here.

The lights are already turned off; only a small table lamp on the nightstand offers light to the large room. He's in bed looking fully at ease. He's not at all bothered by having me take over his house, his bedroom or his bed, it seems.

Does anything get to him?

Somehow, him being so calm and cool makes me even more nervous than I was before.

He glances my way as I approach the bed and he smiles, a warm easy smile, as he flips the covers back for me.

The bed dips as I climb up. It's soft, so, so soft, like a marshmallow, and I sink in, pulling the covers up around me.

Jason turns out the light, and the bed shifts as he settles in. I don't realize that my body is so tense until his hand seeks me out, snaking an arm around my belly and tugging me across the bed, until my back is flush against his front.

"Relax, darlin'," he murmurs, shifting my body, and pulling

me closer. "We're just gonna sleep."

"Okay," I say quietly, not sure if I'm disappointed or relieved by his statement.

Once I'm settled into him, he sweeps my hair aside and kisses my neck. There's something about the gentleness of his lips against my skin that eases my coiled muscles. I feel safe here, with him. Safe, and oddly enough, cherished. His hand slips under my shirt, sliding along my midriff, and my skin tingles from the warmth of his touch.

"Night, darlin'," he murmurs against my skin.

I sigh, content, and press closer to his heat. "Night, Jase."

It only takes about five minutes before I'm dead to the world.

Chapter Fifteen

Jason

I wake up in darkness to the sharp chime of the doorbell.

Elena's warm body is pressed against my side and her hot breath fanning over my chest. Her leg is cocked up, knee draped over my thighs, and my palm is full of a firm, round ass cheek.

I thought it had been the limited space on the couch, but it wasn't. Elena is a full contact sleeper.

I've never enjoyed having a woman wrapped up around me while I sleep. Never really liked them spending the night in my space, either. But this ... waking up to the feel of her soft body wrapped around mine ... I fuckin' love it.

The doorbell chimes again, one, two, three times, in quick succession.

Groaning, not wanting to move just yet, I rub my eyes, and turn my head, blinking at the alarm clock.

Four in the morning.

It's probably Wes. He's the only person I can think of that would ring a goddamn doorbell at four in the morning. He probably lost his keys again. I have half a mind to leave him out there.

Elena makes a disgruntled noise from the back of her throat and blinks her eyes open. My eyes meet hers and the sudden fear in her gaze that greets me makes my stomach coil and my chest ache.

"Who would ring a doorbell so early?" she whispers, her voice trembling over the words.

She has a right to be concerned.

She's been running for so long that I bet the emotion is most likely second nature to her.

Still, I don't like seeing it.

"It's probably Wes," I explain calmly, rubbing a gentle circle onto her back. "He has a habit of losing his keys."

She glances at the bedroom door briefly before her eyes dart back to me, surprised and dubious.

She doesn't believe me.

The doorbell sounds again, this time, long and drawn out. The bastard is holding the button down. It lasts for a few long seconds before the house grows quiet again.

I'm gonna kill him.

I linger there for a moment, enjoying the feel of Elena pressed against me before I gently move her aside, and climb out of bed.

Sitting up fully, she tilts her head slightly to the side. "Why would he be back so soon?"

I cross the room, picking up my jeans from where I dropped them haphazardly on the floor last night. I have no idea why he'd be back here so early. He only just left a few hours ago.

"Jason?" she prompts, when I don't respond right away. Her voice is worried, strained, causing my skin to prickle. I try to unwind the coiling in my gut and pull back my own unease before she has a chance to feed off of it.

I inch toward her slowly, keeping my expression light and unworried, as I watch her face pale and her expression turn tense. She's starting to panic.

"Go back to sleep, darlin'," I say. "It's just the doorbell."

Elena isn't listening. I don't think she even hears my voice. Her eyes are wide and she frantically tosses the covers back, scrambling to get out of bed. "I ... I can't. I have to ... Oh God."

Before she can fully get out of bed, I reach out and grab her shoulder, stopping her. "Settle down, Elena," I say. "Everything's fine. If Peck left New York, we would know it long before he showed up here. Liam's watching him, remember?"

"No." She shakes her head anxiously. "No, I—"

"Darlin'," I call, shifting her body to face me.

"What?"

I place a light kiss on her lips before stepping back. "Please be quiet and go back to sleep."

Elena just stares at me.

And she stares.

And stares.

Her eyes glitter brightly with anger. I feel as though her stare is burning right through me. It is, by far, the longest stare I've ever endured.

She doesn't want to listen to me.

I don't blame her for it, but the fact remains, she doesn't have any other options right now.

And she wants to trust me. She wants to believe that I can keep her safe. I can see it in her gaze. I think that's the part that's freaking her out the most.

She feels comfortable here—with me.

"Fine," she snaps, finally dropping her eyes from mine. She flops back onto the bed, yanking the covers up to her chin. "Fine."

I dress quickly, pulling on my jeans and a tee in the dark, and leave the bedroom without looking back at her. I don't want to see the fury or the fear in her expression.

I'm going to kill Wes. Fucking strangle him for freaking her out like this.

Elena

My stomach is in knots as Jason leaves the bedroom and closes the door with a final click. I hate it. Absolutely loathe it. I wonder if I'll ever be able to let go of the unease that's choked me for the last year.

The alcohol has left my system, leaving me feeling sweaty and gross and a touch sick. Every part of my body thirsts for water just as much as my brain urges me to get up and hide.

Do I really think it's Peck at the door?

No. No, I don't.

Jason's right. We'd know Peck left New York long before he found me and turned up here. But I also don't believe it's Wes.

The bed feels entirely too big without Jason here. And cold. Cold and empty. I'm tangled up in the blankets, the sheets wrapped around my feet all scrunched at the bottom of the bed. I know he's only been gone a few minutes, but it feels as though I've been lying here waiting for hours, maybe even days.

I strain my ears, but the house is silent. I hear nothing. No whispered voices, no footsteps. It doesn't sound as though anyone is in the house other than me, and when he doesn't return quickly, my anxiety grows, making me restless.

I'm agonizing over what to do, wondering if I should go down there and see for myself who it is. I know I won't be able to sleep again until I figure it out. The fear will eat at me. It already is; twisting up my stomach and making me feel sick.

Good God, this constant fear inside me is crazy.

"Yeah, it is," I mumble to myself, burying deeper into the covers. But it's better to be on edge and careful, I think, then to let him find me again.

Despite the relentless urge to know who's here, I stay put because Jason's right; it's just a doorbell.

Jason

I head downstairs, quickly making my way through the house. When I reach the door, I flip on the front light, unlock it, and pull it open right away.

"What the—" I start, and then stop, momentarily stunned.

It's not Wes.

Detective Cruz stands on the other side of the door. His shoulders square as I glare at him, but it's not in confrontation, rather it's as though he's making an effort not to show his exhaustion.

"Cruz," I say and step out onto the front porch, pulling the door closed behind me. "It's four in the morning."

He blinks at me, his blue eyes are bloodshot and ringed with dark circles, and his mouth flattens into a line. "Yes, Jason, it is."

His tone is harsh, and his gaze, critical. He stands there, silent, watching the door as though he's waiting for it to open.

He looks borderline furious.

I don't like it.

Not one bit.

And I don't know what to make of it.

"What do you want?" I ask needlessly, already knowing why he's here. The manila file clutched in his hand gives it away. He did the search, found what I need on Elena's brother.

His tired eyes meet mine, surveying me, studying me, as he holds up the file folder. "I brought the stuff you asked for."

I regard him curiously, shoving my hands in my pockets as I lean back against the wall beside the door. "At four in the morning?"

"Yeah, well, I just finished up at the station," he says and shrugs. "Figured I'd stop on my way home."

That, I can believe.

Cruz is the hardest working detective I know.

I respect him for it.

And at the moment, I'm grateful for it.

"Thanks." I reach out a hand to accept the file, but he doesn't pass it over. Instead, he flips it open, thumbing through the pages.

"Andrew Reed," he mumbles. "A long line of misdemeanors and a felony charge for trafficking two years ago. Seems he made a deal on that one, all charges were dropped." He pauses mid-way through, tapping the page. "Says here that his sister's been missing for a year."

I quash a flinch as his eyes survey me in a way that I suspect he does while questioning a suspect. "Huh."

His eyes narrow angrily at my minimal response as though I've offended him.

Maybe I have.

It's not the first time.

I'm sure it won't be the last.

"She's engaged to an officer," he continues stonily. "Lawrence Peck. A good man. He's top of the chain in his division, active in the community, even coaches a special needs basketball team. Upstanding citizen, it seems. Things went downhill for a bit after his girl disappeared, but that's to be expected."

I gaze back at him, keeping my expression carefully blank, and nod my head to acknowledge his words. "Okay."

He closes the file and glances back up, his eyes cutting to the door and holding there for a moment, before settling back on me. "He's the same officer that uses this Andrew Reed as an informant."

He knows.

I can see it in his eyes.

I don't know how, but he knows she's here.

I stand there, not moving, watching him as he watches me. His lips twitch ever so slightly with a ghost of a smile. He sees my realization. He thinks I'm going to enlighten him without him having to ask the questions.

At another time, I might.

Perhaps if he hadn't just given Peck a glowing recommendation, I would.

But his words make me think that he wouldn't be too keen on the idea that Peck might not be the good guy here.

I hold his stare for a moment longer, before casually asking, "Are you done?"

"No," he says. "No, I'm not done."

"You know," I say. "This is really none of your business."

He looks at me incredulously before the smile returns and he chuckles. "Do I look like a ditchable prom date to you?"

The question stalls me and the way he words it makes me laugh. Shaking my head, I hold out a hand. "Just give me the damn file, Cruz."

"No."

His sharp tone surprises me. "Why not?"

"Is she in there?" he asks, his voice tentative as he jerks his chin toward the door. "Is she the girl Savannah saw with you?"

Shit.

This is not good.

I'm not ready to involve him. I need more time. Time to talk to Elena. Time to warm her up to the idea of talking to a cop.

I glare at him. "Fuck off, Cruz."

He meets my eyes once more and holds the file straight up, taunting me. "Maybe I should show her photo to Savannah," he says. "She'll ID her for me."

I hold his stare.

He holds mine.

"I'm not playing this fuckin' game with you, Cruz," I say. "I don't need your help with this one."

"Right," he says. "So you don't need this file then."

I consider telling him to fuck off again, but I refrain. I don't say a word, merely holding my relaxed stance and his gaze, unflinching.

Sighing exasperatedly, he leans back on the banister, tucking the file under his arm. "Why are you looking into this guy, Jase?"

Offering him a slight shrug, I say, "I already told you, I'm working a case."

He stares at me silently for a moment, before letting out a long sigh. "Tell me right now that you don't have a missing person stashed in your house."

"I don't have a missing person stashed in my house," I tell him immediately. It's not really a lie. She disappeared by her own choice, so she isn't missing, exactly.

He's quiet, his eyes narrowing doubtfully as he searches my face, as though he's trying to find the truth in my expression, but I force myself to keep it blank. After a long moment, he shakes his head and he steps forward. "Then you won't mind if I come in and meet your new girlfriend."

I want to remind him that it's four in the morning. Not really a good time for a meet and greet, but I know that won't deter him. I can see the determination lurking in his eyes, the doubt and the concern.

I wonder if I should let him see her.

Maybe he won't recognize her.

More likely, he will.

I consider it for a moment longer before letting out an aggravated sigh. I'm sure introducing Elena to a cop—detective or otherwise—wouldn't go over well. Especially not while she's already unnerved.

She doesn't trust the police. She made that point impossibly clear as she recounted her story for me.

No. Letting him in without preparing her would not go over well.

I have no idea what to tell him, so I tell him nothing. "We're not talking about this anymore."

His eyes immediately harden. "Yes, we are."

"No. We're not."

He glares at me.

I glare back at him.

"I'm trying to help you, Jase."

"You can help by giving me that fuckin' file and letting me go back to sleep."

My words shock him. He stares at me as though he's never seen me before, as though he doesn't know me and hasn't worked with me for years. I guess in a way he doesn't really know me. I've shown him what I want him to see and nothing more.

I stare at him pointedly, giving him time to come to his decision.

After a few long moments, he finally does.

Shaking his head, his shoulders drop, and he holds out the file. He doesn't accept my response, but he relents in his argument.

"We're not done here," he says as I reach out and snatch it up. "Not even close."

I nod, saying nothing. I don't doubt for a second that this isn't over. He'll be back, poking around as soon as he gets some sleep. I'm sure of it.

Cruz walks away. I listen to his footsteps as he crosses the driveway and gets into his car. Relief eases some of the tension in my muscles as I watch him pull out onto the road.

I go back into the house, locking up the door behind me, and I stand there for a moment in silence, listening.

I don't hear a thing from upstairs.

Not a footstep or a creak or a shuffle.

Satisfied that Elena stayed put as I asked, I move into the living room, taking a seat on the couch, and I glare at the file.

I wonder if there will be anything useful in it.

I wonder how she'll deal with it if there is.

I wonder how I'll deal with it if whatever is in the file leads to her going home.

Releasing a sigh, I flip it open and find myself hoping that Andrew Reed is a dead lead.

Chapter Sixteen

Elena

"You're wrong," I repeat for the hundredth time.

Jason is standing in front of me, and he's doing an extremely poor job of explaining to me why my brother is a useless piece of shit. His words, not mine.

I'm sitting on the bed, legs crossed and hands folded in my lap. It's still early, not yet five o'clock in the morning. I'm trying to wrap my head around what he's found out, but it's not working.

My shoulders sag. We've been at this for half an hour. My head hurts, my eyes are dry. I need a coffee or a drink. Better yet, a coffee with rum or rye or any kind of hard alcohol will do. Really, I'm not overly picky.

"I'm not wrong, darlin'," he says. He rubs a hand over his head roughly, and sighs. He's getting annoyed, but he also appears concerned. His jaw is bunched up, and so are his fists, but his eyes … they hold the same softness as they did the first night we met.

I don't reply and wait for him to say whatever it is he's going to say next.

Steadily, I'm growing more anxious, and I'm hyperaware of everything around me. The chill from the air conditioner. The softness of the sheets against my bare thighs. The scent of his cologne, woodsy and a touch sweet.

He holds up a manila folder then tosses it on the bed beside me. I don't move for it. Don't even look at it.

I'm scared to see what's inside.

I don't want to know.

I don't want to believe him.

I lick my lips; they feel as dry as sandpaper.

"Open it," he coaxes, his tone calm, but his gaze full of anger. I don't believe the anger is directed at me, but still, it makes me uneasy. "Take a look for yourself."

I stare at Jason and attempt to seem uninterested. It's a lie, though. I'm interested. More than interested, but I can't look.

I just can't.

His eyebrows raise in disbelief and he stares at me.

And stares.

And stares.

I can't take it. I want to throw up.

"You're wrong," I repeat curtly. "My brother is not an informant. He is not working with Peck." My words come out evenly, with conviction, but I don't believe them. It wouldn't surprise me if Andrew were working with the police, especially with a cop like Peck. He's done a lot of shady things in the past, knows a lot of shady people, and he's not overly loyal. If it'll save his skin, he'd give up just about anyone.

I've got firsthand experience with that.

He traded a date with me, his little sister, to keep his ass out of jail.

Jason must see the panic building in me because he holds a hand up to me as though to say calm down.

I laugh. I can't help it. It's not an amused laugh. It's wiry, strangled; it sounds like I'm choking.

I feel like I'm choking.

"Come on, Elena," he says, exasperated. "I know you've had to have wondered about that night. Why would Peck take a risk like he did with you? I don't care what kind of shit he's into, I'm sure he's not stupid enough to do something like this randomly. He knew you were a sure thing."

I know what he's getting at. I know, because I'm thinking the same thing, and it's exactly that thought that keeps me from looking in the darn file.

Because if Andrew is really working with Peck, then they knew each other. There's a good chance that he wasn't pulled over at random as they'd both made me believe.

It was planned.

Me going with Peck was the intended outcome of that traffic stop.

When I think about it, truly consider it, I remember the way he looked at me, as though he already knew me, and the familiar way he touched me when he helped me into the back of his cruiser while he questioned my brother.

As though he had touched me before.

As though he would touch me again.

Goose bumps spring up on my arms, but I'm not cold. I'm sweating; my skin grows clammy. I feel myself turn paler and paler until I'm certain that my complexion is ghostly white. I hear my own heartbeat, though, and it's surprisingly calm.

I bristle for a moment. "Yes, I have thought about it, but I didn't come here for you to investigate my brother."

Jason glares at me so thoroughly and hard that it looks as though he's about to burst a blood vessel in his eyes.

"No, you didn't," he agrees, after a drawn out moment. "But here's the thing, it was your idiot of a brother that got you into this fuckin' mess. The same brother who was supposedly arrested yesterday by the man you're running from. Seems to me that starting at the source—"

I don't let him finish. "My brother is not an idiot," I snap. My words are hissed, snarled on my tongue.

Good God, why am I defending him?

Why?

What's wrong with me?

Jason actually rolls his eyes at me. "We've got him working with Peck for a year before that DWI that ended with him walking away and you getting engaged," he says impatiently.

I know what he thinks. That I'm just a senseless girl who

can't see what's right in front of me. That I'm naïve. That I'm foolish. And maybe I am. But I can't … I can't hear this. My brother—the knowledge that he thought he was doing something good for me—was all that kept me going through the four horrid months I spent under Peck's thumb.

I run my hands through my hair, scratching at my scalp. It's a restless motion; something for my hands to do that does not involve looking in the darn file. I need to burn off some of the anxious energy that's sizzling through me.

In the past hour since I woke up, I've gone through a wide array of emotions: contentment, panic, shock, anxiety. Now, though, all I'm feeling is anger. Anger that heats within my belly. Anger that twists my chest and closes my throat.

My heart starts thudding as I watch Jason pace casually, as though he's not sticking a knife into my chest and twisting.

He knows what he's doing.

I see the recognition in his eyes.

He looks like he's struggling with something. Struggling to stay calm? Struggling not to strangle me? I don't know. Right now, I can't really think about that.

"Will you sit down," I say sharply. "You're freaking me out with all this pacing."

He laughs and looks at me disbelievingly for a moment, before his expression goes entirely blank. "Elena," he says, his voice slightly guarded. "Just look through the damn folder. Blind loyalty can only take you so far."

My eyes tear up as my gaze falls to the file. "I don't want to," I whisper. I don't want to see the proof. I don't want to know. I prefer ignorance. It's bliss. Truly it is.

But still, I feel it. I left everything to keep my brother safe and I feel his betrayal cutting through me like a jagged knife.

Jason steps toward me and takes a seat on the edge of the bed. "You know what the worst part of betrayal is, darlin'?" he asks.

I shake my head. What kind of a question is that?

A damn good one, I suspect.

He reaches out, brushing his fingertips across my cheek. "It always comes from the people you love and trust."

I blink, momentarily confused. "What?"

He looks away for a beat, and then his gaze comes back to mine. I can't read his eyes and I don't bother to try. They are dark, far darker than I've ever seen before. "Enemies can't betray you because you never trusted them to start with."

I don't know what to say to that so I decide to say nothing. From the look on his face, it's obvious he knows I'm trying to get my head together.

Jason leans in and kisses my forehead. He's so noticeably angry that I'm shocked by the tender action and I lean back.

"What was that for?" I ask.

He shrugs.

That's it.

He only gives me a shrug.

The room isn't well lit. Only the small table lamp beside the bed is on, but I'm pretty sure he's looking at me with something that resembles longing mixed with a touch of sadness.

I can tell he's uncomfortable and that whatever it is he's thinking I'm not going to like. I can feel it in the air, like pesky static clinging to my hair, and even though I'm certain I don't want to know, I ask, "What's going through that head of yours?"

He smiles at me, but it's entirely fake, no dimples at all. "I want you to meet an acquaintance of mine."

"What kind of acquaintance?" I ask cautiously, feeling every muscle in my body tighten. I don't like the way he's watching me. Cautious and gentle, as though he suspects that I'm going to jump from the bed and hide at any second.

"A detective I work with," he says.

A detective.

I stop breathing.

Um ... I do not think so.

My eyes narrow and my lips thin. "No way," I say. "Forget it."

"Elena—" he starts, giving me a look that is not amused.

Oh my God.

No. No, no, no.

I do not want to hear this.

I will not consider this.

"No," I say. "I am *not* meeting a detective. It is *not* happening."

Jason gets close to me, shuffling on the bed until he is completely in my space, placing his hands on either side of me, trapping me between his chest and the headboard.

I lean back, tilting my head up to meet his eyes. "What are you doing?"

"Do you think I'd put you in a position that would hurt you?" he asks.

My eyes narrow as I try to read his expression. I take in his hard gaze, the relentlessness blazing there, and quickly stammer out a response, "Um n ... no."

He isn't finished. His gaze hardens further. "Do you think I'd do something to alert that prick to your whereabouts?"

I shake my head, unable to find my voice.

"Words, darlin'," he says. "I want to hear the words."

"No." I swallow, shaking my head. "No, I don't think you would."

"Meet him, darlin'," he says. "Feel him out, listen to what he has to say, and then you can tell him whatever you want."

"Why?"

"Because," he says, his voice softening, "to put the guy in jail we're gonna need a cop on our side."

He has a point there. I hate it. I don't want to admit it, but he does.

I sigh, dropping my gaze from his. "Okay," I mutter. "I'll meet him."

His lips curl up into a smile. "Thank you."

I expect him to move back, but he doesn't. Instead, he brings a hand up to my hair, taking a curl and twisting it around a finger. His eyes focus on his hand, watching my hair as it wraps around his finger. His expression changes, softens, warms.

It feels ... nice. Warm and sweet.

But also … uncomfortable.

Intimate.

Close.

Too close.

I stare at him, swallowing hard. "Um, can you move back a little?"

"Yeah," he says, but he doesn't move, still toying with my hair.

"Okay," I say, swallowing again. "Maybe you could do that now."

He grins and chuckles. "Sure."

I wait for a moment, but still he doesn't move. "So shouldn't you move then?"

He keeps grinning, his gaze turning soft and warm. "Kiss me."

My belly flutters. It's not just with butterflies, but excitement and anticipation and lust. Yes, hot, steamy lust.

I laugh, trying to keep my cool. "Um … I … What?"

"Kiss me," he repeats, his voice deepening.

My belly flutters again, so does my pulse. "Jase—"

"Kiss me, Elena," he says firmly, and then his tone softens and he says, "Please."

I hesitate, licking my lips, staring at him. He's looking at me as though he wants much more than just a kiss.

My body heats, my belly buzzes.

Jesus, I want more than just a kiss, too. I know I said it was too soon, that I wasn't that kind of girl last night, but …

I do it.

I kiss him.

I have no idea why. I know I probably shouldn't, but I do it anyway. Maybe it's because his expression tells me he's not moving until I give in, or perhaps it's simply because I really, really like kissing him.

Either way, I do it.

I shimmy closer to him, wrapping my arms around his neck and hesitantly, cautiously, I lick my lips, and then press them against his.

His mouth opens as soon as my lips touch his, and I go for it, parting my lips as well, and I slide my tongue along the edge of his teeth.

Jason takes control of the kiss as soon as my tongue breaches his lips. He leans forward, maneuvering me until I'm flat on my back and his warm weight is pressing me into the mattress. One of his hands comes up to my hair, fisting the curls at the back of my head, while the other slides under my tee, bunching it up at my hips as he cups my bottom, pressing us closer together.

It feels so good, my body pressed in close to his, and I squirm a little, wrapping one leg around his thigh, trying to get closer, as one of my hands finds its way under his tee at his waist.

He pushes my tongue out of his mouth and slides his into mine. His hand slides up my side, groping and fondling my bare skin under my tee, and when his hand caresses the underside of my breast, I moan. It's throaty and soft and it seems to spur him on. His fingertips brush my nipple as his lips work mine, and I moan again, this time louder.

At the sound of my moan, Jason pulls back, only a few inches, and stares at me, his gaze intense, full of lust. But there's something else there too. Something that looks like curiosity mixed with shock.

We stare at each other for a moment, neither of us speaking, both of us breathing heavily.

I feel hot everywhere, my skin is buzzing, and I'm certain my heart is beating somewhere in the imminent heart attack zone.

"Wow," I finally whisper when I get my breathing somewhat under control.

He cups my cheeks in his warm palms, his thumbs brushing along my jaw. "I shouldn't have let you sleep last night," he murmurs. "I should have fucked you until you knew that you weren't going anywhere. Until you never wanted to leave. I came fuckin' close to waking you up to do it. I can't believe I didn't."

Oh my God.

I don't know what to think.

Does he really mean that?

Is it crazy that I want him to mean it?

I swallow hard.

Okay.

Okay, okay, okay.

Just breathe.

He's not serious. He can't be.

So what if we kissed, groped a little, and slept in the same bed?

So what if he wants to fuck me?

It means nothing, right? Just a little fun on the job. He can't really mean what he just said, right?

Right?

But even with all of this, there's something about the way he's stroking my jaw, possessive and gentle, that says something.

Something that I'm entirely not ready for.

Something that scares me more than Peck ever could.

Stop analyzing, I scold myself. *Just enjoy it. Live!*

I swallow hard, and deciding not to acknowledge his comment, I ask, "Um … what was that kiss about?" my voice coming out breathless.

Jason looks down at me, wearing his double-dimpled smile. "You were stressing," he says. "I don't like it when you stress."

I scoff. "And you thought a kiss would fix that?"

His eyes turn soft and sexy, and his grin widens. "It worked, didn't it?"

I choke on a laugh and swat at his chest playfully. "Jesus, you're full of yourself."

Amusement touches his lips, travelling all the way to his eyes, but he doesn't respond. Instead, he leans into me, kisses my forehead once more, and climbs off the bed.

"Read the file, darlin'," he mumbles. "Gonna make breakfast."

And then, he walks out of the bedroom, leaving me alone with the file.

Chapter Seventeen

Jason

"I've got to get out of here for a bit," Elena says, as she swallows her last bite of toast. She reaches for her coffee cup and clasps her hands around it, but she doesn't take a sip. She just stares down into the mug.

My gaze shifts to hers. It's the first thing she's said to me since I left her alone to read the file.

I have no idea if she read it.

I think she must have. It would explain why she seems so withdrawn.

Or maybe she's pissed at me for something.

It could be either. I don't have a clue.

I've been trying to get her to say more than a grunt or mumble for thirty minutes now, and hearing her speak a full sentence is a fucking relief.

"Sure," I say, leaning forward to rest my elbows on the table. "Where do you want to go?"

"Just out," she says and shrugs. She glances back up at me, looking a touch uneasy. "Do you have my car keys?"

I contemplate how to respond to that. The question sounds innocent, but there's something about her shift in attitude that's making me tense.

I don't like it.

I don't like the thought of her going out alone, either.

"You don't need your keys," I say. "I'll take you wherever you wanna go."

She stares at me, blinking a few times as she considers my response. She doesn't say anything, but she doesn't need to. Her lips purse, her eyes narrow, and her back straightens. Her displeasure is clear.

"Don't want you out of my sight, darlin'," I tell her. "Not until this shit with Peck and your brother is sorted out."

She closes her eyes and bites her bottom lip. When she reopens them, there's an uncertainty there that doesn't sit well with me.

"I need some space," she says, looking away. "I need to be alone for a bit."

She needs space. She needs to be alone.

What the fuck does that mean?

I have no response. I don't even want to acknowledge that I hear it.

Fuck. Maybe I did do something to piss her off. Forcing the file on her? I hope that's it. That, I think, she'll get over.

Fine. She needs space. I'll give it to her. Whatever.

I open my mouth to tell her where her keys are when a thought dawns on me. "Where did you get that car?"

She doesn't respond. She only stares at me as though she thinks that maybe I've recently sustained a head injury, and she's not entirely sure that I'm sane right now.

"Where did you get that car, Elena?" I ask again, more firmly.

She scrunches her nose, still looking at me oddly. "Why?"

My brow furrows, surprised and slightly confused as to why she's dodging my question. "Just answer the question."

She glances away. Her eyes are fixed somewhere on the table. She looks lost and uncomfortable. Almost scared.

I hate it.

I thought we were past that nonsense.

"I'm not going to leave, Jase, if that's what you're worried about," she says, her tone edging on spiteful, as though I'm prying into something that is none of my business. "I just want to get out for a bit."

The thought hadn't even crossed my mind.

It should have.

Elena running again wouldn't really be a stretch.

But it didn't.

Taken aback by the bite in her tone and her words, I hesitate, shaking my head. "Did I say I thought you were gonna run again?"

She says nothing. Her lips thin into a scowl and she glares at me.

Swallowing back an exasperated sigh, I grit my teeth. "I just want to know where you got the car."

"Why does that even matter?" she asks, staring at me expectantly, waiting for an explanation.

She doesn't understand why I want to know. She doesn't get why it's a big deal.

Fair enough. It's a valid question. I'll give her what she wants.

"Because if the plates can be tracked to you, you probably shouldn't be driving the damn thing around town."

"Oh," she whispers, dropping her eyes to the table once again. She's quiet for a bit, sitting back in her chair, fiddling with her fork.

"So if you need to go out," I continue, carefully, "maybe you should be taking my car."

Her eyes swing back to mine, wide with disbelief. She shakes her head, her hair bouncing back and forth with the movement. "That's not necessary. The car isn't mine."

"Where did you get it then?" I ask again.

"Drop it, Jase, please," she says quietly. "Stop trying to pick a fight with me. You already know who the car belongs to. I'm sure you ran the plates."

Pick a fight? Is she fucking serious? There's sarcasm in her tone, but the look she's giving me says she truly believes I already know the answer and that I'm trying to be difficult.

"I didn't run your goddamn plates," I grit out. "But I'm

getting the feeling that maybe I should."

She motions toward me. "You're doing it again."

I let out a shocked laugh, shaking my head. "You think I'm being an ass again."

Maybe I am.

But she's being incredibly stubborn.

"Just a little," she says, holding up her fingers about half an inch apart. She doesn't smile, but something flashes in her eyes. It looks like amusement. She thinks this is amusing?

If I weren't so goddamn frustrated, perhaps I'd think so, too.

"Don't be cute, Elena," I say. "It's not gonna work."

She shifts, tilting her head slightly, and she sits up straighter. She stares at me. Seconds pass. Five, fifteen, thirty, and then she smiles. It's soft, hesitant, sweet, and it lights up her face all the way to her eyes. "You think I'm cute?"

I smile, chuckling. I don't mean to, but I can't help it. Her smile is addictive, and I don't want it to fade. "I think you're fuckin' adorable most of the time."

"Now isn't one of those times, is it?" she asks, propping her elbows up on the table.

Sighing, I relax back in my chair and shake my head.

It's a lie and she knows it. I can see it in her doubtful gaze.

She's adorable all the time.

Even when she's getting under my skin like she is right now.

She blows out a breath. "But you'll get scary angry if I tell you."

"I won't get scary angry," I promise. "Just spit it out."

"You will," she tells me, seriously.

"No. I won't."

"Fine." She huffs, tossing up her hands. She hesitates for a second before whispering, "Your dad leant it to me. I'm supposed to give it back to him when this is over. Same as the cell phone."

She's nervous again. She says it as though she's afraid for me to hear it, as though she's scared of my reaction. I guess she's justified, but it makes me flinch anyway. I want to put her at ease, but it's fucking hard when another part of me wants to strangle her.

She doesn't get it.

She doesn't understand the kind of person my old man is.

She thinks he's a goddamn saint, when he's really the devil.

I should probably enlighten her, but I can't.

I can't think about him, let alone talk about it.

When I say nothing, she rolls her eyes. "See," she says. "I told you, you'd get mad."

She's wrong. I'm not mad. Not at all.

Actually, I think I get why she's been so distant since she came downstairs. It has nothing to do with her brother or Peck or me. I'm almost certain it's that she wants to talk to my old man.

I don't like it.

But I'm not mad about it.

She spent months with him. He's probably the closest thing she has to a friend. And I'm certain, one-hundred percent sure that she knows nothing about all the family bullshit.

Perhaps it's stupid of me, but I want to believe she wouldn't do anything to betray me.

I want to believe he isn't using her, too, but that's a stretch.

"I'm not mad," I say. "I just understand why you want to go out *alone* now."

She makes a startled sound from the back of her throat, and eyes me curiously. "You do?"

I nod. "I do."

A flush spreads across her cheeks and down her neck, and she quickly adverts her eyes. "So you'll drop it now?"

She's fidgeting nervously. I wish she'd stop that. I hate that I make her so nervous.

"You don't need to take off, darlin'," I say, an unintended bite comes out in my words. I take a breath, forcing my voice to smoothen. "You wanna call my old man, call him. I won't stop you."

"You won't stop me," she says, blinking with disbelief.

I shake my head. "No, I won't stop you."

The last of her nervousness turns to confliction as though

she wants to believe me, but she's not sure if she should. "Okay. Um ... thanks. I'd prefer you were with me anyway. You can listen if you want. If it'll make you feel better."

I stall, furrowing my brow. I don't know if I'm offended that she'd think that I'd listen in on her calls, or angry about it. Yeah, she showed me her text messages, but I'd never have gone looking for them without her telling me to.

"I ain't gonna screen your calls, darlin'," I say slowly. "Who the fuck does that?"

She smiles sadly. "Peck did."

My hands clench into fists involuntarily and the urge to punch something nearly overwhelms me. Each time I hear something new that that prick did to her, white-hot anger engulfs me.

Goddamn asshole.

Almost as though she can sense my anger, Elena stands up abruptly, and comes over to me. She nudges my shoulder, pushing me to lean back in the chair and slides herself onto my lap, taking one of my rigid arms and winding it around her waist. She doesn't say anything. She only curls her arms around my neck, and rests her head against my shoulder.

"Tell me something," I say after a moment, and she looks up at me, her face tense. "Did my old man ever explain to you why he was helping you?"

Her expression softens, shoulders relaxing. "Maybe it's just because it was a decent thing to do."

I laugh once. "I doubt that."

She shrugs. "Maybe you should ask him."

"Yeah, maybe."

"You won't, will you?" she asks, her voice falling flat.

"No," I say, "probably not."

She sighs dramatically and then leans in, placing a light kiss on my lips. "I'm going to give him a call. Could you set up that meeting with the detective? I want to get it over with."

"Yeah, sure," I say, and with that, she gets up and walks out of the room.

Chapter Eighteen

Elena

I leave half a dozen voicemails and send a dozen text messages to Mr. Chapman and he doesn't return a single one of them.

It's nine-nineteen in the morning.

Two hours and nineteen minutes of waiting for him to call me back.

I don't mind waiting. I've done a lot of it over the last year. Waiting to be found. Waiting for the moment I have to leave again.

Waiting, and waiting, and more waiting.

But these last two hours and nineteen minutes have been the longest wait of my life.

I try to keep myself busy. I shower and dress, spending far too much time on my hair and make-up. I clean the kitchen, the bathrooms, and make the bed. Anything that will keep me from reading the file on my brother again.

And I wait.

I wait for the phone to ring.

I wait to meet the detective.

I wait for Jason to find something—anything—we can use.

I'm in the bathroom, washing my face so I can fiddle with my make-up again. Jason is somewhere in the house doing whatever it is he does. Each time I see him, he's either on the phone or on the computer.

He seems to be doing a lot of waiting, too.

I've been avoiding him as much as possible and he knows it. His concern for me doesn't make me feel any better about my situation. In fact, it's making me crazy. I swear he's acting like he wants me to be his. Like I am his already.

The things he said this morning run a constant loop through my mind … *"I shouldn't have let you sleep last night … I should have fucked you until you knew that you weren't going anywhere. Until you never wanted to leave. I came fuckin' close to waking you up to do it. I can't believe I didn't."*

A part of me wants to tell him that he's wasting his time. That it can't happen. That we can't happen.

But another part of me aches to have his lips on mine again.

I like him. I really, really like him.

He might be bossy and he can be overbearing, but he's also kind and generous, and God knows I love his protective streak but …

My phone rings as I'm sponging the water from my skin with a fluffy yellow towel. Reaching into my pocket, I pull it out and glance at the screen.

Unknown caller.

I don't know why I bother looking. Mr. Chapman always comes up as an unknown caller, but even if he didn't, he's the only person who has this number anyway. I guess it's just an old habit.

Sighing, I answer it, muttering quietly, "I've been calling you for hours."

I'm greeted with silence. So much silence that for a second I think that maybe I let it ring too long and missed the call altogether. I'm about to hang up and call him back, but then I hear it.

A whispered breath.

A rustle.

Inhale.

Exhale.

Inhale.

"Hi, El." The voice on the other end of the line belongs to a man. It's deep and gravelly, whispering my name in a way that sounds familiar and threatening.

My body freezes and my heart stops.

It's not Mr. Chapman.

It's Peck.

I can hear him breathing on the other end of the phone. It sounds so close, rattling in my ear; I can almost feel the phantom warmth of his breath against my cheek.

Chills spread up my back and my hands tremble ever so slightly.

It's not him. It can't be him.

Oh God.

Trying to control my ragged breath, I ask softly, "Lawrence?"

"Yeah, baby, it's me," he murmurs.

Baby. He says it like a caress, but my body jerks and my stomach clenches as though he hit me with the word. I close my eyes. My lips quiver and I feel tears crawl up my throat.

This isn't happening.

This cannot be happening!

I say nothing. I just stare straight ahead in the mirror, unable to process this.

I don't even breathe. It's as though my lungs have forgotten how to expand and my mouth has forgotten how to draw air.

"Come on, baby," he says, his voice deceptively gentle. "Talk to me. I've missed hearing your voice."

My hand trembles, knocking the phone against my cheek. I need to hang up. I want to hang up. Good God, why can't I hang up?

"Don't call me baby." The words are hardly more than a whisper.

He lets out a light laugh. "Almost three months this time," he says. "You're getting better at hiding; although I have to say I'm not happy to hear that my fiancée has moved herself into another man's house."

His words hit me, but they refuse to sink in. My knees are giving out on me, and my vision blurs with tears. I try to understand how he could possibly know where I am or who I'm with. I haven't been here long enough or left a trail. The few people who know I'm here don't have this phone number and the one that does …

I shake my head; tears bead on my lashes. Oh God, no. No, no, no.

"How did you get this number?" I ask, but I already know, don't I?

My stomach sinks and twists, and I swallow hard. I feel like a fool. A stupid, stupid fool.

He chuckles. "You know how I got your number."

My body goes tight, and then wobbles. I brace myself against the counter and I stare at it unseeing as I try to process what he's saying.

"What?" I ask shakily, hoping that I didn't hear him correctly.

"You heard me," he says.

Yes. I heard him, but I wish I hadn't.

I don't want to believe it.

I don't ask again. I don't want to hear the name. Hearing him say it will make it so, so much worse. And I don't think he would answer me anyway. He's never been one for direct answers. He likes to see me squirm. Likes it when he gets under my skin.

So I say nothing. I don't admit that I heard him and I don't deny it. I don't let him hear the hurt and the fear in my voice.

Silence, with a man like him, is better.

"You're being stupid, El," he says, the sudden rage in his voice sends icy terror through me. "Very, very stupid. You think getting yourself a couple of private investigators to dig around in my business is going to keep you hidden? Did I teach you nothing?"

My heart is beating so hard it hurts. I can feel it everywhere, my pulse throbbing in my temples and throat and wrists.

I swallow away the lump in my throat. "Lawrence, I—"

"I'm coming to get you, El," he interrupts, his voice coming out sharp. "It's time for you to come home."

"You know I'll—"

He laughs, a harsh, unamused sound, cutting me off. "Go ahead, baby. Run again if you want. You can't hide forever. Sooner or later I'll catch you. Make no mistake about it."

Oh God ... no.

No.

Hell no.

This is not happening!

Before I can respond, the line goes dead.

My heart is beating so hard that I can hear it in my ears, the frantic beat making the house sound hollow with silence. My entire body is alive; I can feel the fear in every inch of it. I'm terrified out of my ever-loving mind.

The phone falls from my hand, clattering to the floor.

My heart beats faster.

My breath hisses and sputters.

I back up, my back hitting the wall and I slide down, cradling my head in my hands.

It was just a phone call. He isn't here. He's still in New York.

My heart is too loud, my head even louder.

I'm safe. I'm safe. I'm safe.

Jason

I'm lost.

Completely lost.

It's odd feeling this way. It makes me uncomfortable and sends frustration radiating, pulsing, convulsing throughout my body. I haven't felt this way since the day I made the choice to let my father walk away instead of spending years in prison.

How do you prove abuse and blackmail that happened a year ago? At this point, it's all he said/she said bullshit. I have half a mind to drag Elena into the station and force her to file a report. With it all on record, the bastard wouldn't be able to close down her parents' business without drawing attention to himself, but there's still her goddamn brother and her fear of the police to contend with.

At least she agreed to meet Cruz.

Flipping through the file, I mull over the connection between Elena's brother and the cop. At least it's a lead. Maybe he can show us something useful.

Two years … My fingers drum a restless beat against the tabletop. Andrew Reed has been a rat for two years. His file doesn't have much, a list of crimes, petty theft being the most common. It was the trafficking charge that led him to his relationship with Officer Peck. Andrew gave up his supplier to keep his ass out of jail, and Peck took the supplier down.

Other than the proof of a relationship between them, there's nothing.

Where does Elena fall into all of this?

I don't know …

There's got to be more here than what it looks like.

Peck must have known about her beforehand, must have had her in his sights. And her goddamn brother …

"Jason?"

Slapping the file closed, I turn to the sound of Elena's voice. "What's up, darlin'?"

She's silent for a moment, regarding me, before looking away. "I um … I really need my keys back."

Again with the keys? I almost groan, but I manage to swallow it back—barely. I don't believe she truly wants to leave. If she did, she would have. She wouldn't ask for the goddamn keys. She would just go.

I figure I should have expected it. Elena has been … unhinged for the last couple of hours, scrubbing my bathrooms, kitchen, she even vacuumed the fucking house. I thought perhaps it was because of my *fucking her* comment this morning, but I guess I'm wrong on that.

I glance at her, taking in her uptightness. "They're by the door in the dish with mine," I say, and wanting to see if this is just her needing alone time or if she's about to run, I reach into my back pocket, tug out my wallet, open it, and retrieve a fifty.

"You mind stopping to grab some beer while you're out?"

She gapes at me.

Gapes as though she thinks I've completely lost my mind.

I can't argue with her there. I've been thinking the same thing since she walked up to me in that damn bar, but she actually seems distressed that I'm simply agreeing.

Or maybe it's that I'm asking her to come back?

Hesitating, I debate for a second before standing up and slowly moving toward her. I watch her expression, gauging her nervousness. She has her arms crossed over her chest and her chin tucked down, but she doesn't retreat as I stop in front of her. "You okay?"

Elena glances up and nods once, but her gaze flickers to the left as she says, "Yes, I'm fine."

It's one of her tells. Everyone has them. Little unconscious twitches or fidgets that tell when they're bluffing or right out lying. Elena has a few of them, but the jittery eye contact is the most common.

"You wanna answer that again?" I ask softly, reaching out and taking her cheeks in my hands, tilting her head up to meet my gaze.

She reaches up and grabs onto my wrists, pulling my hands away from her face instantly and although I don't want to let her go, I don't resist, letting my hands fall away.

She stares at me.

It's not her usual stare.

This one isn't curious or cautious.

It's right out spooked.

She frowns as she gathers her thoughts, and then meets my gaze again. She offers me a slight shrug and as she opens her mouth, her eyes flicker once more. "I'm—"

My jaw clenches and ticks. "Bullshit," I say, stopping her before she can spew another lie.

Elena makes a disgruntled noise. Her eyes snap back to mine and narrow. They're skeptical and bordering on angry as she places a hand on her hip. "Bullshit? What do you mean bullshit?"

"Whatever was about to come out of your mouth was gonna be bullshit," I tell her. "Give me the truth, darlin'. I think I deserve that much, don't you?"

Stepping back, I lean against the wall, folding my arms over my chest. My eyes trail along her body, spotting each tremor and shake. She's watching me, her brow slightly furrowed, unsure and annoyed all at once.

"How do you do that?" she asks, stepping closer to me, and wrapping her arms around herself. "How do you know I'm lying?"

"You've got tells," I mumble, watching her as she takes another step toward me.

"What does that even mean?"

I stand there for a moment, not responding, and she takes the last step to me, reaching out and placing a tentative hand on my chest, just above my folded arms.

That hand tells me so much.

She trusts me.

She doesn't want to, but she does.

She also like's touching me.

I fucking love it that she does.

I place my hand over hers, holding it against me, and grin. "You give off signals when you lie. It's your eyes. They flicker to the left when you're about to bullshit me."

She frowns. "Oh."

Carefully, I let her hand go, and wind an arm around her waist, holding her to me. She doesn't make a sound, letting me hold her close. We stand there for a moment, not speaking, before I let my arm fall away from her.

Elena looks up at me, her frown deepening. She doesn't move away, instead, she leans further into me, resting her cheek against my chest and tugging my arm around her again.

I fight the grin that itches my cheeks.

I fight it until my face burns with the effort.

Just like I thought, she doesn't want to go anywhere. It's nice to be sure of that.

Actually, it's a goddamn relief.

I press a kiss on the top of her head and ask, "You wanna tell me what's wrong?"

Her eyes glitter strangely, and her jaw ticks. "He called me."

My brow furrows, confused. I'm not sure why that would bother her. She's been trying to reach my old man all morning. "You've been leaving him messages for two hours," I say.

"Not your dad," she whispers, burrowing her face into my neck. A shudder passes through her body, trembling from tip-to-toe. "*He* called me. Peck called me." Her eyes meet mine once more. "Your dad ..." she swallows. "He must have ..."

"Given him your number," I say, finishing her thought. "My old man must have given him your number, I'm not surprised."

"Yes, you are," she accuses. "I think that if you thought he would do that, if you thought he'd give out my location, I wouldn't be here right now."

She's right about that.

Fuuuuck. I'm getting sloppy. I have this girl in my house for a week and ...

"Jason, I have to go," she whispers. "He said he's coming for me."

Letting her go and stepping away from her, I move over to the sink, resting my palms on the counter and stare out the window.

"Jason." She follows me, her footsteps, just a whispered tap on the ceramic floor.

"Give me a minute, darlin'," I say.

I don't have to look back to know that she stops instantly. Her footsteps falter, tripping over each other, and she waits for me to say something. Her breathing hitches and hisses. The rustling sound of her hands running over the fabric of her top and jeans hits my ears.

Groaning, I rub a hand over my face and into my hair, scratching at my scalp. I should have seen this coming. I should have taken her somewhere. I should have destroyed that damn cell phone.

Wait.

My fingers stall.

No. Wait.

This is perfect. Absolutely perfect.

Peck is coming here. Peck thinks she moved in with me. No doubt, he thinks we're together.

I look at her. She looks at me. I feel a grin pulling at my lips.

She carries on, missing or choosing to ignore my grin. "He knows I'm here, Jase," she says. "He knows about you. I can't stay here."

"Yes, you can," I counter, still smiling. "It's exactly what you should do."

Her eyes bore into me. There's so much sadness. So much anger.

I don't like it.

I fucking hate it.

"I can't," she whispers.

I move to her, wrapping my arms around her waist and I quash down my sudden annoyance, managing a gentle tone as I say, "I need you to be smart about this."

"I am being smart," she snaps. "Leaving is smart. Hiding until I have something against him is smart."

"Thought you were sick of hiding," I counter. "Isn't that what you told me?"

Elena doesn't answer. She starts to squirm in my arms and the cutest little growl comes from the back of her throat. "Will you let go. I can't think with you in my space like this."

I chuckle, but I don't let go. It's nice to know I'm not the only one affected here. I look down at her as she squirms, a half-hearted effort to push me away. Her face is flushed pink and she makes another adorable growling noise.

My heart warms.

Holy shit, I feel too much for her. I feel everything. Protectiveness. Possessiveness. I feel her anger, her pain, but I also feel good. I feel good with her.

"Hold still, darlin'," I say, pulling her closer. She freezes mid-twist, and purses her lips, glaring up at me. "It's pretty clear you haven't clued into the situation here, so I'm gonna lay it out for you. I'm gonna do whatever it is I have to do to keep you safe. Which means, you leave, I'm coming with you."

"Why are you helping me?"

I'm not sure how to answer that question.

Silence swallows the room.

I'm doing it because I want to.

I'm doing it because I need to.

I'm doing it because it's the right thing to do.

I smile down at her. "Because I like you, Elena, and you are worth helping."

She smiles slightly and I can tell she's about to argue my response so I lean in, covering her mouth with mine.

Elena stiffens and gasps.

Then she sighs.

She fucking sighs and melts into me, as though my mouth on hers is the best thing that's ever happened to her.

She kisses me back, her tongue swiping against the seam of my lips before darting into my mouth, and her arms wind around my neck, pulling me closer.

Deep down, she needs this contact.

She might not want to admit it, but she does.

It lasts for a whole intense minute, and it fucking hurts to pull away. It burns.

But I do.

I peel my lips away and look down at her. Adorably flushed, her eyes open and she licks her lips. She's smiling, sweet and so innocent, and I watch as the smile falls from her face and her expression changes to one of anxiety.

I watch her, my expression dead serious. "What's wrong now?"

Her cheeks flush brighter, and she pulls out of my arms, turning her back to me. "I like you, too, Jason."

I laugh. I can't be the slightest bit upset about that. "That's not a bad thing, darlin'."

"Yeah," she mumbles. "It is. It's a tragedy, really."

I laugh again. I can't help it. "That's a bit dramatic, don't you think?"

She shakes her head, looking at me over her shoulder. "I'm not being dramatic. It's a tragedy. An epic tragedy."

"And why's that?" I ask, fighting against a grin.

She rolls her eyes, but doesn't respond.

"Trust me, babe," I say. "Life's way too long to go through it alone."

Elena looks torn, unsure whether or not to believe me, and I realize then why this matters so much to her. She's still waiting for me to betray her just like her brother and my old man did. She's looking for justification not to trust me, she's skeptical about my feelings for her, and she's trying to convince herself that she shouldn't care about me.

She doesn't want to care about me.

I don't blame her for that.

Betrayal hurts so much more when you care.

But the fact is she does care.

I can see it. It's written in the softness in her eyes when she looks at me and in the way she melts when I touch her.

The doorbell chimes, and Elena stiffens. She looks at me; I can see the nervous fear swimming in her eyes, and her guard comes back up.

I want so badly to take her in my arms and tell her it's okay, remind her that it's just the doorbell and that she's safe, but I think it would be a waste of breath right now.

Peck knows where she is.

She doesn't feel safe anymore.

Before she can freak out, I smile at her and say, "Stay here. I'll be right back, yeah?"

She nods shakily, forces a small smile, and before she can say anything, I leave her in the kitchen to answer the door.

When I pull the door open, my stomach sinks and my insides coil.

Detective Cruz is back, but he isn't alone.

Chapter Nineteen

Elena

The door slams and I jerk. Instant adrenaline pumps through my body causing my skin and fingers to tingle. I listen hard to hear who it is, but hear nothing. Whoever it is, Jason must not have let them in. That should calm my racing heart, but it doesn't.

Between his words, his kiss, and this blasted interruption, I don't think anything will calm me right now.

I pace.

I listen.

Seconds pass, turning into minutes.

I pace some more.

Where the hell is he?

And then, finally, the door opens again. I hear voices, murmured questions that I can't quite make out, and footsteps—lots of them. I inch toward the doorway, peeking my head around the corner.

Cops.

Oh shit, cops.

Four in uniform, standing behind a man dressed in plain clothes. Jason has his back to me, keeping them all by the door, which is still wide open.

"Where is she, son?"

Um ... what?

My body stills. That voice ... No way. No freaking way.

"Get the fuck out of my house!" Jason shouts, his voice taking on a scary angry tone. His entire body visibly tenses, and red creeps up the back of his neck.

"Baby girl?" Mr. Chapman calls. "Elena, come on out."

A knot grows in my stomach and I squeeze my eyes shut, trying (unsuccessfully) to quill it.

Why is this happening? Why? What did I do to deserve all of this? I must have been incredibly evil in a past life or something.

When I open my eyes, Mr. Chapman stands in my line of sight. His salt and pepper hair is askew as though he's been running his hands through it, but other than that, he looks put together, wearing pressed khaki pants with an olive green golf shirt. He's shorter than Jason is, his face tilted up to look at him, and he's smiling, a full, teeth flashing smile. It's a mocking smile, if not judgmental.

He looks proud of himself.

Proud and amused.

I lose my temper.

I storm out of the kitchen without thought. I no longer notice the police officers, or even Jason for that matter. All I see is Mr. Chapman.

The man I trusted.

The man I cared about.

The man I believed in.

His smile grows and softens when he sees me, his entire face lighting up, and it pisses me off even more. Heat sears through me, boiling my blood, my skin, every inch of me.

I stop in front of him and he opens his mouth to say something, but I don't give him the chance. I hit him. I hit him so hard I hear it. I hit him so hard my palm stings and throbs.

For the first time in my life, I find myself wishing that murder wasn't illegal.

I pull my arm back again, this time clenching my fist. I want to hit him again. Hit him hard enough to break his damn nose.

Mr. Chapman snatches my hand and leans into me. I expect to see rage in his expression, but it's not there. He looks … hurt. Not physically, it's as though I wounded him down to his soul, but I don't care.

I can't care.

He sold me out.

He gave me up to Peck.

"Get your hands off of me!" I shriek, jerking my arm away.

He lets go—instantly—his eyes widening at my outburst. He's never heard me raise my voice, let alone shriek. I was always quiet with him, biting my tongue, too scared to do much more.

I feel Jason's heat hit my back just before his arm snakes around my waist. He maneuvers me, tugging me to his side and tucking me in, so my front is snug against his side. The hold is a mix of protective and possessive as he swivels until he has placed himself between me and everyone else in the room.

Mr. Chapman stares at me, and then stares at Jason, before staring at us both, his eyes wide and mouth open. He finally settles his eyes on Jason. "Get your hands off her."

Jason says nothing and he doesn't let go.

I glare at Mr. Chapman.

I want to tell him to get out. I want to tell him to shut the hell up, but I'm so mad that I can't seem to spit out any words.

"Elena," Jason says, ignoring his father, and I look up at him to find that he is grinning, no teeth, but grinning enough to make both his dimples pop out. "Go wait in the kitchen. Make some coffee, yeah?"

Um … what? What, what, what? He wants me to make coffee? I glare at him. I glare so hard it hurts my eyes. "You want me to make coffee."

"Yeah, darlin'," he says. His eyes flick to the cops, and then back to me. He leans into me, his lips coming to my ear. "I promise I'll let you beat the shit out of him later."

I clear my throat, readying myself to tell him no, but he pulls back and smiles, this time with teeth, and his amused eyes twinkle down at me.

I stall for a moment, taken aback by his amusement. I have no idea what to do. Tell Jason this isn't funny? Yell at Mr. Chapman? Get away from all the cops and make the darn coffee?

I just don't know.

I decide to try and play it cool, but there's one little problem with my plan. I'm not feeling very cool.

In fact, I'm shaking with both rage and nerves.

Shaking so much that I can't seem to make my feet move.

Shoot.

The police officers are watching me. So is the guy in the plain clothes. They're all grinning, some full out smiling.

Oh boy.

This is not good.

Jason squeezes my waist, and then lets me go. And somehow, even though my knees are shaking and my stomach is flipping, I manage to walk back to the kitchen without falling flat on my face.

Jason

"I've got to bring her in, Jase," Cruz whispers as I watch Elena make her way back to the kitchen.

I'm grinning like a lunatic. I can't believe she hit my old man. Didn't think she'd have the guts to do something like that, but I'm so goddamn proud of her.

"You wanna question her, you do it here," I say. "She'll freak the fuck out if you take her into a police station."

He narrows his eyes angrily at my demand, silently telling me that I'm overstepping my bounds. "I don't have a choice. Her fiancée called in her location. He's worried about her. I've got to bring her in."

I stare at him, considering how to respond. "Can't let you take her, Cruz. There's more going on here than you know."

He glares at me.

He looks furious.

Folding his arms over his chest, he leans in until his face is a few inches from mine. I can feel the heat coming from him; smell the laundry soap from his clothes, mixed with sweat. "Enlighten me."

Gritting my teeth, my gaze shifts to the officers. They're all watching me, looking amused and interested. "She'll talk to you, but you've gotta clear everyone else out."

"I'm not leaving here without that girl," my old man growls. "I told her I'd help her."

I turn to my old man. "You're the one that fuckin' gave her up!"

"Son—"

I shake my head. Whatever he's got to say, I don't want to hear it. "Get the fuck outta my house."

"I did this for her," he continues. "The sooner this is dealt with the better. She can bait him—"

His voice is slowly pulling me apart, piece by agonizing piece. I stare at him hard, feeling years upon years of rage and pain and betrayal bubble up to the surface.

I want to lash out.

I want to strike him down.

I want to grab all the shit I have on him and turn him in to the cops filling my doorway.

"What's going on?" Cruz snaps, cutting off my old man. "Bait who?"

My gaze shifts to Cruz, and he steps back, seeing the fury in my eyes. "It's the fuckin' cop she's running from. The one you called an upstanding citizen last night. The one ..." I stop, clearing my throat when my voice catches, because I know I sound just as angry as I feel and I don't want Elena to hear it.

Cruz's brow furrows and he looks at me as though I've lost my mind. "Are you sure?"

I nod. Of course I'm sure. Elena can't lie for shit. I'd know if she were lying about the cop.

My cell phone chimes with an incoming message and I stall in responding, digging it out and opening up the message.

Liam: Lost Peck.

Me: Where did you last see him?

Liam: At the airport. He went through security and boarded before I could get a ticket and follow.

Shiiiit. The prick isn't wasting any time, is he?

Me: He's coming here. What's the flight time from NY to Sac?

Liam: Five hours, thirty-four minutes.

Five and a half hours, with boarding time factored in we probably have six and a half hours before he's here and off the plane.

Six and a half hours ...

Me: Find the brother and wait for word.

Liam: I'm on it.

Me: Call Wes and Vance and tell them to get to my place, yeah?

Liam: Will do.

Sliding my phone back into my pocket, I look at Cruz who is looking back at me, incredulously. "Peck just boarded a plane. We've got five hours and thirty-four minutes to come up with a plan to keep that prick away from my woman."

Cruz raises a brow, smirks, and shakes his head. "Your woman?"

"Yeah," I say. "My woman."

Elena

I'm sitting in the kitchen staring out the window. My feet are on the chair, heels tucked tight to my butt, and my arms wrapped tightly around my knees. The smell of rich coffee fills the air, soothing my frazzled nerves.

Wes is standing in the doorway behind me. I think he's on the *Elena Run Watch*. I find it amusing, really. Jason retrieved the Taser from the car for me, which I have resting on top of my knees. If I wanted to leave, I could easily drop Wes and do just that.

Okay, maybe it wouldn't be that easy. I'd have to reload, shoot Jason again, shoot a detective, four cops, and Mr. Chapman, but I could do it.

Except ... I don't want to go.

What's the point? Peck will just track me down again.

And again.

And again.

He's not going to give up. I'll be running forever. Running and hiding. Hiding and running.

Definitely not the kind of life I want. Not anymore.

Mostly, I want to see Mr. Chapman. Maybe shoot him a few times with my Taser. I can't quite wrap my head around his betrayal. It's too fresh and hurts far too much right now to see his supposedly *good intentions*.

He's somewhere in the house right now. Perhaps that's why Wes is on sentry duty. Jason, with his voodoo mind reading talents, probably saw right through me the second he handed me the stupid Taser.

I've been sitting here for almost thirty minutes now. Every so often, another cop comes in, fills up his mug with coffee, and then filters back out.

No one will tell me what's going on.

But then, I haven't asked, either.

In the background, I can hear Jason. He's angry. He's hurting. I bet he's working hard to not throttle his dad. He's talking to Vance and that detective. They're talking about me. I can hear my name whispered over and over, but not much else.

It's probably better that way, I think.

I don't think I want to know what their plans are.

Not yet, at least.

It's barely eleven in the morning. The clock ticks, ticks, ticks, from its place on the wall above the table. Do these guys ever sleep? Wes looks wiped and I bet Vance is, too. And the detective, he's had less sleep than any of us has had.

Suddenly, there seems to be something happening in the hallway. There's a commotion, voices raised, feet clomping.

I grip the Taser, pointing it at the door while my body curls in on itself, my knees coming tighter to my chest, my chin pressing into my knees.

Wes eyes me cautiously, moving to the left out of the doorway, but he doesn't say a word. I almost laugh. He probably doesn't want to draw my attention just in case I have another accident.

The footsteps get louder.

My heartbeat stays calm, my breathing, even. It surprises me, but I don't give it much thought. Maybe my body is just too wrung out to panic anymore.

My gaze fixes itself on the doorway. I hear Jason let out a string of curses, and then the detective fills the doorway.

I stare at him.

He stares at me.

The guy doesn't appear to notice the Taser or if he does, it doesn't bother him. He looks to be about Jason's age, maybe a year or two older, and he's tall, with dark brown hair and dark brown eyes. His jaw is square. His hair is thick and cut short. He's wearing jeans, a coffee-colored tee, tan boots, and there is a badge clipped to his belt at his right hip.

"Elena Reed?" he asks in a deep voice. He doesn't make a move to come closer, only stands there with an easy smile, watching me.

I nod, my chin rubbing against my knee as I do it. "Yes, that's me."

"I'm Detective Jacob Cruz," he says. "You mind if I come in and chat with you for a minute?"

My brow furrows. He's asking me as though I have a choice in the matter, as though if I say no, he would leave, but I doubt that's the case.

I almost say no.

My mind screams for me to say no.

If only to see if he will in fact turn around and leave.

But I don't. I promised Jason I'd talk to him.

I nod again, tightening my steady grip on the Taser. If he notices, he doesn't let on. He keeps his eyes on mine as he walks into the kitchen. He seems relaxed enough. I wonder if he truly is or if it's an act to calm me. He grabs a chair, turning it around to face me and takes a seat.

We stare at each other, neither of us speaking. Seconds pass, turning into minutes as his eyes study me, his expression serious, and then he smiles a genuine, full smile.

Wow.

He has a great smile. Great teeth. White and straight. That smile makes him look younger and carefree.

"You changed your hair," he says, his gaze raking over my head. "I like it."

I smile back hesitantly. "Thank you."

I hear more footsteps in the hall and my eyes swing to the doorway, just as Jason fills it. His eyes hit mine, and then they drop to my hand and he frowns. "You doing okay, darlin'?"

The question strikes me as odd and I shake my head, half-disbelieving and half-aggressive. "I'm fine," I tell him, because, of course, I'm okay. He gave me the Taser back. I'm fine. Just peachy.

He walks to me, moving in close to my side, and his hand comes to the back of my neck, squeezing gently. "You don't look fine."

Unwinding my arms from my legs while keeping the Taser steady, I look up. As I study him for a moment, I shift on the chair, bringing my legs down and crossing them. His eyes are tight, his jaw ticks. There are no dimples, no lip twitches.

"Neither do you," I tell him, my voice whisper soft.

He chuckles, but there is no mirth in the sound. "I'm not the one pointing a Taser at a cop, darlin'," he points out.

My mouth goes slightly slack-jawed and I blink.

Right, the Taser. Perhaps his question isn't that odd after all.

"You noticed that, huh?" I ask, dropping my eyes from his.

His hand gives my neck another light squeeze and he chuckles again. "Yeah, darlin', I noticed."

Right. Of course he noticed. Jason Pierce misses nothing.

"I ... um ... I ..." I'm stammering, struggling to get out something that might make this situation okay. I don't want to drop the Taser. It's my safety net. I need it. I need that safety.

I look at the detective, pleading with my eyes.

"She's fine," Detective Cruz says, his lips twitching up with another great smile. "I need to ask you a few questions. You up for that?"

I shrug. "Um ... yeah, I guess."

Cruz looks up at Jason and jerks his chin toward the door. "You mind, Pierce?"

Jason moves in closer, his hip pressing against my shoulder tightly and his hand squeezing the back of my neck lightly. His pose feels possessive, but his hand at the back of my neck, and the way his thumb strokes along the side of my throat ... it feels reassuring, comforting, telling me that he's here, that he isn't leaving my side.

"Ask away," he says shortly.

Cruz takes in Jason's stance and shakes his head. "Gonna need you to step out, Jase," he says. "Don't want you influencing what she tells me."

"She won't talk to you without me here," Jason shoots back, giving my neck another light squeeze. He's completely confident in his statement, and he is not wrong. I don't want him to leave.

Cruz's eyes drift over my face thoughtfully, before he says, "She won't tell me the truth about you and her relationship with you while you're standing here."

For some reason, watching them bicker back and forth on whether or not I'll lie to them strikes me as amusing and I let out a sharp bark of laughter. "Yes, I will. And besides that, I'm told I suck at lying."

Detective Cruz stares at me for a moment, before nodding, giving me a soft smile. "Are you sure it was Officer Peck who called you this morning?"

I nod. "Um ... yes."

"Tell me what happened between you and him," he says gently. "Start from the beginning, from when you first met."

I suck in a breath.

This is it.

This is the moment of truth.

He'll believe me or he won't. Either way, Peck will still come for me.

I meet the detective's eyes. They're gentle, caring, watching me as though he wants nothing more than to hear my story.

Another deep breath.

And another.

And another.

Then, I open my mouth and I tell him everything.

Chapter Twenty

Jason

"Jason, stop it and listen to me," Richard fucking Chapman says, planting himself in my path. "I did this for her."

I swallow back a bark of humorless laughter. He did this for her. Doesn't matter how I try to look at it or rationalize it, the words ring false.

My mother stands behind him, eyebrows raised, waiting for me to respond. I'm not sure what she expects me to say. My glare is pretty self-explanatory, I think. It clearly states: I'm in hell.

I've been trapped in the same house with my old man following me around, trying to talk to me for the last three hours, and my mother is in on it.

I'm not sure who called her, but she showed up shortly after Vance and Wes arrived. It was tense at first between them, but somehow in the last hour or so my old man has managed to weasel his way in and gain her support.

They've been reminiscing.

They've been laughing.

They've been acting as though they're the best of friends, as though nothing happened.

It's making me think about things that I have no place thinking about anymore. Making me remember things that I wish would stay buried.

It's fucking hell.

My old man was a lot of things, some good, some not. When he was there, he was a good father and an attentive husband. He doted on my mother. He did all the father/son bonding stuff.

We were his everything.

But things changed. He changed.

He became someone I didn't know. He became a cheater, not just with Mona, but in life. He started looking for the easy way out. Want a promotion? Make a deal with a criminal for a fake bust. Need money? Rip off the same douche bag you just made a deal with.

But the easy way—at least for my old man—set off a chain reaction of bullshit.

Before I knew it, our basement had become a place for his *friends* to store their drugs and guns and my old man was sneaking out in the middle of the night to clean up crimes scenes, sweeping them clean of evidence.

He jeopardized his career and my mother's safety to make a few quick bucks.

If he'd have kept it away from home—away from my mother—I might have ignored it. I want to think I could have pretended it wasn't happening.

But he didn't.

He brought it into our home.

Brought his buddies there, too.

He exposed my mother to danger, when he should have been protecting her from it.

But there are still days that I regret not pretending. Some days I wonder what would have happened if I'd kept what I found between him and me. Maybe I should have talked to him, helped him get out of the mess he made. Other days I wonder if it would have been better if I just turned him in.

This is one of those days I regret it.

Seeing my mother smile, hearing her laugh … Five years and she still loves him. Despite everything, he is still the only man for her.

It fucking rips me apart.

And to top off the goddamn family reunion, each time I turn around, there's another cop in my house.

Don't get me wrong, I welcome the help, but this is over the top. I like quiet operations. Less people, less chance for fuck-ups.

But this … this is a goddamn circus.

"Jason," my mother says, annoyed by my silence. "Hear him out. He may be able to give you some insight on this whole mess."

I snort, cutting her an incredulous look, which only serves to earn me a disappointed glare.

"Let me help, please," my old man begs. He's speaking loudly, making a big scene. It draws the attention of a few officers and they glance our way, wondering why he's begging me like he is.

I step toward him, giving him a look that makes him shut up. I don't have time for this shit. Peck's plane will be landing in a little over two hours and Elena … Elena has gone into hiding somewhere in the house.

She's stressed.

She's nervous.

I should be with her right now, coaching her, getting her ready to face her ex, not standing here listening to my old man tell me he gave her up for her own good.

Gritting my teeth, and keeping my voice low, I say, "You gave up her location to a prick that beat her, forced her into a relationship, and blackmailed her to stay with him. How the fuck was that for her?"

He blinks at me and his jaw begins to drop, before he steels his expression. "The sooner they get near each other, the sooner this shit can end, and whether you like it or not, it's better that shit happens here, away from people who might be inclined to protect him and discredit her."

I laugh, shaking my head. I don't want to see the logic there, but even if I did, the fury building within my chest won't let me.

"Are you fuckin' serious right now?"

Holding out his hands, he lifts his shoulders slightly. "What do you want me to say?"

I want to know why he did it. Why did he bother hiding her for two months only to call Peck as soon as she left, but I know that there is nothing, *nothing*, he can say that will make what he's done this time okay.

"Nothing," I grumble. "I think it's better if you say nothing."

"She knows more than she's saying, Jase." His tone and comment rubs me the wrong way. Is he saying she's lying to me or hiding shit? He must see where my mind is going because he quickly continues, "Don't think she knows she does, but she does. He's into more than just beating up a little girl. Taking her like he did ..." he shakes his head and sighs. "It shows me that he's sure of his safety and he knows people will back him, but no cop would back this shit. So ask yourself, where's that safety coming from?"

"You would have backed it," I say, and instantly regret it when I see my mother's face fall.

It's not entirely true.

He wouldn't have ignored the abuse, but the rest ...

"She lived with him," Dad continues, ignoring my comment. "She probably went to meetings with him or held dinner parties, shit like that. Show her some mug shots of the guys he's busted in New York. Bet she'll have seen them. It might help jog her memory on things she heard, too."

"How the fuck do you know she could ID anyone?" I ask, aiming for sharp, but my words come out sounding eager.

He might be onto something here.

My gut has been telling me there was more to this than I could see.

He leans in close and drops his voice to a whisper, "Because your momma could have ID'd most of the guys I worked with. You could have, too." He sighs. "Look, you're gonna need something more than abuse that was never reported to bring him down. Unless you plan on using her to bait him into doing it again, which from the way you've been hovering over her, I'm thinking that's not an option, you're gonna need something else."

I stare at him hard.

If he's trying to pull some bullshit, I can't tell.

He's watching me, face straight, sincere even, waiting for me to respond.

When I don't say a word, he drops his eyes, and mutters, "You get her through this and I'll give you what you want."

I let out a sharp bark of laughter that holds no humor. "And what exactly is it that you think I want from you?"

His pained eyes meet mine once more. "You want me out of your life once and for all. I'll give you that, Jase. Get her through this and I'll give you that."

I don't expect the stab of pain in my chest that his words cause. I don't even know how to process it. He's right, that's exactly what I want, but if that's true, then why does it hurt hearing him say it out loud?

"Of course I'll get her through this," I say, my voice sounding thick even to my own ears. "Not gonna let that prick get anywhere near her."

"Thank you," he mutters. "She's a good girl. Kills me to see her messed up in this shit."

I stare at him. He seems sincere. He sounds genuine.

It makes no sense.

This isn't my old man. My old man doesn't care about some random girl. He wouldn't try to help her either.

"Why do you want to help her?"

He laughs, but there's no humor in the sound. "She's my second chance, son. She's giving me the chance to make up for all the shit I did wrong."

"You're using her to clear your conscience," I say, incredulously.

He stares at me for a long moment, saying nothing, before glancing back at my mother. She looks as though she wants to say something, but swallows it when he tips his head and says, "Come on, Mona. The boy's got a lot of work to do."

I stand there, not moving, watching as my old man puts an arm around my mother and they start toward the door. As they reach it, he glances back at me. "I'll be staying at the Embassy until this blows over. Elena's got my number if you need me."

I gaze at him in silence for a moment, and then nod when no words come out.

"See you later, honey," Mom calls out, shooting me a brilliant smile. "You give me a call if there's anything I can do, and tell Elena the same, okay?"

Then, they're gone.

What the fuck just happened?

I hear someone come up behind me and a hand falls on my shoulder. "He makes a good argument, although I would have liked to know what we were dealing with before he set it all in motion."

Turning to Cruz, I let out an exasperated sigh. "He isn't known for thinking shit through before acting."

"You think she'll try it?" Wes asks, coming over.

"Not sure," I say and shrug, glancing around the room, before bringing my gaze back to Cruz. "You think you can get that emergency restraining order in place before the plane lands?"

"With her story," he says, his brow furrowing, "yeah, I should have enough to get one, but she'll have to come in and fill out an application soon."

"Good, do that," I say. "Is there a reason there's so many cops in my house?"

Cruz snorts. "Missing person, engaged to a cop, and that cop decided to call in a bunch of reports of her whereabouts."

Nice. Just fucking perfect.

Who knows how many more will show up?

"I'm gonna go pull her out of hiding and give her the options," I say. "I'll give you a call once she decides how she wants to go with this, yeah?"

Cruz nods. "Sure. We've got just over two hours before the plane lands. I'll be sending over an officer to pick him up so I can probably stall the arrival time a bit more."

"I'll call," I tell him, and then turn my attention to Wes. "Round up Vance and get everyone out. I need some quiet space to talk to her. Lock up behind you, yeah?"

Wes nods, but he also winks and gives me a shit-eating grin.

I don't acknowledge the grin.

All I can think about is getting my girl in my arms and making sure she's okay.

I go off to find Elena.

I hope she's not freaking out.

And if she is, I hope she doesn't shoot me with the goddamn Taser again.

Chapter Twenty-One

Elena

I'm in hell.

I feel like a rock star, that is, if rock stars have an entourage of straight-faced police officers.

There are too many people here, poking around, talking to me. Everyone's looking at me with pity and offering me things. Tea, coffee, food, pop, beer. Each time I turn around, someone else—someone in uniform—is standing there, trying to get my attention.

It's making my skin crawl with unease.

I know they're all trying to be nice.

They're trying to make me feel comfortable and safe.

But it's just too much.

I'm not used to this many people and the fact that they are all dressed in uniform; well … it's quite simply hell.

I'm alone now—finally—in Jason's bedroom, hiding away from the mad house downstairs.

I feel better by myself, being alone and not worrying and checking my surroundings every few seconds.

I feel safer.

But even in solitude, I'm still a mess. A sweaty, jittery mess, and it makes me sick.

I haven't always been this timid, weak woman. I never used

to be nervous all the time. I was outgoing. I liked to have fun and I was always up for meeting new people. I had dreams. I had plans. I was going to have a bright future.

And then Peck happened.

Things changed.

I changed.

Sighing, I cross the room and take a seat on the bed, setting the Taser down beside me. I'm surprised they let me keep the thing so long with all those cops hanging around.

Even with the door closed, I can hear people everywhere, moving through the house. I'm not sure why so many officers are needed or why they all have to be here. Maybe it has something to do with the fact that Peck is a cop, too?

Ugh, I don't know.

After speaking with the detective for well over an hour, he disappeared downstairs with Jason, Wes, and Vance to *review the case,* and it was shortly after that people started showing up.

Mona is here, too—somewhere. I spotted her talking to Mr. Chapman just before I came up here. She looked ... happy to see him, which is confusing.

So confusing.

Actually, I'm surprised Jason even let him stay. I figured he would have forced him out once I finished talking to Cruz, but he didn't. Jason didn't even glance in his father's direction.

I think I'm supposed to be happy or excited. Detective Cruz believes me.

He believes me!

I should be thrilled about that. I should be jumping up and down, doing a happy dance or something. For a year now, all I've wanted was to get my life back and soon, with the help of Jason and Vance and Wes and the Sacramento police, I'll be able to get back to those dreams and plans, and live out that bright future, except ... those dreams and plans ... I don't think they are what I want anymore.

I'm no longer that person.

Good God, I'm not even sure I want to go back to New York anymore.

Peck's plane is going to land in two hours and twenty-three minutes. I'm not really sure what the plan is, but with the amount of cops here, I'm guessing this will end quickly.

And then I'll be going home.

Suddenly, I feel rushed. I want more time here. More time with Jason.

I'm lost in my thoughts, my mind drifting back to last night, when I hear a light tap on the door before it opens. My hand goes to the Taser as I glance up, and seeing Jason standing in the doorway, I quickly take my hand back, knotting it with the other in my lap. He's not smiling. Actually, he looks tense and perhaps even slightly angry.

"Hey, darlin'," he says. "What are you doing up here?"

I shrug. "Just needed some quiet."

He watches me with a curious expression for a moment before he cracks a smile. Crossing over to me, he pauses right in front of me. His arms snake around me, his hands go to my ass, and he picks me up.

I gasp and instinctively wrap my arms and legs around him, holding on tight.

I don't bother asking him what he's doing.

I know.

He's told me enough that he likes me in his arms and at the moment, that's exactly where I want to be.

Jason settles down on the edge of the bed with me straddling him, my knees on either side of his thighs, my chest pressed to his chest, and he wraps his arms around me.

Once he has me settled where he wants me, he leans down to kiss me. His lips are soft against mine, not frenzied like before. He holds there for a moment, his lips tasting mine, before he pulls away, and curves an eyebrow at me. "You doing alright?"

"Um ... yeah," I say, licking my lips. "I'm good."

He doesn't look convinced. "What's going on in that pretty little head of yours?"

I sit there for a moment, clutching onto him, before I respond. "I was just thinking about going home."

He freezes as he stares down at me, a look of surprise

passing across his face. His body stiffens and his arms tighten around me. He shakes his head after a second, loosening his hold, and tries to smile at me. "Yeah?"

Taken aback by the sharp bite in his voice, I furrow my brow. I know he's trying to hide it, but he seems almost agitated with me.

I don't understand it.

"Yeah," I say quietly, and duck my head, resting my forehead against his collarbone. "I guess I'm just trying to figure out what I'm supposed to do when I get there."

"You have tons of time to figure that out, darlin'," he mumbles and before I can get anything else out, he says, "We gotta talk about Peck."

I say nothing, because what is there to say? I'm sure he knows that I don't want to talk about Peck, but I also know that I really don't have a choice.

Not with the asshole on his way to get me.

Jason's hands leave my ass and come up to my cheeks, lifting my head, and forcing me to look at him. He stares at me for a moment, his expression turning serious. "Promise you, darlin', I won't let him take you away from me."

Wow.

He sounds serious, he looks it, too, one-hundred percent certain, and oh God, but seeing it, hearing it, causes my belly to flutter and warm.

I nod, and whisper, "Okay." It's all I can think of saying.

"We've been working this last week, trying to find some dirt on him," he says carefully, watching me closely. "Liam's been following him. Wes and Vance have been checking in at the department he works at. I've been running checks on him, his bank accounts, phone records, credit cards. We've found nothing."

Nothing? I don't even know what to say to that.

There has to be something.

There has to be.

I swallow thickly. "Um ... okay."

"It's gonna be hard to prove the abuse unless he right out

admits to it," he tells me, his fingers stroking along my hairline. "It's been a year. There are no reports. Not even the hospital records show hints of violence. All accidents."

I nod again, not sure what to say. I knew there would be nothing in my medical files. The few times I ended up in the hospital, he was with me, flashing his badge around.

People believe the badge.

They believe that cops are here to keep you safe, not cause harm.

"So," he says slowly, drawing out the word. "We've got a couple options. First one is, you can get a restraining order. We've got enough for that. Hopefully, he'll honor that and stay the fuck away from you, but if he doesn't, he can be pulled in for breaking it."

A piece of paper?

He wants me to get a piece of paper to keep that bastard away from my family and me?

"You're suggesting I let a piece of paper keep him away from me?" I ask. My voice cracks as I try to hold back a sudden well of tears. That sounds like an entirely useless solution. "What about my parents? My brother?"

"It's an option," he says. "And it wouldn't be easy for him to act against your parents since you gave your statement to Cruz. You've got it on record that he used it to blackmail you now. It would shoot off red flags if he tried, darlin'."

I sniffle. "Is that my only option?"

He lets out a sigh. "You could meet with him, wearing a wire, and try to get him to admit to the shit he did to you. We can have your brother pulled in. He can give a statement on the DWI and the trade for you, but I gotta say, babe, with his record that statement might not do much."

Tears gather in my throat and dribble down my cheeks. I know it's stupid to cry. It's ridiculous. He's only giving me options. It's not like I have to agree to them.

I can always leave.

Run again.

But I thought this was going to be easy. It was supposed to

be simple. Meet Jason, and then let him do his thing. I had this delusional thought that I'd just be sitting in the background, doing nothing, and after a couple of days, I'd be home.

It wasn't supposed to be this complicated. I wasn't supposed to have to face Peck again until he was in handcuffs, and I definitely wasn't supposed to care about the private investigator.

I shift on his lap and wipe away some tears, trying to pull myself together. "I don't know if I can do that."

He nods as though he expected that response. "Another option is that you can come down to the police station with me, go through some mug shots and see if you remember anyone." He hesitates for a moment, and lets out a long drawn out sigh. "Dad seems to think that if he was doing anything shady, you'd probably have met some of the guys he was working with. If you can point us in the right direction, we could nail him for something else and get him put away."

My brow furrows. He talked to his dad?

How would Mr. Chapman even know this?

I want to ask, but I don't. There's something about his expression that tells me now is not the time to get into it, and if I try, he won't be giving up any answers.

Jason takes in my furrowed brow and leans toward me, quickly kissing my lips. "We'll get this sorted, darlin'. I promise you that."

I stare at him for a moment, contemplating on what to do. Honestly, none of the options seem great to me. "What do you think I should do?"

He considers my question for a few seconds, his hand running up and down my back. "I'd like you to try and ID some of his associates."

I hesitate. I'm not sure what to say. My instincts say, *yes, whatever you think is best,* but that means trusting Mr. Chapman again, and do I really want to do that? Something tells me that Jason is feeling the same way.

"How am I supposed to do all that in two hours?" I ask.

"You won't," he says. "If you want to try that, we'll go in tomorrow morning to look at the mug shots."

"But he's—"

"He ain't gonna get near you, darlin'," he says, cutting me off. "I swear to fucking God, he won't lay eyes on you if you don't want him to. Cruz will serve him with the restraining order when he shows up at the station to get you."

I don't know what the restraining order will do. Most likely, it'll just piss him off. But if he tries to break it, at least they'll be able to pull him in for that.

My lips curve into an involuntary smile and I nod. "Okay."

A smile slowly spreads across Jason's face and his amazing dimples make an appearance. He runs his hands down my back, slipping under the hem of my tee and sliding back up. He leans in to me and I think he's going to kiss me, but he pauses and holds, a mere inch from my lips. "Glad that's settled."

He kisses me then. His lips are so soft, and his kiss is so, so gentle. His hands caress my back, making my skin tingle, and then they're back on the hem of my shirt, pulling it up.

"What are you doing?" I ask, wiggling away, and tugging my shirt back down. I don't get far, his hands go back to my ass, holding me on his lap. "There are a bunch of people here."

Jason grins. "Wes and Vance cleared everyone out when I came up here to talk to you about the options," he says. "Listen. The house is quiet, darlin'."

The butterflies in my stomach flap wildly as I listen to the silent house.

We're alone.

Oh God, we're really alone.

I pull my bottom lip between my teeth, biting down on it. I'm nervous. So, so nervous, but whatever it is that's happening between us … I want it.

I want more.

"Told you this morning I shouldn't have let you sleep last night," he says, his lips teasing and nipping along my neck. "Don't want to wait another minute to make you mine."

A shiver ripples down my spine, and I feel a tinge of excitement.

His.

Oh God, I like how that sounds.

I'm blushing. He sees it. I know he does. That cocky smirk tells me so.

I say nothing, though I do lean in and kiss him. That seems to be enough for him. His hands capture the hem of my shirt, and I lift my arms, letting him pull it off.

Leaning back slightly, he tosses my shirt to the floor. His hands drift down my arms, down my chest, and stop at my breasts. He gropes them a bit over the fabric of my bra and his mouth comes back to mine.

The kiss is frenzied.

His touch is firm.

He tastes like mint and coffee.

It's intoxicating.

When he pulls back, I'm gasping, I'm dizzy.

Jason makes quick work of removing my bra, before his hands grip my hips and he stands me up, positioning me between his thighs. His hands run down my body stopping at the button of my jeans, his eyes following them, and he unbuttons my pants, pulling down the zipper, and tugs them off of me, along with my panties, leaving me bare.

Slowly, his eyes scan me from top to bottom before trailing back up again. "Beautiful," he whispers. "Fuckin' gorgeous."

He meets my gaze, stands up, and steps right in front of me. I can feel his heat; smell his cologne. It's a heady scent. I lick my lips and he groans, watching my tongue as it peeks out.

And then he's on me, his hands pulling me into him, his lips melding with mine. He lifts me up, his lips trailing my jaw, my throat, as he places me on the bed, before he undresses himself, and climbs in next to me.

I swallow hard, my eyes drawn to him. I only get a quick glimpse of his sculpted body and impressive cock, before he shifts his body so he's on top of me. He nuzzles my neck, trailing kisses and licks and nibbles, as his hand slides down my body between us, and when his fingertip grazes over my clit, my back arches and I gasp through the shock of pleasure.

My heart is hammering in my chest and my eyes drift close as his fingers play against my clit. "Love that flush on you, darlin'," he says. "Fuckin' gorgeous."

My body is heating, tightening. I can feel the pressure building, my orgasm coming as his fingers work their magic.

I'm close.

So, so close.

And then … he shifts. His hand pulls away; his lips leave my skin.

I make a sound. A whimper? A moan? A frustrated growl? Ugh, I don't even know. It doesn't sound natural, that's for sure.

Jason chuckles, shifting ever so slightly. "Want to be inside you when you come," he says, as he reaches over to the nightstand, and pulls out a condom. He tears the wrapper open with his teeth and leans back, gripping his cock, and rolling it on.

"I want that, too," I hear myself say, blushing furiously.

I'm nervous.

Oh God, I'm nervous, watching him fit the condom in place, but I'm also excited and needy.

I want him so, so much.

"You want me to stop, you just tell me, yeah?" he says, leaning back down, and rubbing his cock against my opening.

"I don't want you to stop," I say. "I want you. Oh God, I want you."

Jason pushes inside me then, filling me deeply. I gasp, my hands going to his hair and pulling his mouth to mine. It doesn't take him long to find his rhythm, his thrusts are slow, deep, and every part of my body clings to him as pleasure sears through me.

His hand comes between us, his thumb circling my clit as his cock fills me, over and over again.

I'm gasping.

I'm moaning.

I never knew sex could be this … good.

This amazing.

Pleasure bursts inside me. It's unlike anything I've ever felt before, and hearing the deep moans coming from Jason's lips increases it.

I move my hips, thrusting up to meet him as he thrusts down, urging the pace faster, harder.

"You're close," he tells me; his voice is strained as he quickens his pace, his thumb still working my clit faster and faster.

He is not wrong.

He groans against my lips, and orders, "Come with me, darlin'. Now."

And I do.

I come with him.

It's beautiful. The pleasure and the long groan he lets out as his body stills and my body clenches around his cock …

I don't know how to explain it.

Beautiful.

So unbelievably perfect.

I'm so definitely not in hell anymore.

Chapter Twenty-Two

Jason

Elena sings in the shower.

I'm lying on the bed, listening to her. She can't hold a tune for shit and when she doesn't know the words, she hums. Her humming is even worse than her singing, but I swear it's still the most beautiful sound I've ever heard.

She's happy.

I made her happy.

And that makes me fucking ecstatic.

Elena screeches out a high-pitched note and I laugh, glancing over to the bathroom door, which is hanging open. All I see is steam and her foggy silhouette behind the frosted shower curtain.

I haven't felt this good in a long time. It's not just the sex, though that was incredible. And the way she flushed ... Goddamn, I want to see that rosy flush coloring her skin again.

And again.

And again.

Hell, I don't think I'll ever get tired of seeing that flush.

But it's not just that. It's Elena. She makes me feel good. She makes me feel needed. She makes me ... feel.

Elena's singing comes to an abrupt halt as the shower turns off. The curtain slides open and she reaches for a towel.

"Jase," she calls out. "Are you still here?"

"Yeah," I say right away, sitting up. I climb off the bed and glance around the floor, looking for my boxers. I spot them in a pile at the foot of the bed, snag them up, and tug them on.

Elena steps out of the shower after a moment, wrapped up in a fluffy white towel. She eyes me nervously, fiddling with her wet hair.

She takes a deep breath, and then another. "I want to be there when Peck gets handed the restraining order."

I stall, not sure what to think or where exactly this is coming from. Not even an hour ago she was freaked at the thought of having to face him and now she wants to be there when he gets the piece of paper that will most likely piss him off?

Has she lost her goddamn mind?

"Not sure I heard you right, babe," I say slowly, pushing the words out. "You want to be there when Peck gets the restraining order."

She nods, looking at me anxiously, but determined. "Yes."

Sighing, I turn my head, looking away from her. I rub a hand down my face, before bringing my eyes back to hers. "Not sure that's such a great idea, darlin'."

Hesitating, she opens and closes her mouth as though she's lost for words, before she manages to whisper, "I don't want him to think I'm running again. I want him to know that I'm done hiding from him."

I regard her for a moment, before casually strolling toward her, stopping a mere foot away. My gut and my brain are telling me to shoot the idea down, but my heart seems to have entered the playing field and it's telling me to give her whatever she wants.

Anything.

Everything.

She's under my skin, so deep under it's as though she's always been there.

I open my mouth, ready to tell her no, but her sincere expression causes me to swallow it back. "You sure you wanna see him?"

Her smile grows a bit and her shoulders relax. She thinks I'm agreeing with her, that I think no harm could come of the asshole laying eyes on her.

She's wrong.

I don't agree.

Actually, I think her being there could cause a hell of a lot of harm, particularly to her mental health.

"Yes," she says. "I'm sure."

She steps over to me, wrapping her arms around my neck, and she lifts up to her toes, kissing me quickly. My arms snake around her waist before she can step back, and I trail my hands up her back, stopping at a patch of bare skin at the top of her towel.

Her skin is damp and warm.

Goddamn, I love touching this woman.

"Please, Jase," she says. "I've got to face him sooner or later and I'd really prefer it to be on my own terms."

I consider it for a moment, before letting out a resigned sigh. Saying no will only piss her off, and really, what real danger could she possibly be in at the police station. It's probably the safest place for her to confront him, if that's what she feels she's got to do.

"I'll give Cruz a call," I say. "Have him set up an interview room for you, yeah?"

She smiles and kisses me again. "Thank you, Jase."

I hope she'll still be thanking me after she sees him.

Elena

Detective Cruz wasn't as easy to convince as Jason.

He scowled at me. He right out told me no. He even threatened to throw me in a holding cell if I didn't get my butt out the door and back to Jason's house.

But he relented.

Finally.

It took thirty-eight minutes of arguing while I filled out the application for a restraining order, but he gave in.

I almost wish he hadn't. But it doesn't matter now. Peck is here and I'm not going anywhere.

I'm standing in an interview room with a long wooden table and six chairs, waiting for him. I tried to sit, but I couldn't keep still, and standing feels better.

Easier to bolt if I have to.

Wes and Vance are sitting, both with their backs to the door, and Jason has pulled a chair away from the table, lounging beside where I stand. His hand is hooked around one of my thighs, a silent reminder that he's here and I'm okay.

They're all so relaxed.

It's crazy if you ask me.

I continually glance at the window, forcing myself to stay still and not pace, as I watch for Peck to come down the hallway. I'm a bundle of frazzled nerves.

Wes and Vance are talking about … cars? Football? A case, maybe? I don't know. Their voices are barely a whisper, and their heads, tilted toward each other. I'm watching them, distracting myself with reading their lips, when I feel Jason's hand squeeze the inside of my thigh.

My head jerks up, spotting Cruz first, and then Peck. He hasn't noticed me yet, his head turned away, talking with the detective, but I can see a hint of a smile.

A smile!

Breathe. Just breathe.

This is what you wanted. You wanted to be here when he got the restraining order. Of course he's smiling. He thinks he's coming to get you.

Pushing back the swell of panic, I swing my eyes to Jason's. "You've got this, darlin'."

He sounds so certain of that.

I almost believe him.

"Right," I mutter. "I've got this, but …" I reach down, drifting my hand over his fingertips. "Don't let go, okay?"

He smiles up at me—full dimples—and he says, "Won't let go. Promise."

Five, ten, fifteen seconds pass, before the doorknob turns, and the door opens. Wes and Vance don't turn around. They keep their eyes on me, centering me, reassuring me.

I'm safe.

Safe.

Safe.

Safe.

Detective Cruz comes in first. He blocks the doorway, God love him, as he scans me from tip-to-toe, assessing me. On his way back up, his gaze pauses on Jason's hand, wrapped around my leg, and he shakes his head, disapproving.

I get it.

Why poke the bear, right?

But I need his hand right now, and I lean closer to him, silently begging him not to let go.

He doesn't. He gives me a soft squeeze, and then lifts his chin, signaling Cruz to get out of the way.

With one last scowl, Cruz steps aside, and there he is.

Officer Lawrence Peck.

His eyes come to me and my breath catches on the nerves crawling up my throat.

I swallow hard.

Peck sees it.

He likes it. Likes it when I'm nervous.

I can see the excited glint in his eyes as he watches my throat work, but it doesn't stay there long, as he quickly fixes his expression to one of concern.

His gaze stays fixed on mine as he enters the room, closing the door behind him. He doesn't seem to notice the guys. He doesn't seem to notice anything other than my face and the fear it is undoubtedly showing.

He steps toward me and I force myself not to flinch. There's a table between us still. A table and Wes and Vance.

Jason is right beside me.

Cruz is beside Peck.

I'm safe.

I swallow again.

The excited glint returns to his eyes, and then vanishes once more, and for just a moment, I have to admit, Peck looks good, even if panic tears through me at the sight of him.

The concerned fiancée look really works for him. He's in a suit, white shirt with the top couple buttons undone, and a green tie hanging loose around his neck. His blonde hair is spiked and gelled, and his emerald eyes glow with concern.

He was always a great actor.

Looks as though he still is.

"Baby," he murmurs, holding out his arms and motioning me to him.

I don't move.

I blink a few times, caught off guard by the softness in his voice. Even when he was being kind, his tone always held an unspoken threat that's missing right now. "Um ... Hi, Lawrence."

He takes another step in my direction, and I quickly hold up my hands, warding him off.

The room falls silent.

Jason squeezes my leg, reminding me he's there.

I can barely hear the others breathing over the sound of my racing heartbeat.

Peck frowns. "Jesus, El, I've been out of my mind worrying about you. I thought you were dead. I can't believe you're really here." He smiles, although there is nothing nice about that smile, and he motions again for me to come to him. "Come here, baby. I need to touch you."

He needs to touch me?

He thought I was dead?

Oh God.

Is anyone believing his bullshit?

I want to look at Jason, to see what his expression holds, but I don't.

I can't.

"No," I say, shaking my head. I lean in closer to Jason, and he gives me a reassuring squeeze. "No, I don't think so."

Peck notices Jason then. His carefully put together

expression falters and hardens. "You mind getting your hands off her?"

"Why don't you take a seat, Officer Peck," Jason says coolly, his tone almost bored, keeping his hand firmly in place. "Elena's got a few things she wants to say to you and I'm sure she'd feel a lot better if you weren't trying to creep into her space."

Peck says nothing, but he does laugh when Wes grabs the chair beside him and pulls it out. He looks at it briefly before his eyes fly back to mine.

There's hatred in those eyes.

There's contempt.

There's confusion.

It rattles me.

"Please sit, Lawrence," I say, keeping my voice as calm as possible. "Just for a few minutes."

He ignores me, his gaze going back to Jason. "Who are you?"

"Jason Pierce," he says. "Elena's man."

"Elena's man?" Peck asks, his brow pulling together as though confused, but I'm not fooled. The vein in his neck is pulsing, throbbing.

He's pissed.

Beyond pissed.

"Yeah, that's right," Jason says, his hand slipping from my leg as he stands. He gestures to the chair. "Have a seat, Officer."

He let go!

He promised he wouldn't let go.

He promised.

My heartbeat picks up, thrumming so quickly it hurts.

"Jase," I whisper, reaching for him as he takes a step closer to the table.

He doesn't hear me. Oh God, I barely hear me.

I want to move after him, but I can't. I'm frozen in place. Unable to move.

The skin around Peck's eyes grows tight and he looks at

Jason. "She's engaged," he says, his voice agitated.

"Jase," I try again, louder this time, though still a whisper.

Jason chuckles, shaking his head. "No, not yet. Don't think we're quite ready for marriage just yet."

Peck stares at him and his jaw goes tight. The muscle in his cheek jumps, the vein in his neck pulses.

Then his gaze comes to mine.

"Jason!" It comes out as a shout, and Jason swings his head back to me.

"What is it, darlin'?" he asks, his tone clipped.

My feet come unstuck and I move in close. So close that I'm pressed up against him, my front, to his side. "You promised," I say. "You promised."

"Hey." His arm comes up, snaking around my waist, and he pulls me in closer. "I'm sorry, darlin'. You're okay. You're okay."

His other arm comes around me, squeezing me tight, and he leans down, pressing a kiss to my forehead.

Suddenly, with his arms around me, I don't feel all that freaked out anymore.

I wrap my arms around his waist, hugging him just as tightly, feeling his solidness and his strength, and my heart slows into a steady rhythm.

"You're okay," he whispers against the top of my head. "Not gonna let anything happen to you, babe."

"Right," I say against his chest. "I know that. I've got this. Just a little—"

"What the fuck is going on here?" Peck shouts, before I can finish my thought.

Chairs scrape and clatter against the floor and I pull my head from Jason's chest, to see Wes and Vance blocking Peck's path to me. He's glaring at them, glaring so hard it looks as though his eyes are about to pop out, but he doesn't try to get past them.

Smart, I think.

Wes and Vance are big guys, and with their arms folded over their chests, standing at full height, they look huge.

Tension chokes the room.

The silence is just as thick.

Seconds pass, though they feel like hours, before Peck finally takes a step back, and it feels as though the room itself takes a deep breath.

"Elena," Detective Cruz says, drawing my attention. "You ready, honey?"

I nod, keeping my tight hold on Jason.

Cruz steps toward the table, picking up a manila folder and hands it to Peck.

Peck takes it and steps away, his face studiously blank as he flips it open and scans the contents. "A restraining order?" he says and laughs, his eyes coming up to mine. "What crazy lies have you been telling these people, El?"

"I won't press charges," I say, ignoring his comment. "I just want you to leave me alone. Please, please, just leave me alone. I'm happy here. I ... I ... I want to stay here."

He regards me for a moment, a swarm of emotions passing across his face. Anger, pain, more anger, shock, fury, sadness. "El, baby—"

"I'm not your baby," I say, cutting him off. "I never was."

He opens his mouth, and then closes it, seemingly at a loss for words, and his eyes fall back to the folder in disbelief.

"Officer Peck," Detective Cruz says. "If you'll come with me, I can answer any questions you have about the complaint that's been filed against you."

Peck's eyes drift over my face and he murmurs, "Christ, El, what have you done?"

Jason's arms give me a squeeze and he answers for me, "She did what she should have done a long time ago."

Chapter Twenty-Three

Jason

My phone rings.

I open my eyes. It's morning; the sun is seeping through the cracks along the blinds, lightening the room.

I'm on my back with Elena at my side, her cheek to my chest, arm slung around my middle, and one of her thighs thrown over mine. Her breathing is even; her muscles don't contract.

She's out cold.

I reach out, slapping my hand against the nightstand, searching for the phone and trying not to disturb Elena. She hasn't slept much, probably only a couple hours. After we got home from seeing Peck, and the initial shock passed, she was wired, talking for hours before sleep finally took her.

I feel the phone and snag it up, tapping the screen and bringing it to my ear. "Yeah," I say, keeping my voice low.

"Her brother has been picked up again," Liam says. "Had enough coke on him for a trafficking charge."

Goddamnit!

My stomach coils.

Peck. Goddamn Peck.

"You've got to be fuckin' shitting me," I say, my tone coming out sharp and loud with a sudden spike of anger.

Elena's body goes tight against me, and she blinks her eyes open, looking up at me.

Shit.

I school my expression, keeping it blank, and give her a little squeeze as I mouth, "Sorry, darlin'."

Her lips twitch ever so slightly, a hint of a frown pulling them down, and I force a smile, attempting to reassure her.

"Nope," Liam says. "Pretty fuckin' sure it was a setup, Jase. He took a call, and then booked it to a warehouse. He barely made it out of the doors with his stash before he was surrounded."

I'm very aware of Elena's eyes on me, watching me, assessing me. I consider getting up and slipping out of the room, but I know that will only cause her to panic and stress.

I stay put, stroking a hand along her spine, and say, "Okay. Thanks for the update."

Liam lets out a shocked laugh. "Did I miss something?"

He doesn't sound annoyed by my brush off.

He sounds confused; as though he's worried he fucked up somehow.

Glancing back down at Elena, I see the questions burning in her eyes. I let out a sigh. She's going to ask. She looks like she won't let it go until she gets an answer, too.

"Yeah," I say after a moment. "Elena got a restraining order on Peck. Met with him yesterday and asked him to leave her alone."

"Huh," he says. "What about her parents? Do they know she's turned up yet?"

"No, not yet," I say. "She hasn't brought it up and I ain't gonna push her to call them."

He's silent for a beat. "Fair enough. What do you want me to do here?"

Damn good question.

A part of me wants to tell him to leave it. If Andrew was found with the coke on him, there's not much we can do, especially since Liam watched him pick it up.

It's not like he was forced to do it.

But I can't do that.

Elena would be crushed if I did, I'm sure of it.

Reaching up, I run a hand over my face and sigh again. "Stick around for a day or two. If bail comes up, post it. If not, go home. Not much more we can do for him."

"Will do," he says. "Keep me posted, yeah?"

"I will," I say and hang up, tossing my phone onto the nightstand. When I glance down, I find Elena regarding me wearily, her eyebrows curved up in question.

It's a question I don't want to answer.

"Morning, darlin'," I say. "Didn't mean to wake you."

"What's wrong?" she asks, right away.

No good morning.

No pleasant greeting and sleepy smile.

She's coiled tight, her body feeling like dried cement against mine.

I hesitate for a moment, considering what to tell her, before I mutter, "Nothing, darlin'. Go back to sleep, yeah?"

"Jase!" she snaps.

She's unhappy.

Rightfully so, but I know that she won't take this well, and she's got enough on her plate to deal with already. Worrying about her fuck-up of a brother … not really something I want to add to the mix when there is nothing we can do about his situation.

Truthfully, I think a little time in jail might do him some good.

At the very least, it'll sober him up.

"Relax, darlin'," I say. "It's nothing for you to worry about."

Her cheeks flush and her eyes flare with anger. "Don't tell me to relax," she says, jabbing a finger into my chest. "Tell me what's happening."

I blink at her, stunned by the authority in her tone. Goddamn, she's hot when she narrows her eyes at me like this.

Challenging me.

Pushing me.

Smiling, I look down at her, taking in her spark-filled eyes looking up at me, and I bend my head, kissing her throat, as I consider whether or not to fill her in.

I have a feeling someone will tell her sooner or later, and I know it will be worse if she hears it from someone else.

Elena shoves at my chest, pushing me back. "Tell me."

I tuck her back against my chest, holding her tight. The feel of her warm body against me has my mind wandering and my cock hardening.

Tell her. Get it over with.

Move on to something more … enjoyable.

Yeah, right. I doubt she'll let me touch her after I tell her about her fuck-up of a brother.

"Your brother's been arrested for trafficking again," I say. "Liam will post his bail if one is set."

"What!" she shrieks. "You think that's nothing? That is not nothing! And why are you smiling?"

"There is nothing you can do about it," I say calmly. "That makes it nothing. And I'm smiling because I like seeing that fire in your eyes. Don't get to see it that much."

She purses her lips, her eyes narrowing further. "But you said—"

"I said it wouldn't be easy for him to close down your parents' bakery."

"But—"

"Your brother was caught with a lot of coke on him," I say, my tone matter-of-fact, almost clinical. "Liam watched the whole thing go down. He might have been setup, but the bust happened."

She seems to consider this; I can see it in her eyes as her mind works through the situation.

I also see it when she decides that I'm right.

She flicks her eyes to mine, a flash of helplessness shining there, before she pouts, full on, dramatic, droopy lip pouts at me. "I really don't like it when you cut me off."

I chuckle. "You gonna get some more sleep?"

She shakes her head, and as she opens her mouth to say something, I reach over, running my hand up her inner-thigh.

She snaps her mouth closed as my fingertips run over the thin cotton covering her pussy, dancing over her clit, and she gasps.

I'm surprised she doesn't swat me away.

But I'm not complaining.

I circle there, a little harder, and watch as her eyes drift closed, and that beautiful flush rushes up her neck, coloring her cheeks.

Love that fucking flush.

She lets out a breathy moan, wiggling her hips, seeking more, and I shift on the bed, making quick work of ridding her of her underwear and T-shirt. She says nothing, watching me with hungry eyes, licking her lips as I kick off my boxers. She doesn't move an inch as I come back to her, kissing down her chest until I reach her breasts and capture a nipple with my mouth.

"Oh God," she cries out, her hands coming up to my head, holding me to her as I suckle and nibble. My hand finds its way back between her legs and she lets out a long moan. "Feels so, so good."

I nibble and suck on her breast, pumping two fingers inside of her, grazing my thumb over her clit. Her orgasm comes quickly and hard, her pussy clenching around my fingers as she cries out. I keep going, drawing it out, waiting for her shudders to completely subside, before I move on top of her, rip open a condom, sheath myself, and push into her.

She wraps her arms and legs around me, welcoming me, holding me. Her cheeks are flushed and her lips are curved into a sweet smile, as she looks up at me.

I lower my head and kiss her, as I start to rock my hips, pulling back and thrusting in. "Love being inside you, darlin'."

She gasps and moans. "Love you inside me, too, Jase. Love it so, so much."

Elena

"I don't recognize anyone," I mutter under my breath. I'm back in the interview room with a stack of photos before me. I've been here for an hour, maybe two, and I haven't found a thing.

Nothing.

Maybe if they showed me images of the officers who worked with Peck, I'd get somewhere, but these images ... they all look like hardened criminals.

Peck's friends wore suits.

They had good hair.

Good teeth.

Great smiles.

They were friendly enough, even if they never seemed to notice the bruises marring my skin.

They were ignorant.

But I don't think they were criminals.

Maybe if I picture these people smiling? A smile can really transform someone's appearance. Why don't people smile in mug shots?

"You only just started, darlin'," Jason says, from his seat beside me. "Just keep looking. You knew this wasn't gonna be a quick solution."

"Yeah, I know," I mutter, and I let out a dramatic sigh, causing him to chuckle, before turning my focus back on the photos.

We sit in silence, me flipping through images and Jason working on his phone.

Another hour passes.

And another.

When Cruz comes in, Jason slips out for a bit. I wonder if they're discussing Peck. The jerk is still in town, staying at the Apex Hotel. He even tailed us to the station this morning.

I guess I knew he wouldn't just pick up and leave like I asked.

But I hoped.

Good God, did I hope.

Or maybe there's something new on my brother.

Ugh. My brother. I don't even know what to think about that. Jason's right. There's nothing we can do. Logically, I know he was bound to get thrown in jail sooner or later.

And really, it shouldn't be bothering me so much. He traded me to Peck. He put me in this mess.

But ... he's still my brother.

Jason comes back in, and gets right back on his phone. He's texting, I think, and suddenly, I find myself thinking about Mr. Chapman.

I turn to Jason curiously. "Um ... Jase?"

"What's up?" he asks, prying his eyes away from his phone to glance at me.

I consider my words carefully before opening my mouth, and he watches me with a curious expression on his face. "Did Mr. Chapman ... I mean, your dad, is he still around?"

Jason's expression falters. "Yeah."

That's it.

That's all he says, before turning his attention back to his phone.

I should probably let it go.

He obviously doesn't want to talk about it, but ... I'm curious.

So, so curious.

"What happened between you two?" I ask.

He glances back up at me; his expression turns hard, the warmth I'm used to seeing when he looks at me, gone. "It's in the past," he says. "Better to leave it there."

"Don't do that," I say. "I know you care about him, even if you don't want to. Maybe talking about it will help."

He keeps his hard expression fixed on me and for a moment, I'm worried that he's mad at me. I'm not trying to push, but I want to know.

I need to know.

"It'll change the way you see him," he says seriously. "You sure you wanna know?"

I hesitate. How bad could it really be? My gut tells me that whatever Jason has to say won't change anything.

Mr. Chapman has betrayed my trust one too many times.

Not much can be worse than that, right?

And I want to understand. A small part of me is looking for

a reason, any reason that could explain why he's done everything he has.

I nod. "Yes, I'm sure. I want to understand why all this crap with him is happening."

Jason closes his eyes for a moment, and when they open again, a speck of warmth has returned to his gaze. "Fine," he says softly, and nods as though he's trying to convince himself that telling me this is, in fact, fine. "Richard Chapman was a good cop, and then he wasn't. He was dirty, rubbing palms with a few different gangs who sold drugs and guns. He welcomed them into our home, used our basement as a storage unit, and when he got too deep, he started cleaning up their messes."

I gape at him. Mr. Chapman was a cop? A dirty cop? I was living with a dirty cop?

Good God, I'm not sure what to say.

My lack of response prompts him to continue. "I missed it for a while. I was in college, not home all that much. It wasn't until I finished school and was about to apply for the Police Academy that I really noticed the changes. I followed him one night, got footage of him destroying evidence at a crime scene. It was an attempted murder. Rival gangs and he was working with both of them."

I gasp. I don't mean to, but it slips out and I bring my hand up to my mouth. "Oh my God."

"He was bringing his buddies home to meet Mona," Jason says, shaking his head. "Invited criminals into our house to have dinner with our family, playing them off like old college friends. He could have gotten her killed. Sooner or later they would have clued in he was working them both."

Oh God.

Oh God.

I don't want to believe him. It seems … impossible.

Mr. Chapman wouldn't do this, would he?

I study Jason, looking for something to tell me that this isn't true, but I see nothing. Nothing but hurt, as though what he's telling me stings him to say out loud.

I don't know what to say. I'm sorry your dad did that? It

doesn't seem appropriate. Doesn't seem right.

He closes his eyes and stays like that for a bit, as though he doesn't want me to see him hurting. He doesn't want me to see the pain in his eyes.

But I see it.

It's clearly displayed on every inch of his body.

When he finally opens his eyes again, he takes my hand, bringing it to his thigh and holding it there. "I decided not to be a cop after that. I also decided he shouldn't be one either, but I couldn't bring myself to turn him in. He's my old man and Mona ... fuck ... he's still her world. She loves him like crazy."

My chest aches from his words and guilt nags at me. I want to apologize for even bringing it up. "Jase, I'm sor—"

"Stop," he says, cutting me off. "Don't be sorry. You've got no reason to be, darlin'."

His words should make me feel better, but they don't. "It bothers you to talk about it. I'm sorry I brought it up."

"I made him quit the force," he says, choosing to ignore my apology. "I've been holding the evidence against him to make sure he doesn't go back."

Oh my God.

The bar. The parking lot.

It all makes sense now.

I stall, mulling over what he's told me, trying to pick my words carefully. "You thought that's why I was here? Wes said I wasn't the first person Mr. Chapman sent to you."

"No, you weren't," he confirms. "He's been trying to get the evidence for five years now. He's not a fan of me holding it over his head. But you were different. You're not what he usually sends to get my attention."

"So this case, my case, did you take it because of him?"

"At first, yeah," he says and lifts his shoulder in a half shrug. "I guess it had an influence. I thought he was jerking you around."

I furrow my brow. "Does that mean you don't think he's, um, jerking me around anymore?"

"What I mean is, before you shot me with a Taser and I saw

that panicked look on your face, I was taking the case because of him.　You seemed so sweet, innocent, and you were desperate.　I couldn't stand by, knowing he could be using you."

What about after I shot him?

"And now?"

He doesn't respond, instead he leans toward me and presses a soft kiss on my lips, before pulling back.　"Give it another hour, darlin', and then we'll go grab something to eat."

Jason stands up, tapping the screen on his phone and bringing it to his ear as he slips out of the room.　Sighing, I turn back to the photos, and get back to work, not even a little bit sure of what to make of everything he just told me.

Chapter Twenty-Four

Elena

Days pass … a week … two weeks.

They just keep slipping by.

I've fallen into a routine. Every day, the same thing. Wake up, go to the station, look at photos, come home.

Wash, rinse, and repeat.

Jason is always with me, and the odd times he can't be, Wes or Vance takes his place.

I'm grateful for that.

I'm relieved.

Peck is … missing.

He followed me around for two full days after my brother was thrown in jail, and then, he just up and vanished. He didn't go back to New York. The official story from his department is that he took a sabbatical. Supposedly, the false lead he chased on his missing fiancée crushed him.

But it's not true.

According to Cruz, he's been suspended with pay, pending an investigation of my complaint against him. The whole thing is being kept quiet. I don't know if it's for my benefit, or Peck's.

Either way, I don't really care.

No one's heard from him.

No one's seen him.

And the only person back home that knows the lead on my whereabouts wasn't false is Peck's captain.

I like to believe he gave up, but the guys don't share my optimism.

They believe he's still here.

Waiting.

Watching.

Biding his time.

Jason told me he feels it in his gut, and his gut is never wrong. I think he's being slightly overprotective.

The kitchen is quiet. Jason is sitting at the table. He's reading. Reading my case file. He reviews it daily, combing through Peck's financials and my medical reports, looking for something he may have missed.

I'm beginning to think that we're never going to find something to put Peck in jail, and oddly enough, I'm almost okay with that. In a sense, I've gotten what I wanted. He's leaving me alone.

I stand at the island, wrists deep in ground beef. It's Saturday and we're having a small party tonight. A few friends, good food, and drinks. More importantly, we're all supposed to be taking the day off. Something that I think all of us could use right now.

Jason doesn't share my thoughts on that. No matter what I try, I can't get him to forget the case, even for a day.

The guys have worked on a couple other cases over the last two weeks. Favors for Cruz. It's the only time Jason took a break from my stuff. He chased down a few skips with Wes and Vance, brought them to Cruz, and got right back to work, reviewing my file.

His phone rings and I look up as he reaches for his cell, answering it. "Yeah?"

He's silent, listening. Whatever the call's about doesn't make him happy. He tenses, and his jaw ticks.

I sigh. I feel so drained. It's driving me insane. It's like I'm back in hiding, waiting again. Waiting for something to happen.

I'm starting to wish I'd gone with the wire option, and I

think Jason is, too. He's been ... unsettled the last few days. Restless.

"Don't care," he growls into the phone. "I want that fucker found before Elena and I leave."

I flinch at his words, at the reminder that I'm going home next week, and dig into the ground beef, mixing in the oats vigorously.

Jason notices and he curves an eyebrow at me in question, but he stays on the phone. I hesitate before shaking my head and offering up a small smile.

What am I supposed to say?

That I'm worried about seeing my parents again? He'll most likely laugh at me and tell me I'm worrying about nothing.

And besides, I'm the one who made a big deal about going. Jason wanted me to wait until Peck is found. He tried to get me to call them instead, but calling my parents just didn't seem like the right thing to do.

I need to see them.

It's time.

And the restraining order is there to protect me.

The argument lasted three days, but in the end, he agreed as long as he goes with me.

But now that the plane tickets have been purchased, I can't help but wonder if they will believe me when I tell them what happened.

What will they do?

What will they say?

Will they expect me to pick up and start right where I left off?

And where does that leave Jason and me?

I think that's the thing that's eating at me the most.

"Don't care about the cost, Wes," Jason says. "Find him. Whatever it takes."

He hangs up, tossing the phone down, his eyes never leaving mine, as I beat the ground beef into a pulp. It feels as though an eternity passes as he watches me, trying to get inside my head, before he says, "Are you okay?"

"Yes," I whisper. "Of course. Why wouldn't I be?"

But I'm not okay.

I ache.

I ache so, so much.

I want to see my parents again. I really do. I miss them like crazy. But each time I think about going, I feel as though I'm about to lose my life all over again.

Jason's coming with me, but he won't stay.

He'll make me safe.

Then he'll go home.

At the end of the day, I'm just a case.

He lifts a hand and motions me forward. "Come here, darlin'. I wanna talk to you about something."

I don't respond as I turn away from him and go to the sink. I wash the meat from my hands as quickly as I can, and then make my way over to him.

When I stop in front of him, Jason brings his hands to my hips and tugs me down onto his lap. His arms come around me, pulling me close, and he kisses me, a barely there press of his lips against mine.

"You give any more thought to changing your major?" he asks, his tone soft.

I blink. That's what he wants to talk about?

"No," I say. "No, I haven't."

He smiles, amusement flashing in his eyes. "The guys and I have been thinking about opening an office."

"Uh-huh," I mumble. I don't have a clue why this conversation needed me to stop getting the burgers ready for tonight, but I'm not complaining.

I love his arms around me.

I tuck my face into his neck, snuggling close. Have to enjoy the contact while I can, right?

"PRG Investigations is gonna need an office manager," he says. "Someone to book cases and keep shit organized."

"Mmmm-hummm."

"CSU has a campus here," he tells me. "They have a great business program. I think you'd like it. There's still time to register for the fall semester."

My flesh springs with goose bumps.

Is he …?

Is he really asking …?

Oh my God.

I meet his eyes. "What are you saying?"

"I want you to come back with me," he says. His voice is so earnest, his gaze, pleading. "When I leave New York, I want you to come home with me."

I can tell he means it; his voice is genuine. I close my eyes and when I open them, Jason is staring at me expectantly. "You want me to come back with you?"

He nods his head very slowly, his smile faltering. "Yeah, darlin', I do. Not sure what this is between us and I don't know where it's going, but I'm telling you right now, I sure as hell want to find out. I love having you here, going to sleep with you in my arms. I love waking up with you, and coming home to you. Don't want that to stop. Don't even want to think about it stopping."

My breath catches, and I swallow hard. "Do you really mean that?"

He doesn't respond right away, glancing down at his arms circling me. When his eyes lift to mine once more, I can see he means it.

He looks so vulnerable.

So nervous.

It's odd.

It's unsettling.

My chest burns. I inhale a harsh breath, but it feels as though no air enters my lungs.

My heart screams at me to say yes, my brain hollers to proceed with caution. I've only known him a few weeks. Yes, we've spent every second together and we already live together, but there's still so much more to learn.

What if it doesn't work out?

What if it does?

Is this something I even want?

Yes. I want him. I want this.

All this time I thought I lost my life when I ran away, but now that I may actually go back to it, I realize that perhaps it was never really lost.

Maybe I just hadn't found it yet.

At some point in the last few weeks, I've made a life here. A life that I want to keep.

"I mean it," he says. "I want you to move in with me. Haven't been able to think about anything else since I bought those plane tickets. It's driving me insane thinking I could lose you in just a few days. Don't wanna let you go, darlin'."

He pauses, smiling down at me, waiting for me to say something, but I don't. I can't seem to push a single word past my lips.

Oh God, I freeze.

His arms squeeze me, before he places me back on my feet. "Just think about it, yeah?" he asks, and before I can form a response, he stands up and walks out of the room.

Jason

I should have goddamn waited.

The plan was to talk to her about it after we got to New York. I thought I'd meet her parents, let her get a feel for her old life, and let her decide if it was what she wanted.

I meant to give her time.

I wanted her to experience what she'd been missing out on before she made the choice to give it up for something else.

But that flinch …

I didn't miss it. I also didn't miss the dread in her eyes when I mentioned our trip.

Maybe I'm delusional, but I swear, at least for a second, she looked as though she didn't want to go.

Or perhaps it's only that I don't want her to go.

We've been living together, sharing a bed, fucking, and playing at being a couple for weeks. And I want more. I want all of her.

I feel like an ass. A selfish, stupid ass for putting her on the spot like that.

Fuuuuck. I need some space. I need to give her space. I don't want her to feel like I'm hovering, or pushing for an answer, so I pace around the house, sitting in one room for a bit before moving on to the next, making sure to avoid the kitchen.

I don't know if I can take an answer from her right now anyway.

I look at the case file some more.

I make a few calls, following up on leads for Peck's whereabouts.

I even consider calling my old man. Elena's been on my ass about talking it out with him. They've been talking again for about a week now, and just as he did with my mother, my old man has weaseled his way back in and convinced Elena to forgive him.

She told me the other day that his heart was in the right place and you can't be mad when he meant well. She thinks I'll feel the same if I'd just talk to him.

I don't know if I believe it.

I also don't call him.

An hour passes, or maybe it's been three.

Elena bangs around the kitchen. She's gone all out for this. Last I counted there were eight different kinds of salads and she said she still had one more to make.

We only have six people coming.

It feels like a lifetime drifts by before people start to show up. I greet them. I smile. It's pointless, though. One look from Wes, and I know he sees right through me.

So naturally, I avoid him.

Seems to be my game today.

Avoid Elena.

Avoid Wes.

I work the grill. I chat with Cruz and his wife. Vance gives me a heads up that there was a Peck spotting earlier today in town, which I store in the back of my mind to check up on later.

My mother talks to me about the salon. My old man shoots glances in my direction.

And through it all, I watch Elena, while not allowing Wes to get me alone long enough to talk.

The two things sound easy, but it's a lot of goddamn work.

My gaze scans the yard, picking her out. She's wearing a yellow summer dress. It's thin, cotton, I think, with little straps, rounded neck, and hangs just above her knees. She's laughing. It's a real laugh. Her cheeks are rosy, and her arms are wrapped around her belly as though she's trying to hold herself together.

It's my old man that's making her laugh like that.

It puzzles me.

She puzzles me.

I just don't understand, no matter what his intentions were, how she can so easily forgive him for letting Peck know where she is.

"Surprised you invited him."

Wes.

Shit.

I look at him. He's watching me peculiarly, as though he knows exactly what's eating at me and doesn't have a clue why I haven't stepped in and fixed it.

Except, he has no idea.

"I didn't," I say. "Elena did."

He laughs, amused that she took the liberty to butt in where she really shouldn't have. I'd laugh, too, if I weren't so twisted up about Elena's lack of comment after I asked her to move in with me.

"She's really doing good here," Wes says. "She looks relaxed, happy. Never thought I'd see that look on her."

He's right, she is.

My gaze goes back to her. She's still laughing, smiling huge.

Fucking gorgeous.

Perfect.

That smile … it lights her up like the crack of dawn.

"You two have a fight?" Wes asks casually. "Or is it your old man that's got you moping around?"

I slowly shake my head, pulling my gaze away from Elena. If he were someone else, I'd brush him off, make something up, but he's not. He knows me far too well to believe some bullshit. With a frustrated sigh, I grumble, "Told her about opening an office today."

He frowns, looking right at me. "Thought you were waiting on that," he says.

"I was," I tell him. "Ended up asking her after you called. Thought the time was right, guess I was wrong."

A look of genuine surprise crosses his face. "She said no?"

"Nope," I say, letting out a humorless laugh and shaking my head. "She didn't say anything."

Elena

"Should have warned Jase about letting you loose in the kitchen."

I glance up, finding Mr. Chapman standing beside me and I blush, cutting him an embarrassed look. "I think I made too many salads," I mutter. "Everyone needs to eat more salad."

It may be possible that I haven't quite gotten over the whole starving homeless thing.

When we first met, Mr. Chapman refused to let me cook because I would make enough food for an army and we could never eat it all before it would go bad. He used to threaten to lock up the food and only give me enough to last me the day.

His eyes flash with amusement as they scan me over, and I stall for a moment, taking them in. I never noticed before how similar his eyes are to Jason's, the way, even straight-faced, you can see the humor dancing within them. "Not sure that's gonna help, baby girl."

Looking over the table again, I can see he's right. There's so much salad that we'd all have to eat at least five platefuls, and still, there would most likely be leftovers.

I glance around the yard. It's getting dark. Music plays softly, country, I think. Everyone seems to be having a good time, relaxing, chatting.

It's exactly what they needed.

I spot Jason standing by the grill. He's talking with Cruz, drinking beer. I haven't spoken to him since he asked me to stay. He hasn't given me the chance.

He's in full on avoidance mode.

It sucks.

He looks so good tonight, dressed in jeans and a light gray polo shirt. It's snug across his chest and hugs his biceps. He has a ball cap on, blue, I think.

His eyes drift my way. He always seems to know when I'm looking at him. He stares at me, his gaze trailing along my entire frame, before shifting back to Cruz.

"Gotta say this, baby girl," Mr. Chapman says, his voice low and gruff. "I want you to really listen to me, yeah?"

Pulling my gaze away from Jason, I glance at him. "Okay."

"Don't think you should be going back to New York," he says casually. "Think you should stick around here."

I don't know what I expected, but this was not it. I furrow my brow, surprised. "I—"

"Not done yet," he says, stopping me right away. "Haven't seen you this happy before and you make my boy happy. I like that look on both of you. I like it a lot. You wanna go visit your parents, go visit, but I'm pretty sure you know that this is where your home is at now."

I don't know what to say. Truth is, I've been thinking close to the same things.

"Has he talked to you yet?" I ask, attempting to shift the subject.

He sees right through me.

"Don't try and weasel your way out of this," he says. "You know I'm right."

I nod, hesitate, and then whisper, "He asked me to stay."

He stares at me for a moment, taking in my panicked expression, and then laughs. "Knew he would, baby girl."

"I didn't say yes," I inform him.

He stops laughing and stares at me.

"I froze."

He continues to stare.

"He's been avoiding me since it happened. He thinks I don't want to stay, but I do. I'm ... I ..."

Ugh. I'm stammering. I'm shaking. My chest aches. I'm an overall mess, and I can't see a way to fix it. He won't even talk to me.

Mr. Chapman grasps my shoulder and looks down at me. "Spit it out, Elena."

"I think I love him," I blurt frantically.

"Calm down, baby girl," he says. "This is a good thing. You should be happy. He's a good man, and he'll treat you right."

I know. I want to shout it. This is a great thing. Amazing. And Jason's ... the best. Better than the best.

"Richard," Mona calls, and walks over to us. "Stop upsetting the girl."

"He's not," I say quickly. "I'm good."

She doesn't believe me.

Good God, the look she's giving me ... she's just as intuitive as her son.

Mr. Chapman chuckles. "She's in love with Jase."

Mona looks at me, a soft smile on her lips. "Of course she is. I spotted that the first time I saw them together at my shop. Why in the world is that upsetting you, honey?"

I'm surprised at the ease and confidence in which she says it. I'm not sure how to respond, and I whisper, "Because he wants me to stay."

She blinks at me, confused. "And?"

And ...? I don't know. This whole thing is ridiculous. I should just march right up to him and tell him how I feel.

I should.

And I will.

Just maybe after everyone leaves.

Yes. Tonight when we crawl into bed, I'll tell him.

I smile. "I'm being ridiculous, aren't I?"

Mona doesn't answer, but she does take my hand and squeezes it, before pulling away and taking a long sip from her beer.

Mr. Chapman starts rambling. I take a bite of food, looking around the yard. As I glance around, my eyes catch onto something. A movement by the gate. A shadow. I lower my burger back to the paper plate in my hand and I stare, squinting my eyes in the darkness.

It's Peck.

Peck is slipping through the side gate!

No one seems to notice him.

He looks right at me. His arm raising up in front of him and for a second, it looks as though he's pointing at me, beckoning me.

Something strange and unpleasant crawls along my skin. My brain focuses, my gaze zeros in.

Oh my God. Oh my God. Oh my God.

I blink and blink again.

He's not calling me over.

No.

He isn't …

He wouldn't …

He doesn't have a …

But yes, yes he does.

Peck's holding a gun and he's pointing it right at me.

Chapter Twenty-Five

Jason

Gun.

The single word forms on Elena's lips, but she doesn't make a sound. Her eyes are wide, fear filled, and even from my place across the yard, I can see her body tremble.

Instinctively, my hand reaches for the butt of my gun at my hip. She glances my way, just a brief flick of her eyes and she mouths the word again.

I have no idea what's gotten her so freaked out. I usually don't carry it around the house, but since Peck showed up in town, I've had it with me.

She knows that.

She never seemed bothered by it before.

I start toward her, making it one step, two, three, before I watch as Elena shoves my mother hard, knocking her to the ground. My old man grabs Elena, shoving her behind him as he pulls a gun from his back and trains it toward the side of the house.

"No," Elena shouts, struggling and pushing to get past my old man. "Get away from me."

What the fuck?

Adrenaline hits me hard and fast. It rushes through my system and a chill sweeps over me. My heart skips a beat before it picks up speed, hammering in my chest, and I pull my gun from my hip holster. I don't think about it. I don't hesitate. I grip my gun, my finger hovers over the trigger, and I pivot, searching the place my old man is aiming.

"Put it down," my old man growls. "Put the fucking gun down."

It only takes seconds for my eyes to find who he's speaking to. Peck. He's standing under a light by the gate to my backyard. He holds a gun, gripping it tightly with his finger on the trigger.

Fucking suicidal idiot.

"Fuck you," Peck says, his aim staying steady.

I aim my weapon, pointing the muzzle of my gun right at his head.

The yard turns silent. It's as though everyone stops moving, stops breathing even. From the corner of my eye, I see both Wes and Vance draw their weapons and take aim. Wes moves in front of Cruz's wife; Vance moves to my mother.

Cruz is … I don't know where the fuck Cruz is. He was beside me a minute ago …

Fuck. Fuck. Fuck.

I take a step toward Peck.

He doesn't notice, or if he does, it doesn't faze him.

"I'm surprised you're here," I say calmly, taking another step in his direction, hoping to draw his attention away from my woman. "Figured you crawled into a hole somewhere."

He stares at Elena, watching her as she struggles to get past my old man, unfazed by the gun I have pointed at his head. I don't even think he sees it.

"Came for my fiancée," Peck says. "Hand her over and I'll go."

"I'm not your fiancée," Elena shrieks, frantic. "I never was. I never will be."

My stomach clenches and my lungs squeeze. My eyes dart to her, only a quick glance, before bouncing back to Peck. She's pale. She's panicking. But she also looks as though she's ready to charge him and rip him apart.

Peck's hand is steady; his gaze is hard.

He's going to shoot, I think.

This isn't an empty threat. Anger, hatred, desperation … he's soaked with the emotions, seeping from his sweaty pores.

He means to kill her. He means to take her and kill her.

I can see it. I can feel it.

And I'm not going to let that happen.

I'm not letting her go.

Elena screams in frustration. "Get the hell out of my way, Richard!"

My muscles tighten at the sound of her voice. So do Peck's. His body seems to snap straighter, his jaw clenches, and his grip on the gun tightens.

"Elena," I bark, my tone sharp. "Stop."

She makes a sound, somewhere between a growl and a whimper. Another quick look in her direction, though, shows me she's frozen solid, shooting daggers at me.

Whatever. Better her mad than dead.

"You're not getting near my woman," I tell Peck. "Put the gun down."

He laughs. His eyes dart between Elena and me, and a second later his aim shifts slightly and he squeezes the trigger.

Elena

A gunshot goes off, loud in my ears. Mr. Chapman shouts out and his leg buckles. He weaves on his feet, crumples to the ground.

My world stops.

It stops moving, stops spinning.

No. Oh my God, no. No, no, no.

He shot him. Peck shot him.

Someone screams.

Others shout out orders.

"Get over here, El," Peck says, his voice calm, controlled. His gun moves, his aim going to Jason. "Or your fuck buddy is next."

This isn't happening.

This isn't happening.

I put my hands up. Someone's going to die. I can feel it in my gut, in my toes, my fingertips. Someone I care about is going to die.

I have to do something.

I go to move and Jason's gaze hits mine instantly.

"Stay where you are, darlin'," Jason orders, his voice like whiplash. "Get down; put pressure on Dad's leg."

I freeze.

My gaze swivels between the two of them, and without hesitation I drop to my knees, putting pressure on Mr. Chapman's bleeding leg.

He hisses as I do, but he raises his gun and aims it back at Peck.

"Why are you doing this?" I shriek. "Why?"

Peck doesn't answer. Not that I really thought he would. He does look at me though, and what I see there, confuses me.

There's fear.

There's affection.

There's hatred.

How can one person show so many conflicting emotions at once?

"Drop the gun or I'll shoot," Jason says, taking another step, this time to the left, getting in front of me.

"Baby, come here," Peck murmurs, ignoring Jason, his voice shaking ever so slightly. "I'm not going to hurt you."

I blink at him, pressing on Mr. Chapman's leg a little harder. He grunts. I can feel his warm blood coating my hands.

My stomach turns.

My chest tightens.

And then I lose my temper.

"Hurt me?" I snap loudly, my voice bordering on hysterical. "All you ever did was hurt me. You're hurting me right now. You just shot Mr. Chapman!"

Peck jerks back a step and his eyes widen with surprise.

I've never raised my voice to him before.

I've never had the guts.

He shakes it off quickly, his expression changing from shock to regret in a blink. "It'll be different this time. I swear it, El. Come here, baby."

"Stay where you are, Elena," Vance says. My gaze snaps to him. He's behind me and a little to the right, standing in front of Mona, who's still on the ground, keeping still and silent. He has a gun, too, leveled on Peck. "Drop the fuckin' gun."

"I'm not fucking around here, El," Peck says. "I'll shoot him and it won't be in the leg."

"Don't fuckin' move, Elena," Jason growls, moving forward closer to Peck.

Everything is happening so fast. Everyone's shouting, giving me orders. I don't move, though, keeping the pressure on Mr. Chapman's wound.

Jason takes another step.

"Don't come any closer," Peck yells. "I'll shoot if you take another step."

He's breathing heavily, quickly. I can hear the pants, see his chest rise and fall, quicker and quicker.

My eyes immediately go back to Jason. His face is hard, his focus steady. He's not panicking. He doesn't look fazed by the gun pointed at his head.

It rattles me.

Seeing him so calm scares the hell out of me.

"Lawrence, please don't," I beg, my voice hitching on the words. "Please. You don't have to do this."

Peck looks at me, his face twisting with anger. "You're my fucking fiancée. You're mine. I only want what's mine and we'll go. No one has to get hurt here."

Jason laughs, a humorless and unnaturally sharp sound. "You shot my father. You pointed a gun at my woman. You have a gun pointed at me. You ain't fuckin' going nowhere but jail."

"I just want my fiancée back," Peck yells. "I bought her. She's fucking mine."

Bought me?

Bought me?

Oh my God.

What does that even mean?

"Bought me?" I ask, my voice louder than I meant it.

"Doesn't matter, baby," Peck says. "Not anymore. I love you. That's all that matters, and as soon as you tell my captain that your complaint was bullshit, we can move on. It'll be better. You'll see."

"Bought me?" I ask again. I should probably feel fear, but I don't. I don't feel anything. Not even the blood on my hands or the breeze in the air.

Peck raises a hand, pinching the bridge of his nose, keeping his aim with his other hand. "Forget it," he says, his voice steady, even though he looks as though he's ready to lose it. "Come here, baby. Let's go home."

I barely even hear him. Anger. Blinding, white-hot anger courses through me.

All I see is red.

I shift my body, facing Peck fully and scream, "Bought me!"

"Elena, stay where you are!" It's Wes this time, ordering me, but I don't look at him. I keep my glare fixed on Peck.

He hesitates. *Hesitates.* He's looking at me as though he can't believe I even have the gall to question him. It lasts a moment. A long, eternal moment, before he mutters, "Your brother sold you to me for a clean slate and a get out of jail free card for as long as I'm on the force."

For the second time tonight, my world stops.

I don't even breathe.

I stare at him, blankly, my chest aching, and my body turns numb.

I can't process this.

I don't notice Cruz moving in behind Peck until he says, "Drop the gun. You're under arrest."

Peck spins around, waving his gun wildly. He pulls the trigger, and two separate gunshots ring out, one after another.

Jason

I'm a killer.

I should feel something. I should be unsettled, or angry, or sick, or something. Anything. But I don't. I feel nothing.

I killed Peck.

Shot him in the head.

I've had to shoot people before. It's not like this is the first time I've used my weapon, but I've never killed anyone until now.

Non-fatal shots.

Wounds don't kill.

Elena is huddled in my arms. She isn't talking. She isn't crying. She isn't ... anything. She just clutches onto me, holding me, stroking her fingers through my hair, down my back.

I think she's trying to give me comfort.

I find that almost ... amusing. My scared, timid girl is trying to comfort me.

We're standing by the grill, with Wes and Vance, watching as Cruz directs traffic as people arrive at the scene. They're oddly quiet, too.

The yard is swarming with officers and paramedics. I don't know when they arrived or how long they've been here. Statements are being taken. My yard is being secured with police tape.

It's chaos.

Controlled chaos.

Peck is on the ground, covered with a sheet. I'm told I won't be charged with anything. It was self-defense. I was protecting my property and the people on it.

I think my case was helped by the fact that Cruz took a hit. Nothing severe, just a graze on his right shoulder when Peck spun on him and pulled the trigger. The cops aren't too keen on charging a man that saved one of their own.

My old man is being loaded up in an ambulance. My mother is holding his hand, climbing in with him.

My old man took a bullet for my woman.

I don't even know what to think about that.

I'm grateful. So goddamn grateful.

I glance down at Elena. She's staring up at me, her gaze, troubled. "Cruz needs stitches," she says. "Shouldn't he be getting treated or something?"

Yeah, he probably should be, but he won't. He right out refused treatment, saying he needed to be here until the scene was dealt with.

"He's fine, darlin'," I reassure her, placing a kiss on her forehead. "His shirt took more damage than he did."

"What about you?" she whispers. "Are you okay?"

I smile down at her. It's weak, I know, but I try. "Yeah, darlin', I'm good. It's over. He's gone."

I don't think she believes me, but she doesn't push it. She gives me a slight smile and turns her head back to the yard. "Yes," she says quietly. "He's gone."

Chapter Twenty-Six

Elena

The plane rocks through turbulence as it starts its descent over the city. Jason groans beside me, squeezing my hand in an almost painful hold.

The man can stare down the barrel of a gun without breaking out in a sweat, but flying ... let's just say he's not a fan.

"We should have driven," he grumbles.

I merely laugh. I lost count of how many times he's said those words somewhere around the first hour of the flight.

"Relax," I say. "We're almost on the ground."

Jason doesn't respond, though he does give me an unamused look that causes me to giggle.

Yes, giggle.

I'm giddy.

I've been giddy since we woke up this morning. It's odd. It feels wrong with everything that's happened. But I can't stop it.

I'm excited.

I'm going to see my parents.

And my man is coming with me.

It's Friday. Six full days since Peck died. The first couple of days were ... tense. We gave statements. We answered questions.

And questions.

And questions.

But by the third day, things settled. We began healing. We started to move on.

The man who haunted me for the last year is gone. No more hiding. No more running. All that's left to do is live.

Good God, I want to live.

And Jason … Jason's okay.

He's better than okay.

I was worried that killing someone would hurt him, but it hasn't. He told me it was either Peck or me and that he'd always choose me.

Always.

He still hasn't spoken to his father. I'm not sure what's stopping him. He won't talk to me about it. All he says is that he will.

He's just not ready yet.

Mr. Chapman is doing fine. The bullet went straight through the side of his leg. He hasn't left town yet, and I find myself hoping that he won't.

He may have made mistakes, but he's got a good heart.

The plane lands and we make our way to collect our bags. There's no real plan to the trip. We don't have a clue how long we're staying or what we're going to do while we're here.

Surprisingly, it's nice not to have a plan.

When we reach the baggage area, a strange thrill settles in my belly. It's nerves. It's excitement. It's all consuming, tumbling together, causing my heart to flutter, my belly to flip, and my knees to tremble.

I'm here.

I'm really back home.

I hesitate, staring at the bags. I want to grab mine. I want to reach out and take it, but I don't. For a brief moment, I don't move.

Jason notices.

He always notices.

A hint of a smile takes over his face. "You sure you don't wanna call them first?" he asks, grabbing both our bags. "Give them a heads up?"

I shake my head. "No. I want to surprise them."

He looks at me peculiarly, before chuckling. "We're here, darlin'. Whether you call or not, I ain't letting you back out of this."

I laugh. "You've got it all wrong, Jase. I was just thinking about whether we should go straight to the bakery or wait until they get home."

That almost sounded believable.

He smiles, flashing me those amazing dimples, and winks. "Almost believed you that time, darlin'."

The drive across the city drags. We take a taxi, and I look out the window, not seeing a thing. Jason never once lets go of my hand.

When we finally reach my parents' bakery, my palms are sweating and my fingers shake. I'm so excited. I'm so nervous.

What if they don't recognize me with the new hair?

What if they don't want to see me?

What if …?

Stop it. This is ridiculous. I'm being ridiculous. They're my parents. They love me. They'll be happy I'm back.

Right?

Jason pays the driver and folds out of the taxi, coming around to my side and opening my door as I get out. I breathe a sigh of relief as he reaches over, taking my hand and giving it a little squeeze. "I've got you, darlin'."

The door chimes overhead as we walk into the shop, and the first thing I see is my mother. She's bent over the counter, cloth in hand, cleaning up what looks to be spilled coffee. Her white blond hair is pulled back in a tight bun, and her white apron is crisp and clean.

She's humming.

She always hums while she works.

It's like nothing has changed.

The shop is busy; the scent of fresh pastries and bread baking fills the air.

I walk up to the counter, never once letting go of Jason's

hand. He doesn't say anything, just holds on tight, giving me his support.

Mom looks at me when I stop in front of where she works. She's silent. She's smiling. I don't think she recognizes me.

My grip tightens on Jason's hand.

He squeezes back.

That's when it happens.

Mom blinks. Silent tears fill her eyes and slowly begin to streak down her cheeks as she continues to stare at me.

It's like she's frozen.

My stomach coils, my heart races.

"Hi, Mom." My voice sounds awkward, squeaky and raw.

At the sound of my voice, she gasps, and rushes around the counter. She collides with me, almost knocking me over, and pulls me into a bone-crushing hug.

She loses it.

She cries; deep, sniveling sobs.

"What's going on out here?" my dad calls, his gruff voice sounding just like I remember it.

I pull back from my mom, only slightly, just enough to see my father. "Hey, Dad."

And just like that, he's on me, too.

I'm crying.

I'm laughing.

I'm being crushed between my parents.

And Jason still has a firm grip on my hand, holding me steady.

I love every second of it.

My eyes meet Jason's. I grin. He smiles.

In that moment, I can see it. I know exactly who I am.

I'm a daughter, a sister, a woman.

I'm a fighter, a survivor. I'm strong.

I'm loved and I'm whole.

I am Elena Reed.

Epilogue

Jason

Four weeks.

It's been four long-ass weeks since I left Elena in New York. The first few nights without her were hard; the last few were fucking torture.

I swear I haven't slept in days.

I'm standing at the door, peeking out the window. A mix of fear and excitement curls through my gut. She called me ten minutes ago and told me she was five minutes out.

How does that work?

Why didn't she fly? It would have been quicker if she flew.

Christ. Look at me. I'm acting like a little girl waiting for her first date to pick her up.

What the fuck is wrong with me?

But I miss her.

I miss her so goddamn much.

And I can't get rid of the sickening feeling that my woman isn't coming home.

It's crazy, I know.

Of course she's coming home ... I hope.

I never wanted to leave her in New York. I stayed with her for a little over two weeks before I had to come back home.

A case. One that the guys needed me for.

She needed time alone with her parents anyway. She needed to heal.

And I had to see my old man.

It was time.

Elena told me weeks ago that if I hear him out I'd understand why he did what he did. She was wrong. I don't understand. He said he did it for us, that we needed the money with me in school and Mona not working. He told me it was never supposed to go so far. Things just got out of hand.

The thing is, my school had nothing to do with him. I paid for it. Every cent.

In truth, I don't think he knows why he did it anymore.

We came to an understanding of sorts.

He's still here. He's planning on sticking around. And that makes both Mona and Elena happy.

If they're happy, I'm good with that.

I look out the window again. Where is she?

A minute passes. Five. Ten.

My stomach coils tighter.

I need my woman back in my arms. Now.

We talked almost every day while she was gone. I missed calling her a few times because of work, but even when missed, I always sent a text message and she always responded as soon as she woke up.

I've never been a phone person. Always hated long, drawn out conversations. But those calls with Elena. Fucking loved every one of them.

We talked about everything. Shared childhood stories. Favorite memories. Worse memories. We talked about our dreams and our plans. We talked about our future.

We got to know each other without all the bullshit swirling around us, and I swear I fell for her all over again.

The only thing that we never discussed was Peck. I'm good with what I did. I'd do it again if it meant keeping him away from her, keeping her safe, but I don't want to talk about it.

I killed someone.

I can live with it.

I *will* live with it.

And I know she's done hashing out the past.

Elena wants to move on, and I'm fucking thrilled to give her that.

It's done.

The rumble of a truck draws my attention back to the window.

She's home.

She's finally fucking home.

I throw open the door and pause, when my eyes come in contact with a black F150 sitting in the driveway, and I watch her through the windshield as she cuts the engine and hops out, letting the door slam.

She turns around to look at me, leaning against the truck, crossing her arms over her chest. She lifts her chin, a small smile curving her lips. "Hey."

"Hey, darlin'," I say quietly, my voice gruff and low, thick with emotion. "You get lost?"

She blushes. Fuck, I've missed that blush. "Um … yeah, I did."

I chuckle. "You should have called. Would have been quicker."

"Well, I would have," she says, and offers a small shrug. "But my phone died after we hung up."

I stare at her for a moment, taking her in. She looks so good my mouth goes dry. She's not wearing anything special, jeans and an off-white tee. Her hair is half up, half down, a mess really, falling out of the elastic, and she's not wearing a stitch of make-up.

But still, she's beautiful.

Gorgeous.

She's watching me, her eyes running along my frame, before she uncrosses her arms and pushes off of the truck. Wordlessly, she strolls over to me, coming up the steps, stopping right in front of me.

Her eyes meet mine, she puts a hand on her hip, and she smiles. "Are you going to help me with my bags or what?"

I pull her to me, laughing, and kiss the top of her head, before I tuck my face into her neck, holding her tight against me. "Fuck, I missed you."

Her arms come up, wrapping around my neck. Her hands digging into my hair. "I missed you, too," she whispers. "So, so much."

She gasps as my hands run down her sides, sliding over her hips, and settling on her ass. I lift her, and her legs go around me instantly, holding on tight.

"What are you doing?" she asks, laughing, as I carry her inside, kicking the door shut behind us.

"Welcoming you home," I say, as I move through the house, going for the stairs.

She laughs again, this time louder. "But my bags."

I grind her against me, letting her feel how much I want her. "They can wait, darlin'."

She doesn't say a word, but her lips hit my throat, licking and nipping along my jaw, up to my ear lobe.

I groan. Fuck, it feels so goddamn good to have her back in my arms.

We reach our bedroom quickly, and I have to force myself to slow down, savor the moment, as I lower her to the bed and strip her from her clothes. I stare at her, taking in every inch of her peach skin, running my fingers along every curve and dip.

I love her slowly, thoroughly, and as I watch her come apart in my arms, I feel … complete.

Elena

Oh God, it's good to be home.

I curl into Jason, my leg going over his thigh, my arm draping across his middle, and I feather kisses across his chest. "I missed you so, so much, Jase."

"Glad you're back, darlin'." His voice rumbles through his chest and his arms tighten around me holding me tight.

"I meant to ask you," I say, trailing my fingertips along his abs, "how much do I owe you?"

"What?"

"For taking on my case," I say. "I told you I'd pay you as soon as it was over."

"Forget about it," he says, nuzzling into my neck. "Let's just forget the whole thing happened, yeah?"

"I'm serious, Jase. You guys spent a lot of time on this. You need to get paid."

Jason knifes up to a sitting position and he stares at me.

And stares.

And stares.

"Jesus, you really are serious," he mutters, and he gives me a funny look, one that I don't understand, and says, "Don't want your money, darlin'."

I furrow my brow. "What do you want then?"

Jason chuckles and flat out smiles. He lies back down, pulling me into his arms. "You," he says. "Just you."

Butterflies dance in my belly at his words and I kiss him, smiling wide against his lips. "I can give you that."

We lay there for a while. I can't say how long. I think I even dose off for a bit. I didn't sleep much during the trip, driving as much distance as I could before stopping, and it's left me drained.

Seeing my parents again was amazing. Handling their misplaced guilt, not so much. They took my story with Peck hard and they took Andrew's involvement even harder.

They blamed themselves for not seeing it.

When I left, they were actually looking into a legal way to disown him.

He's still in jail. From what I've been told, he was sentenced to ten years, but made a deal and will only serve three.

As it turns out, Mr. Chapman had been right. Peck was dirty, but it was other cops he was working with. I guess that explains why I never recognized anyone from the mug shots in the two weeks I spent combing through them.

There were three others he partnered with. My brother fed them leads, they'd make a bust, and only turn in half of what they found, keeping the rest to sell or for personal use.

Andrew gave them up.

A door slams, causing me to jump, sitting straight up. Jason mutters a few curses as footsteps hit the stairs, thump down the hallway, and someone raps against the door. "Yo, Elena! Jase! Get your asses dressed and down here. It's barbeque time."

Wes. Oh God. I flush. I can feel it, creeping from the tips of my toes all the way to my cheeks, causing my skin to blaze with heat.

Jason chuckles and I look at him. Amusement touches his eyes and he smiles wide, giving me the dimples.

Good God, I missed those dimples.

"Barbeque?" I croak out.

He didn't tell me we'd have company tonight. Honestly, I hadn't even considered that he'd invite the guys over.

"I tried," Jason says, his smile faltering. He runs a hand down his face, letting out a groan. "I fucking tried to put it off, but they missed you."

They missed me? Something inside me soars at those words. I knew they didn't hate me, but I always held onto the idea that I was just a job to them.

Well, to everyone but Jason, that is.

I smile wide. So wide that my face burns and my lips hurt. "I like barbeques."

Getting dressed, we head downstairs. The guys are already out back, the barbeque fired up and beers open.

I hesitate for a moment, reaching the patio doors. Jason stops with me, his hand settling at the small of my back, and he leans in, his lips coming to my ear. "I'll get them to bring it inside, yeah?"

I quickly shake my head, "No. I'm good. This is good."

It's safe back there. I know that. Jason had a new security system put in while I was gone. New locks on the gate. No one's getting back here without us knowing.

And Peck's dead.

No one's after me anymore.

Pulling in a breath, I push the door open and step outside. I barely make it onto the deck before Wes and Vance are on me, arms around me, squeezing me so tightly that I can hardly breathe.

"Jesus," Jason mutters. "Let her go. You idiots are gonna suffocate her."

They let me go, grumbling something about Jason hogging me as they do.

"You ain't allowed to leave for four weeks again," Vance says seriously. "Not unless you take him with you. Can't handle the fuckin' moping."

"Shut up," Jason says.

Wes laughs. "He barely slept."

"Shut up," Jason repeats, louder.

"He wouldn't go to the bar with us because he didn't want to miss a call with you," Vance continues, grinning like a fool.

Jason's arms come around my waist, pulling me to his side, and he groans and mutters, "Shut the fuck up."

I laugh, tilting my head, looking up at him. He watches me, brow cocked as though daring me to say something, but I don't. I just laugh and hug him back.

"Yo, Piper," Wes says after a moment. "Come over here, babe."

I pull my face out of Jason's chest, untangling myself from his arms, just as a young woman steps over. She's stunning. Heart-shaped face, rosy cheeks, a slight nose, speckled with freckles. Her hair is bone-straight and red, the brightest red I've ever seen, and her eyebrows ... she has fantastic eyebrows.

"This is Piper," Wes says. "Piper, meet Elena."

She smiles, offering a little wave. "Good to meet you. I've heard so much about you."

I let out a groan at her words. I can only imagine what they've told her about me. "Whatever they said, don't believe them," I say. "These guys are the best liars I've ever met."

She laughs, a sweet little Tinkerbell laugh. "It was all good. I swear."

The guys laugh, making their way over to the barbeque. Jason hands me a beer, before joining them. They joke around, laughing and carrying on like a bunch of teenagers, while Piper and I sit on the deck.

She doesn't talk much, just watches.

I get lost in my own head, mulling over what to do about school. I never got around to registering for classes, but I want to. Maybe for the winter semester.

We eat and drink and laugh, and again, I find myself thinking how good it is to be home. After stuffing ourselves, Vance pulls out his guitar. Turns out, he really wasn't lying. He can play.

And he's good.

Really good.

"Oh my God," Piper whispers, setting her beer down. She jumps up from her chair and makes quick work of crossing over to where Vance sits, guitar in his lap.

He looks up at her, a big shit-eating grin spread on his lips. "Hey, Piper."

"Play it again," she blurts. "That was amazing. Please, play it again."

I nudge Jason in the ribs, and look up at him, confused. "What's her story?"

He grins, winking at me. "She's a new case."

I look at her, at Vance, at both of them, and then I laugh.

It looks like a little more than a new case to me.

Acknowledgments

An enormous thank you goes to my family and friends. You all are the best support group. Thank you so much for your encouragement and patience as I worked through the writing process. I love you all.

A special thank you to my mom. I don't know what I would have done without all our phone calls. Thank you for being there, day and night.

To my editor, Kathryn, I couldn't have finished this book without you. Thank you for being an invaluable member of my team.

And to my husband, Jordan, thank you for having so much patience and understanding, especially when I ignored you for weeks while writing this book. You are the best!

Last, but not least, a big, huge thank you to all of my wonderful readers. You guys are the best and I couldn't have done it without you all!

About The Author

Ashley Stoyanoff is an author of romance novels for young adult and new adult readers, including The Soul's Mark series and the Deadly Trilogy. She lives in Southern Ontario with her husband, Jordan, and two cats: Tanzy and Trinity.

In July 2012, Ashley published her first novel, The Soul's Mark: FOUND, and shortly thereafter, she was honored with The Royal Dragonfly Book Award for both young adult and newbie fiction categories.

An avid reader, Ashley enjoys anything with a bit of romance and a paranormal twist. When she's not writing or devouring her latest read, she can be found spending time with her family, watching cheesy chick flicks or buying far too many clothes.

Ashley loves hearing from her readers, so feel free to connect with her online.

www.ashleystoyanoff.com
www.facebook.com/AuthorAshleyStoyanoff
www.twitter.com/AshleyStoyanoff
www.goodreads.com/ashley_stoyanoff